Books by Nicola Skinner

NICOLA SKINNER

Illustrated by Flavia Sorrentino

HarperCollins *Children's Books*

First published in the United Kingdom by
HarperCollins *Children's Books* in 2022
Published in this paperback edition in 2023
HarperCollins *Children's Books* is a division of HarperCollins*Publishers* Ltd
1 London Bridge Street
London SE1 9GF

www.harpercollins.co.uk

HarperCollins*Publishers*
Macken House, 39/40 Mayor Street Upper,
Dublin 1, D01 C9W8, Ireland

1

ISBN 978-0-00-842248-6

Nicola Skinner and Flavia Sorrentino assert the moral right to be identified as the
author and illustrator of the work respectively.

A CIP catalogue record for this title is available from the British Library.

Typeset in Goudy Old Style 12pt
Printed and bound in the UK using 100% renewable electricity at
CPI Group (UK) Ltd

This book is produced from independently certified FSC™ paper
to ensure responsible forest management.

For more information visit: www.harpercollins.co.uk/green

This book is dedicated with love to my father,
Keith Skinner, who always loved the satisfaction of
finding just the right word.
Thank you for passing on the thrill of the chase to me.

THE GREAT WAR OF 1803

Once there were no giants. It was just us, and we lived peacefully on a little island in the middle of the ocean, surrounded by one or two other little islands, which we didn't bother, and which didn't bother us. Life was good and quiet, and our people went about their business.

Then the giants came. They sailed over the ocean in their ships. They landed on the shore, shouting threats and saying nasty things, and they invaded the island and tried to rule us. They came because we were smaller than them. They thought we were weak, and therefore could be conquered.

They were wrong. We did not want to be ruled by giants. We did not want to be conquered by outsiders. So we fought back.

The war between us – the humans – and them – the giants – began.

Fighting raged for so long that both sides lost track of time. Bodies, both small and big, piled up around each other. The stench of death filled the land.

Then the earthquakes began. Just like us, the island didn't want the giants either. Their thundering footsteps had disturbed the earth, so it responded with destruction. Every tremor was violent, as if the island wanted to shake off both the war and the invaders.

Still the war raged on. The longer we battled, the more the island shuddered. Each quake caused another. These shocks became a part of island life, as much as the war and the death were; a never-ending line of tremors that rippled through the streets and valleys. Some were so small they were barely felt. But once in a while a quake shattered neighbourhoods, brought down great trees, and filled the roads with rubble. There were so many earthquakes, and there was so much fighting, that soon all the buildings on the island had been smashed to pieces. So the islanders lived in ruins and bedded down in wrecks, with no roofs to keep them dry and often no walls. They slept on the ground, with their swords in their hands, for there was no other way.

And still the war stormed on, for years and years. Many islanders died with valour. They battled through every quake, barely stopping to brush the rubble dust off their shoulders before going back to the important business of plunging sword into flesh and slamming fist against fist. Neither side was prepared to stop, for all knew that their future spun on who would win. Our people fought for their way of life, while the giants fought for their stomachs, greedy for the green land they had seen from their large, scavenging ships.

Each side had separate weapons.

The giants had their strength, and against this the islanders were helpless. But the greatest weapon of all was the island itself, and our people knew how to use it best. They lured giants into swamps, trapped them in secret valleys, and dazzled them with light so they fell from mountain tops. Thanks to our brains and our bravery, after many years of fighting and death, we islanders won.

It was a glorious victory. A good victory: the right side had won.

So the giants admitted defeat. After mourning their dead, they in turn prepared to die, as punishment for their invasion.

But our people were merciful. They did not wish to shed one more drop of blood. Everyone had lost their appetite for death. Also, they had seen what the giants could do with their hands. The islanders looked around the shattered landscape, at the broken houses and streets. 'You must stay and rebuild this,' they demanded. 'Lift the rocks. Repair the walls. And make good what you have broken.'

The restoration took a long time. The sight of the

giants slowly putting buildings back together became so familiar that, after many years had passed, the children of the island stopped being frightened of them.

They liked to watch the giants at work. They would laugh and try to help. They would beg to be carried on their shoulders. At first, the giants resisted. They concentrated on their work. But the laughter of the children made them smile, and the giants and the children grew secretly quite fond of each other.

And the rebuilding seemed to take for ever. In fact, it seemed to be impossible.

Because even though the war was over, the earthquakes were not. The minute a giant finished putting together a nice row of houses, an earthquake would come along and pull them all down again. This went on, and on.

At first, the giants had bricks and stones to work with. But the repeated shock of the quakes made the bricks and stones crumble, eventually, into dust.

'It's like building with sand,' they would explain, worriedly, to the humans. 'We cannot restore your homes if there is nothing to make them with.' They would hold out their hands and let the brick dust run through their fingers. The children would dance underneath the dust, laughing, not understanding how serious this all was.

This dreadful business of stone shortage and brick dust made the islanders very distracted. They didn't watch over their children very closely. The children continued to ask to play with some of the giants.

One day, a giant finally gave in to a little boy's entreaties and bent down and picked him up. After spending a day together, the giant took the child back to his broken street. The giant bent low to put the boy down on the ground. Before the giant straightened up, the little boy leaned forward and, overwhelmed by affection for his new playmate, kissed him, for a moment, on his cheek.

This little kiss, innocent as it was, did something peculiar to the giant's skin. It began to harden, then crack, like bread in the oven. Then it began to turn a distinct shade of grey.

'Wh-what's happening?' stammered the little boy, looking up into the eyes of the giant in front of him.

'I – feel –' the giant gasped, and then he clutched his throat, and he could not say what he felt any more, for he had turned to stone.

In front of the frightened little boy, the eighteen-foot-tall giant, who just a minute ago had been alive, turned into a large stone statue, frozen to the spot: half-crouched, his hands around his own throat as if he was trying to pull words out, staring down at the boy with a permanent expression of surprise and dismay in his large stone eyes.

At the sight of the playmate he'd accidentally petrified, the child sobbed, utterly heartbroken. But his tears were not necessary. Because he had, entirely by accident, done something magical. He had turned flesh into stone. Most importantly he had turned giant flesh into giant stone.

After experimenting with one or two other giants that they didn't particularly like, the islanders discovered that the giants had one fatal flaw. They looked invincible – indeed, you would think that nothing could destroy them at all, but they were allergic to human kisses. There was something within the lips of our people that, when pressed against giant flesh, caused an instant toughening of not just their skin but every single part of their body. Their insides turned to stone, too. The islanders knew this because, when they broke open the giant to check, they discovered a stone heart within.

In much the same way as a flame, when held against a pile of dry wood and newspaper, will catch fire and burn brightly, so too would a kiss cause a blaze of grey to ripple across giant flesh. And just like a fire turning wood to ash, turning flesh to stone was as impossible to stop and as hypnotic to watch. It was the most wonderful and strange chemical reaction anyone on the island had ever seen.

'This is fascinating,' our people cried, staring at the stone giants in front of them, transfixed for ever into mute effigies. 'A giant can be turned to stone with a mere kiss? Wish we'd known that years ago! We'd have won the battle much earlier!'

Captivated by the discovery, forgetting, for the moment, that meals needed to be cooked and children cared for, the islanders conducted more experiments with a few more giants they thought they could spare. They learned that, while an adult could turn a giant's flesh to stone, the process was incomplete, and just resulted in the giant walking about with extremely thick skin. The process only worked all the way through when a child kissed a giant. No one was entirely sure why, but they had fun guessing. 'Their lips are less dry and cracked?' they suggested. 'Less caked in lipstick?'

Someone clever said: 'Perhaps the children's kisses are more powerful because they are innocent.'

But the reason, they all agreed, didn't really matter.

In any case, they didn't mind if adults didn't have to do it, as they had plenty of other things to do, and adults kissing giants seemed somewhat foolish. So they made the children do it instead.

They discovered that the process worked better when the children were told that what they were doing was a marvellous thing.

Once or twice, if a child protested and said they didn't want to turn a giant to stone, but kissed the giant anyway, the procedure didn't fully work, as the kiss didn't last long enough. This resulted in some truly dreadful statues, with some parts that were still alive; their eyes, for example, or their mouth, or – in one horrible instance – an entire hand, which flapped about helplessly in the air. Like a fire, the process had to be tended and believed in, wholeheartedly, if it was going to work.

The islanders would have thrown these badly made statues into the sea if they could, but they were too heavy. Instead, the defective stone giants were left exactly where they were, as a lesson to the children to do their job properly.

Once they had perfected their technique, the islanders began to scheme, and plan.

'So our children can turn giants to stone,' they said,

at a very important meeting. 'How can we make this work for us?'

Their minds whirred. They thought of their shattered streets, and their lack of building material. They thought of the time-consuming business of parenting, and how well the giants and the children seemed to get on. They realised that one stone giant alone was more effective, and solid, than a thousand island bricks.

They whispered: 'The giants can look after our children, just like nannies, and give us more time to ourselves, and when our children grow up and their nannies are no longer needed, the giants can be turned into statues, which we can use as columns and walls and all sorts to fix our island.'

Everyone looked at each other, very impressed by how clever they were.

The minutes of the meeting have been lost to the ravages of time, but some fragments remain, and these say:

'They'll solve our material shortage!'

'We can sell the giant stone to other islands, for a huge fee!'

'We'll be rich!'

'We'll have babysitters and servants on tap!'

'Using giant stone statues to prop up our buildings

will give everything a very grand look!'

'We can break them up into smaller pieces if we want to make cobbles!'

'We'll be the talk of the archipelago!'

'We'll never have to worry about keeping the giant population in check!'

'And best of all, they deserve it completely, because they started the war!'

In this way, the Giant Management Company was born. They created traditions, and wrote down rules and guidelines. The island was given another chance at life. And the new laws came to pass.

From: *The Island Chronicles: For the Good of the Island.* Reprinted with the kind permission of the Giant Management Company.

- 1 -
THE LAGOON

THE FIRST TIME Minnie Wadlow broke a rule from the
*How to Manage Your Giant – a Giant Ownership Manual
for Children* she blamed the heatwave. The second time,
she blamed her giant. By the third, fourth and fifth times,
she had run out of excuses.

It all started in the lagoon, a vast body of water so dark
it was like swimming in ink. It was in the west, only a
short stroll from Minnie's home, Quake Quarter.

Minnie loved that lagoon. Unlike the toxic sludge of
the Five Bridges river, whose length spanned the island,
or the wreckage-infested ocean that surrounded it, the
lagoon itself was clean, safe and not as likely to poison or
kill you. Its attractions included a rusty waterslide, a kiosk
for ice creams, and hordes of huge, feathered screecher
birds, who were either screaming grumpily at each other
about when they were going to eat next, or feeding lumps
of meat to their young and screaming happily about that.

Despite the screams of the screecher birds, the lagoon
was Minnie's second favourite place. (The bakery in

Quake Quarter was the first, and if you were lucky enough to try their almond and honey pastries, you'd know why.)

On this particular day, Scarred Island was exceptionally hot. The sun showed no mercy to the island, or its inhabitants, that day. Metal seats left outside for too long caused huge blisters on bare legs. Flies droned in and out of windows, stunning themselves on the glass. Babies grew flushed and feverish. And the caged jackals down at the meat factory, whose cries could normally be heard all over the island, were too hot to do anything but whimper.

Usually on such a day the lagoon would have been crowded with Minnie's classmates whizzing down the waterslide, telling their giants to fetch them an ice cream, or throwing rocks at the screechers for fun. But Florin Athelstan was having his ceremony that day, with Sandborn, his giant. Florin's family was the most powerful on the island. No expense had been spared on the feast. So the islanders were excited. They wanted to look smart. They were too busy getting ready. Despite the heat and the sun, the lagoon's dark waters lay almost empty.

There was only one child swimming in its shallows: Minnie Wadlow, a small feeble girl who'd slither about in your arms like a slippery trout if you tried to hug her. This was on account of the greasy sun cream she was always slathered in, even when it rained. Her tangled, unwashed brown hair grew down to her waist in a ratty, knotty clump, and she had a nose that some people privately thought was a bit too big for her face. When it was school photo time, Minnie Wadlow was always asked to stand at the back.

While she swam in the lagoon, sending plumes of oily sunblock into the water, her classmates from Quake School were otherwise engaged, walking into beauty salons and barber shops so they could get primped and preened for Florin's ceremony. But Minnie had nothing like that planned at all. Her parents didn't believe in any of that stuff on ceremony days, or on any other day for that matter. Quite the opposite, in fact. If anything, they practically *encouraged* her to look scruffy and dirty.

'You don't need to brush your hair too much, or wash your face, or do any of that nonsense,' they'd say. 'Just be yourself Minnie. Pick that lovely distinctive nose of yours whenever you want, and don't *ever* feel you need to use too much soap, darling.'

Minnie's neighbours all agreed that Minnie Wadlow was as free as a screecher bird, as smelly as a jackal cage, and as grubby as the river path. They never said that to her face though, because they had manners. They also said awful things about her parents, but that doesn't concern us now. (Oh all right. If you *must* know, they said her mother was an ageing beauty who contributed very little to the moral backbone of the place, and her father's earthquake-prevention designs were next to useless. They said terrible things about the state of the Wadlow house too, which we shall not repeat here because we're not gossips.)

So greasy, grubby, little Minnie Wadlow had the lagoon all to herself! For the first time *ever*! All that water, all that *space*, all to herself, made her giddy. She grinned in the direction of the shallow end and then said something very, very bad.

'You should get in here too, Speck.'

She was rewarded with a stern look from the giant sitting cross-legged on the grassy bank of the lagoon.

'And if I do, those screecher birds will be picking over my bones by the end of the week,' said the giant, peering down her nose at her charge.

'Just for a little bit?' said Minnie.

'I don't believe I am scheduled to die this week, thank you.'

Minnie was struck by a sudden thought. *Maybe Speck couldn't even swim . . .*

She wouldn't be surprised. There were lots of things Speck couldn't do. She couldn't pick up a plate in the kitchen without accidentally snapping it. She couldn't sit in a chair without breaking it. She couldn't walk past a bin without looking in it for cast-off treasures, like scraps of fabric, stubs of lipstick. She couldn't walk past a fruit stall without licking her lips, or tuck Minnie into her bed at night without looking a bit soppy.

And there was no denying Speck was a runt: the shortest giant in Quake Quarter, measuring in at a mediocre twelve feet. When she stood, she was only twice the height of the fridge freezer in Minnie's kitchen. When she sat on the banks of the lagoon, she was merely the height of a tall Christmas tree. She was much shorter than all the other giants on the island. They were usually around eighteen feet high; or, to put it in more sensible terms, the length of three rhinos standing in a row.

No one in Quake Quarter could remember what Speck's real name was. Speck was just a nickname. It was Florin Athelstan himself who'd given it to her, at Minnie and Speck's pairing party, back when Minnie was three. 'Call that a *proper* giant? She's tiny,' he'd lisped, pointing at Speck in the Wadlow ballroom, back when they'd used it for parties. 'She's so much smaller than *my* giant! She's a speck of a thing. That's what we should call her.' Everyone laughed, because Florin was an Athelstan, and the Athelstans were high up in the Giant Management Company, and very powerful.

From then on, the name had stuck.

'Please get in the water with me,' said Minnie from the lagoon. 'One tiny dip. In and out, very quickly. Like a posh teabag. It won't even count.'

Speck rolled her eyes, which was very naughty of her, but which secretly Minnie rather liked. 'If I get in there, and someone sees, you know what will happen to me,' she said quietly.

'The dungeon,' whispered Minnie, thinking of the dark space in the middle of the old castle. A shudder ran through her that had nothing to do with how cold the lagoon was.

'Exactly,' said Speck, stretching her legs, which were the length of oak saplings, out on the grass. 'Then who'll listen to your teasing or bring you here on sunny days?'

There was an awkward pause. They had just skirted the truth of their relationship: that it was going to end. Speck probably wouldn't get thrown in the dungeon – that was a punishment only given to very bad giants. But Minnie would lose her another way. She even knew when: on the day of her twelfth birthday. She could feel *her* ceremony getting closer every week, like a stranger walking towards her. Ceremonies had begun many years before Minnie was even born and she didn't dare question them. Even so, she had mixed feelings about her own, which she was clever enough to keep to herself.

Before Minnie knew what she was doing, she was at it again.

'Aren't you tempted, though?' she said. 'I can see you're hot.'

'I am indeed hot, Minnie,' said Speck, turning her huge yellow eyes towards her and raising one eyebrow. 'Top marks for observation.'

'Have you *ever* swum, Speck?' Minnie said.

'Of course. We servant giants are taught to swim in case of an emergency, to rescue any children we're caring for. It was part of my training, before you and I were paired.' Whenever Speck mentioned the time she spent learning how to be a servant, before she came to the Wadlow house, her face took on a frightened, haunted look. 'But I've never swum for fun, Minnie,' added Speck. 'You know the rules.'

GIANT OWNERSHIP:
A Guide for Children

Dear Child,

Now you have been paired with your giant – congratulations!

We hope that the next nine years are wonderful for you both. Having a giant as your servant is an honour. But it's not all fun and games. Giant ownership is a big responsibility. You could say it is a GIANT responsibility. And you would be right.

Every child must learn how to manage their giant. To make things as safe as possible, learn the rules inside this manual inside out. We recommend reading it every night for the rest of your life, and twice on Sundays for a treat.

From your friends at the Giant Management Company

On the Subject of Rest and Relaxation

These are the hobbies giants are allowed to enjoy:

NONE.

An unreasonably happy giant is a dangerous giant, who may get funny ideas about freedom, and nobody wants another war. So remember: <u>no fun</u>. Giants have one occupation, and one alone: to look after you. And they should count themselves very lucky they can do that, quite frankly. What a privilege – look at you!

Giants <u>must</u> look after you in public spaces, but they absolutely <u>must not</u> take part in any activities you can enjoy with your peers, but they may not participate in any activities with you.

SWIMMING, SUNBATHING, OR DANCING WITH YOUR GIANT ARE ALL <u>VERY</u> FORBIDDEN.

REMEMBER: GIANTS ARE YOUR SERVANTS, NOT YOUR PLAYMATES.

'I do,' said Minnie. 'I do know the rules. Inside out and back to front.'

The family copy of the manual hung from a rusty old nail next to the fridge in the kitchen. Minnie had another copy by her bedside, and there were at least three more copies in the house. The Giant Management Company were very generous when it came to handing out manuals, and so the rules were as much a part of Minnie as her muscles and her bones.

Minnie trod water, noticing for the first time how, in the sun, Speck's uniform was beginning to look a bit shabby. Her long-sleeved shirt was more grey than white, and the embroidery on the shirt that said THIS GIANT IS ON LOAN TO THE WADLOW FAMILY was beginning to fray.

Minnie knew Speck was not allowed to swim with her for *fun*. But what her brain knew, her heart fought against. It wasn't like Minnie was asking *all* the giants on the island to get into the lagoon with her. Just Speck. Surely one tiny paddle wouldn't be so very bad? Who would it harm?

She checked the lagoon entrance: no newcomers rustled the green fern leaves that lined the path, no one made the white butterflies dart up into the sky. They were alone. This had never happened before, and there was no guarantee it would ever happen again. And one day, soon, in just a matter of months, Minnie would look over and Speck would not be in her usual place on the bank. She would be somewhere else. She would be *something* else. She would not be Minnie's any more.

A lump the size of a lagoon pebble appeared in her throat. She swallowed it down. Then she had an amazing idea.

- 2 -
MiNNiE'S IDEA

WHAT HAD SPECK said? That she had been taught to swim *in case of an emergency*?

'Well then,' muttered Minnie to herself, 'an emergency it shall be.'

She turned and paddled clumsily to the middle of the lagoon, where she could not see or touch the bottom. 'Help!' she said in a very quiet voice. She stared straight at Speck as she said this. Three screecher birds, nesting on the top of some nearby trees, looked down at the girl with sudden interest. They liked it when they heard people say 'help'. It normally meant dinner was on the way.

But to their disappointment, Minnie seemed quite alive.

So they tucked their vast black wings back under themselves and carried on feeding lumps of meat to their young.

'Help!' said Minnie, again.

'What's wrong?' said Speck, scrambling to her feet and looking alarmed.

Minnie was good at winking, and now realised it was a useful skill to have. She winked twice then said: 'Emergency. I have a cramp and I must be saved by you, which means you have to get in the water—'

Speck's yellow eyes stared straight at her. She had caught her meaning, Minnie could tell. But Speck stayed right where she was; her training went deep.

Minnie frowned. 'I *said*, "Emergency".'

Speck bit her lip a little. 'Minnie Wadlow, you listen to me—'

'No, *you* listen to me, Speck. What about the first rule of all the rules, Speck? What about *that?*'

The first rule of all the rules was a very important rule.

In the event of an emergency, giants must do everything they can to save the lives of children in their care.

There was an entire chapter on the punishments giants would receive if they failed in this duty; some were quite inventive. Some were so dreadful that Minnie could never bring herself to reach the end of the sentence.

But however they varied at the start and in the middle, they all ended in the same place: the dungeon.

'Minnie,' said Speck, softly. 'I can't swim with you. I'm not allowed to. I don't think it's a good idea.'

'You're my *servant*,' snapped Minnie, frustration making her nasty. 'It's what *I* think that counts.'

'Why don't you wait until your mama or papa can bring you to the lagoon?' muttered Speck. 'There are no rules against you swimming with them.'

Minnie frowned. 'They're too busy to swim with me.'

The giant and the girl stared at each other for a beat. The water lapped against the edge. And then, quietly, Minnie said, 'Please, Speck.'

Because one day soon, we won't be together any more.

'Do you know what?' said Speck, after a moment.

'What?' muttered Minnie.

'From where I'm standing, you look like you're in the middle of an emergency.'

They grinned at each other.

'Looks like you're in trouble, in fact,' said Speck.

'Oh, I am! Terrible trouble!' Minnie cried, liking the sound of it. 'Terrible, terrible trouble!'

They stopped smiling for a moment. For at the same time, without putting it into words, they'd both realised that this was their way of dealing with their approaching ceremony. They wouldn't win the fight, but at least they could say they'd fought.

'Hold on tight,' said Speck. 'I'm coming in. To, um, *rescue you.*'

Speck took off her uniform with the excessive care of someone who didn't own another set of clothes. First, she unpinned the faded grey bonnet on top of her head. The white shirt, black skirt and brown shoes came off next. These were carefully folded and placed on top of a towel. She stood in a knee-length, threadbare cotton slip, with strange red flowers embroidered on the hem.

Minnie had never seen Speck without her servant's clothes on, nor without her bonnet. She blinked in astonishment at the strands of pure gold that ran through Speck's brown hair. Some of the women on Quake Avenue wore solid gold bracelets made from giant hair, but Minnie's mama said that was vulgar and allowed Speck to keep her golden strands, which Minnie thought was very kind.

'Hold on,' said Minnie. She lifted a dripping finger in the direction of Speck's uniform. 'That's too tidy.'

Speck frowned. 'Too tidy? There's no such thing, Minnie, not according to the Giant Management Company.'

Minnie explained: 'But . . . that pile of carefully folded

clothes looks like you cared more about keeping your uniform neat than actually *rescuing* me. They'll think you took too long to jump in. They'll say: "Why were you folding clothes, when you should have been swimming extra fast to save the child you are responsible for?"'

Minnie didn't need to spell out who *they* were. On the island, everyone watched the giants, all the time. Everyone was ready to report anything that seemed suspicious, in order to prevent another war. 'They' was anyone who wasn't Minnie or Speck.

Speck's eyes went wide, and she gasped as Minnie's words sunk in. She turned back to the clothes. Then it was Minnie's turn to gasp. For the first time ever, she saw the scars snaking around Speck's shoulders and upper back, narrow white rivers tracing their way through her pale, freckled skin.

'Speck?' she said, softly. 'How did you get—'

'Is that better?' said Speck.

Minnie tore her eyes away from her giant's scarred back and looked at the clothes on the grass. Speck had kicked them a little. Now they looked like they had been flung to the ground.

'Much better,' said Minnie.

Speck walked towards the lagoon again. The only other bodies Minnie had seen were those of her parents.

Her mother was so slender she looked like a gust of wind would blow her over. Her father had the hunched shoulders and soft belly of someone who spent hours at his desk. Her own body, with its weakened muscles, didn't feel like anything special.

But Speck . . .

All the giants in her picture books had guilty faces and bloated bodies. Yet Speck looked nothing like those giants. In the light, she was dazzling. Literally dazzling: the tiny yellow freckles on her skin were brightening into a sparkling gold in the sunshine. She didn't walk as if she knew this, though. She didn't move as if she was aware that she was covered with a glimmering sheen of gold. Like all the other servants, she had a shy, tentative way about her; as if every step had to be permitted.

Speck dipped one foot, and then another, into the lagoon. At the sight of her giant walking towards her in the water, gasping and smiling, wild wings of reckless jubilation stretched out to their full width within Minnie's chest. Under the cloudless sky she laughed and laughed.

- 3 -
IN DEEP WATER

Speck waded deeper into the lagoon.

'It's cold,' Speck gasped.

'I know.'

'It's soft,' Speck shrieked.

'That's the mud at the bottom,' said Minnie, wisely.

'I can't feel the bottom now,' said Speck, a few minutes later. 'I'm – I'm swimming, Minnie! Here goes! I'm really doing it!'

'Can you swim out to me?'

'I can try! It's been a while.'

Speck's swimming was good and fast. Once she reached the middle of the lagoon, where it was deepest, she began to tread water. As Speck was about eight feet taller than her, Minnie was used to always looking up into Speck's face. Now, in the lagoon, with both their faces just above the dark water, they were eye to eye for the first time in their lives.

For a moment, all they did was look at each other, each totally amazed by what they were doing. It was as if

their brains were being given endless electric shocks.

'Your face is big,' said Minnie, after a while.

'Yours is small,' said Speck. 'Although it has grown since I first met you, when you were three. Back then it was *really* small. I could barely see it.' Speck's voice had a rare teasing quality to it. Perhaps the water was making her reckless too.

Minnie giggled. 'Barely see it?' She liked it when Speck was in this sort of mood.

'Unless I crouched down and peered right into your face, and if I did that too quickly you would cry. I was basically looking after a tiny, pink, blotched crying blob with a mouth.' Speck looked right into Minnie's eyes with a boldness that would have got her into trouble if anyone else had seen. 'It was all quite unrewarding.'

The laugh that erupted from Minnie sent the screecher birds flapping from the nearest tree.

'Luckily,' Speck said, her smile growing a bit wider, until she was daring to show a tooth or two, 'you've grown more interesting, over the last few years. So I decided I wouldn't trade you in for another child.'

Minnie gave a delighted gasp at the joke. Trading Minnie in would have been impossible; giants had no choice about who they were paired with. As if *giants* had any sort of freedom like that! 'Very funny,' said Minnie.

'I'd like to see you try. Who would you have traded me in for? Hester? *Florin?*'

Speck gave a tiny grimace, and Minnie spluttered with happiness. At the sound of Minnie's laughter, Speck began to smile. At first, she did it with her lips closed, as all the servants were told to. Then her smile grew some more, and to Minnie's surprise she bared her teeth in a huge smile: the biggest Minnie had ever seen.

Minnie stopped laughing and began to whimper. Giant smiles *were* a lot to take in; so big, so beaming, so much emotion, so all of a sudden. And those teeth were *massive*, each one the size of an encyclopaedia. She stared at the teeth, a little frightened. How well, after all, did she really know her giant? What if Speck wasn't smiling, but grimacing? What was it the manual said? *A relaxed giant is a dangerous giant . . .*

She whimpered again. Had she done something incredibly stupid? Would Mama and Papa find her corpse in the lagoon later that evening?

Speck's eyes widened in concern. Immediately she stopped smiling and tucked those teeth safely away behind her lips. 'I hope I didn't frighten you.'

'It – it's okay. I just wasn't used to it.'

'I should get out,' said Speck, looking mortified, swimming to the edge. 'I should never have got in—'

'Please stay.' Minnie swallowed. 'I just wasn't expecting a smile that size, that's all. Not used to servants smiling. Come back.'

Speck glanced back at Minnie. 'All right,' she said.

For a blissful few moments, they said nothing, and floated in the lagoon as happily as lily pads. Minnie stretched out and sighed with happiness under the sun. 'How long can this emergency last for, do you think?'

'Well,' said Speck, instantly clicking into servant mode, 'you asked for help at exactly 11.05 a.m., and I told your mother we'd be back by 12.30 p.m. to get ready, and it takes us precisely twenty minutes to walk back, but we must allow for drying and dressing time, and depending on how your legs are feeling we should factor in some extra time for rest stops along the way—'

'Urgh,' said Minnie, shooting under the water. When she reluctantly resurfaced, Speck was still talking, but she heard the words 'forty-five minutes'.

That was ages! They could practically paddle around the entire eastern point of the lagoon, and she'd still have time to show her the baby turtles she'd seen in the roots of the yellow-moss tree.

Unfortunately, those were forty-five of the most deceitful minutes Minnie had ever known. They'd barely begun when it was time to get out. They dressed in the sun quietly, each reflecting on what had just happened. They had got away with it; they had swum together. Minnie hugged the secret to herself like a present.

They turned away from the lagoon, side by side, and started down the fern-lined path that would take them back to the main road. Minnie took in deep, appreciative breaths; she loved the perfume of the lagoon, the way the earth smelt when it met the water, the wildflowers and ferns that edged the entrance. In the winter, the island could be forbiddingly cold, and the lagoon froze over, but summer days by the water were her favourite, and, with her skin still pleasantly cooled, she felt miraculously comfortable. Even her limp was less pronounced.

At the end of the path were two things: a cheerful sign that declared the temperature of the lagoon that day. And a vast stone statue with ferns growing over her feet. The statue was of a female giant in a simple stone dress. She was nearly sixteen feet tall: taller than Speck. One of her arms was propping up a bent lamppost, righting it into position, and the other was stretched in the direction of the lagoon in an inviting gesture, as if to say, 'This way, please! Isn't life wonderful?'

Yet Minnie was still very careful not to look up into her face as they passed beneath her. For the statue had not been properly made. The child who had kissed her had not wanted to do it, had not had enough time to prepare. And so the statue's eyes still moved frantically, left and right, up and down the path. She saw Minnie and Speck, and stared at them both as they walked away from her, but she didn't say a word, for her mouth and teeth and tongue were stone.

- 4 -

'THERE'S BEEN ANOTHER ONE'

WITH EVERY STEP away from the lagoon, the air grew warmer. As Speck and Minnie turned towards Quake Quarter, heat pushed against them. By the time they approached the city gates, Minnie's limp was back, and Speck was no longer walking next to her but two steps behind, as law dictated.

Quake Quarter was their home: a gated, walled city built around the ruins of a large castle. There was only one way in and one way out, and that was through gates guarded by vicious dogs and men holding axes. The gates were made of thick reinforced steel. Both the walls and the gates were thirty feet tall.

This gated city was perhaps the only truly lovely part of the island left. So much of it had been destroyed by the Great War of 1803, and the earthquakes that had affected the island ever since. Compared to the rest of the island, Quake Quarter was a shining jewel of beauty, and the inhabitants worked hard to keep it that way.

Once or twice Minnie had gone with her parents to

visit Black Sand Beach, but beyond admiring the glittering dark shingle there was little else to do. Swimming in the ocean was out of the question: it was constantly churning and roiling, the water was freezing and there were shipwrecks in the treacherous depths from which planks of timber could come loose and knock you unconscious if you were foolish enough to risk a dip.

Those wrecks were all that remained of that long-ago giant invasion, and although Minnie gazed at the remains of their rotting hulls with fascination, she also found them difficult to spend too much time around; a permanent reminder of the invasion that had nearly destroyed the island. Mama and Papa clearly felt the same, and never wanted to linger either.

And so, beyond her lagoon visits, Minnie never left Quake Quarter. But she was used to her gated existence. Life was harmonious, if a tiny bit dull. Sometimes, privately, Minnie found the occasional small tremor, if it only brought down vases or pictures on the walls, a welcome distraction.

Besides, Minnie thought, glancing down at the shining cobbles beneath her shuffling leather sandals, there was beauty everywhere, even though her world was small. Wherever she looked in Quake Quarter there were bright flowers hanging from every wall and beam. There were working fountains which made nice splishy-splashy noises, and narrow side streets where you could play hide-and-seek.

They had just entered her favourite part of Quake Quarter – the part known as the Old Town. This was the bustling collection of cafés – including her favourite pastry shop – and restaurants and shops arranged in a pleasing circle of cobbled streets.

In the middle of the Old Town, rising above it, was a huge grassy mound. On this lay the ruins of a castle. Within the castle was the dungeon. As the sun moved slowly around, the shadow of the castle crept stealthily over the shops and cafés and the people.

The shadow served as a reminder that *it* – the castle, the dungeon, the darkness within – was constantly there. Despite the heat, the shadow brought Minnie's skin out in goosebumps as she limped in and out of it.

Yet at the same time, and this was what made it all bearable, the air was full of the scent of flowers, and the freshly baked almond and honey pastries Minnie loved so much. There were friendly things within the Old Town – the shiny cobbles, the friendly pastry chef, the splishy-splashy jets, and they were just enough to distract from the shadow, the castle and the knowledge of the large white bones within.

And, of course, there were the statues to admire, too.

These, unlike the woman by the lagoon, had thankfully been properly made. There was nothing to fear, none had eyes that moved, and so she liked to look at them.

Minnie had her favourites.

She liked the statue outside the pastry shop, which held out a large baking tray just over the entrance and created a nice shaded place where one could wait in comfort on a hot day for a bun.

In particular she liked the statue which had been used to repair the fountain in the middle of the square, from whose mouth erupted an endless stream. She had fond memories of dancing underneath it as a child, enjoying its cooling jet while her parents drank cocktails with their Quake society set.

Sometimes she even caught herself smiling at the statues, which was silly she knew, but was something she had done ever since she was a baby and couldn't bring herself to stop. As they passed it, she gave the statue in the fountain a tiny wave, for old times' sake.

In the late afternoon sun, the cobbles of the old streets seemed to gleam with excitement. Everyone in Quake Quarter was looking forward to Florin Athelstan's ceremony later that day, and it showed. There were fresh roses in the restaurant windows and everything gleamed and shone.

Minnie and Speck walked past a cramped shop, squished at the bottom of a bent brick building. This was the Old Town newsagent's, where everyone bought their papers and sweets.

Minnie cast a quick glance at the newspaper stand on the way past and stopped. 'There's been another one,' she murmured, in an awed voice.

The Evening Standard

LATEST KIDNAPPING ATTEMPT!

BEASTS FROM THE EAST TARGET SMALL DEFENCELESS MILTON YELLOWTONGUE

The seven-year-old Quake Quarter boy survived the savage attack, but barely. We gained an exclusive interview · · ·

Underneath the headline was picture of a small boy from her school, sitting squeezed between two shocked-looking parents on a large sofa.

'It says that the giant "forced open the shutter and got as far as putting his hand on Milton's bed before he was stopped by their guards".' Minnie shuddered.

'I expect he's lost that hand by now,' said Speck, flatly.

'Yes,' said Minnie, reading on. '"Mrs Primrose instructed for it to be chopped off this afternoon."'

Mrs Primrose, who all the islanders agreed was a sweet, loving and generous woman, was the boss of the Giant Management Company.

Minnie read on. 'Oooh – listen to this: "The fiend from the mountains, hellbent on his devilish plan, pressed his face up to the window, stared at Milton with his deadly criminal eyes, and called the boy a 'wrong un',"' she read.

She glanced over at her giant, and was surprised to see how panicked Speck looked. Mountain giants trying to steal children was nothing new; this was the seventh attempt this year, at least. So why did Speck suddenly look so fearful?

Minnie turned back to the newspaper.

'It says here that Mrs Primrose is considering enlarging the dungeon,' Minnie said. 'And installing a few more instruments of torture. And then she's going to post those hands back to the mountains, to send them a message. Clever Mrs Primrose,' she said. 'Do you think that might work, Speck? Do you think they'd stop trying to steal children, if they all knew that their hands would get cut off?'

'I don't think so,' said Speck, in a voice so quiet that it was almost a whisper. 'I think they're determined to find a child.' She looked as if she wanted to say more, then stopped herself.

All her life, Minnie had been fascinated by the immense difference between the mountain giants and the servant giants. For there were two types of giants on the island, and one could not be more different from the other.

There were the good ones – the servant giants, like Speck; born in captivity, trained to obey, decent and obedient and easy to control. These were the ones who did as they were told and never complained or fought back, not even when they were turned to stone.

Then there were the bad ones; who wormed their way into her nightmares and made her wake up in a hot, tangled mess of fear. The ones who escaped from the Giant Management Company's training compound (where all the giants lived, and were bred and then coached before they were paired with human children). They fought off every attempt at capture and hid away in the No-Go Mountains. It was these bad giants who kept trying to steal human children. No one knew why. Several times a year, they slithered down their mountain paths, scaled the city walls and attempted to kidnap a child. To date, none had been successful. But this didn't lessen the horror of every report, not least because the bad giants from the mountains, whenever one got caught, would never reveal *why they kept doing it*, or what they planned to do with the child if they were to get their thieving hands on one.

And they were clearly gluttons for punishment, because every single mountain giant who attempted to steal a human child was thrown in the dungeon, where they starved to death before being picked over by the screecher birds.

Yet this never seemed to deter their kin from trying again, a few months later. It was the sheer mystery behind it all which captured the feverish imaginations of the residents of Quake Quarter, who were desperate to know *why*.

'I wonder if this one confessed . . .' murmured Minnie, stretching out a hand to turn the page.

'You going to buy that, Minnie Wadlow?' snapped the grumpy shopkeeper, hunched over his crossword at the back of the booth. 'Otherwise you can keep your greasy hands off my goods, thank you.'

Minnie smiled apologetically, for she had no money on her that day, and she and Speck turned to go. As they walked, Minnie listened for the inevitable sound that always filled the air after a No-Go Mountain giant was caught.

Sure enough, within a few seconds they caught it; the moans of a giant in agony, coming from the dungeon at the top of the mound. The sound seemed to touch every shop and café beneath, just like the shadow.

Even though Minnie knew that the giant from No-Go deserved its pain, the moans were still dreadful to hear.

'Let's go home,' begged Minnie. 'It's awful to listen to.'

'It is,' said Speck, horribly pale.

They turned towards Quake Avenue, where the sobs of the giant grew mercifully quieter, until the sounds disappeared altogether.

- 5 -
MEDICINE

Quake Avenue was a wide, elegant street with the largest houses on the island. The roses that grew round the windows were fat and glossy. Here lived the island's grandest families, and within every house was someone who worked for the Giant Management Company.

There were twelve mansions in all, six on each side. The biggest belonged to Mrs Primrose and came with its own moat and drawbridge. She lived inside, with a wardrobe full of jackal-fur jackets for company. Her family had made its fortune, back in the day, by selling surplus giant stone to the neighbouring islands.

The second biggest mansion belonged to the Athelstans. It had sweeping lawns that ended at a large lake, where they held parties in the summer.

The third biggest mansion belonged to the Pershings, whose daughter, Hester, was Minnie's best friend. Mrs Pershing was involved in the training side of the Giant Management Company. She sometimes came home flecked with tiny droplets of blood. Mr Pershing worked in the finance department and was responsible for giving out large sums of money to various people, depending on what they did.

The fifth biggest mansion belonged to the doctor, Mr Straw, who delivered all the giants' babies, gave the servants medicine, and looked after the families who worked for the Giant Management Company. Strange scents would come out of his basement windows, where it was rumoured he had a laboratory filled with a thousand test tubes.

The sixth biggest belonged to the Lloyds, who owned the jackal-meat factory. They had neither a drawbridge nor a moat or a lake, but large, golden, snarling jackals on either side of their door.

Right at the end of the avenue was mansion number 12. This was the twelfth biggest mansion, also known as the smallest. Compared to the grand halls and manors around it, this house was but a stained tooth in the gleaming white smile of the avenue. It was smaller, shabbier, dirtier, covered in moss. The ceiling height was a mere fifteen feet. Weeds sprouted up through the drive. The carriage house was missing several roof tiles. All the windows had rotting wooden frames.

Here lived the Wadlows. Mr Wadlow also worked for the Giant Management Company, but not very successfully. His job was to invent something that might, one day, stop the earthquakes for good. None of his designs ever worked, and Mr Pershing from the finance department didn't seem to want to give him much money to improve them.

Minnie opened the door and went inside. They walked into the kitchen, and Speck reached for the can of coffee beans to make coffee for Mr and Mrs Wadlow.

'It's too tight,' muttered Speck, putting down the canister. 'Can't open it.'

'Let me try,' said Minnie.

'It's very stiff,' Speck said doubtfully.

Minnie reached for the canister, twisted the lid and popped it open.

'Easy,' said Minnie. 'Now don't forget to put the kettle on for the coffee. And I'll have some biscuits, when you're done. Bring them up to Mama's, will you?'

'Yes, Minnie,' said Speck, obediently. 'Thank you.'

Then, wincing a little from the pain in her legs, Minnie walked to the medicine cabinet in the downstairs bathroom. She took out a glass bottle on which was written in Mr Straw's narrow handwriting the instructions:

Minnie Wadlow: Painkiller and Muscle Strengthener.
To be taken _twice_ daily.

With movements that spoke of years of practice, Minnie put a syringe into the medicine bottle and pulled the plunger until its plastic barrel was full of a thick, murky brown liquid. She placed the needle against the slightly greased skin of her forearm. Then she quickly pushed the contents of the syringe into her arm.

Minnie counted for five seconds. She put the medicine bottle back in the cabinet and threw the needle in the bin. Then she limped through the dark hallway and up the large sweeping staircase towards Mama's dressing room. It was time to get ready for Florin's ceremony.

WHAT IS THE DRESS CODE FOR CEREMONIES?

FORMAL. These occasions are a chance for the entire island to come together and celebrate the triumph of humans over giants.

We urge every child to wear smart clothing that mirrors how special the day is.

- 6 -
'PERFECT FOR WHAT?'

THE DOOR TO her mother's dressing room was slightly ajar. Minnie pushed it open and walked into a large, wood-panelled room, which was elegant if you didn't look too hard at the moth-eaten rug on the floor or the long strings of cobwebs in the shadows. The shutters on its window were bolted against the sun. Only a tiny beam struggled through. In this spotlight a woman sat at a dressing table in a silk robe, plucking her eyebrows with slightly trembling hands.

'You're late,' she said, over her shoulder.

'Sorry, Mama.'

Mama sniffed. 'I can smell the lagoon water on you.'

'Sorry,' said Minnie, again. 'Shall I shower?'

'Absolutely not,' said Mama quickly. 'That's perfect,' she muttered, as if to herself, before smiling a little. 'No need to be anything but yourself, my delicious island pear. Wild and free, as nature intended.' She gave one final solemn look at herself in the mirror, then crossed the room to the wardrobe, from which she pulled out Minnie's dress.

Normally, girls attending their first ceremony got a new dress from the Old Town. But that wasn't possible for the Wadlows. *Not yet*, Minnie thought stubbornly. Instead, Mama had slashed and restitched an old silk gown of hers for Minnie. She draped it now over Minnie's head.

'You've got a little thicker around the waist since you last tried this on,' Mama mumbled through a mouthful of pins.

'Sorry,' said Minnie, again.

'I'll have to unpick this seam. Stand still.'

For a time they stood in silence in the one beam of sunlight.

'Are you cold?' said Mama. 'You're trembling. Did you spend too long in the lagoon?'

'No,' said Minnie. 'We – I wasn't in for long.'

Mama pulled back and looked deep into Minnie's eyes. Minnie felt like she herself was a lagoon and Mama was peering for something in her depths.

'Mama?' said Minnie, after a while. 'Is everything all right? Why are you looking at me like that?'

'Have you taken your medicine?' Mama said softly.

'Yes, Mama.'

'And did you wear sunscreen at the lagoon? I can't have you—'

'Burning. I know. Yes, I put lots on.'

'Good *girl*.' Mama's face softened. She reached down and tucked a strand of hair behind Minnie's ear, and Minnie felt a beat of love between them. Mama rarely touched Minnie, always saying she didn't want to make the pain in her body any worse, but once in a while she would put her arms around her for a light, brief hug. Minnie wondered if today might be a hug day.

Someone coughed behind them. The opportunity for a hug seemed to vanish. A thin man, his black hair standing on end, slouched in the doorway, despondently holding up a box Minnie faintly recognised.

'Well, that's that,' said the man, shaking it gently with a rueful look. 'My seismograph has finally given up the ghost.'

'But that's your most valuable possession, Papa,' said Minnie. She'd always loved watching it when she was a young girl, sending up messages from the earth, heralding the earthquakes with long black jagged lines.

'It was,' said Papa, smiling tiredly at her. 'But it was old when I brought it to the island, and that was fifteen years ago. And I can't afford a new one.'

'Maybe the finance department will lend you the

money to buy a new one,' suggested Minnie.

'There's a higher chance of screecher birds learning to sing like nightingales than that happening, Minnie Moo,' said Papa, ruffling his hair a little. 'Never mind. I'll try and fix it tomorrow. I think I can afford to wait a while – we haven't had any tremors for five months. Perhaps we've entered a dormant phase.'

'Can I help you fix it?' said Minnie.

'Of course,' said Papa. 'After we've all recovered from Florin's ceremony. What time does this one start again?' he said.

'Really, Keyton!' sighed Mama. '*Really?*'

'Six?'

'*Eight.*'

'Ah, yes. I thought it was eight.' He winked at Minnie. 'Nice time at the lagoon?'

'Yes, Papa.'

'Does it still have that badly made statue with the eyes?'

'Yes,' said Minnie.

'Dreadful business,' he said absent-mindedly, checking his watch. 'Well, I have an hour to add the finishing touches to this new design. I want to show it to a few of the chaps.'

'You *can't* take work to the ceremony,' Mama said. 'It

will make you look desperate—'

Papa shrugged. 'I *am* desperate. But I want to talk to them about this one. It wouldn't cost as much as the last one they rejected—'

One day, Minnie thought, as Mama pinched at the dress around her, Papa's luck would finally turn. All his inventions would get made, and they would stop the earthquakes on their island for good. But until then, his most recent design would probably remain on his desk along with all the others. *One* day, though, he'd come up with an earthquake-prevention machine that the Giant Management Company actually approved of.

Yet that was easier said than done. Mrs Primrose and the board of executives kept spotting things wrong with Papa's designs that Papa had not seen. One design was too complicated. One was too simple. One design was rejected because Papa had hastily sketched it in black ink, not blue.

But soon he'd get it right, Minnie was sure. The island would be safe, and the quakes would stop, and Papa would get paid that bonus he was always being promised. Then Mama and Papa would turn the ballroom, which had, over the years, become Papa's study, back into a beautiful room with a polished floor, and they would throw big parties like they used to when Minnie was tiny, and eat nice food instead of tinned jackal meat all the time, and the ceremonies would end and—

'Lift up your arms,' said Mama.

Minnie lifted her arms.

In the meantime, Papa kept scratching away on his ideas in the cluttered, dark, dusty ballroom, surrounded by papers and prototypes of his machines, getting by on the tiny Invention Allowance that they gave him.

Mama flapped a hand in the direction of Papa. 'Work if you must, but at seven thirty sharp I want to see you dressed smartly outside by the carriage house, with no ink marks on your face.'

He and Mama looked at each other then. Papa said softly: 'Nothing too fancy for Minnie.'

'Yes,' said Mama. 'Plain and simple.'

'Yes,' said Papa.

The air grew thick with secrets. Minnie looked from Mama to Papa, confused.

After Papa left, Mama braided Minnie's hair tightly, without bothering to brush it. Then she seized her by the shoulders and rotated her to face the mirror.

'Perfect,' said Mama, sounding delighted.

Are we even looking in the same mirror? thought Minnie sadly. In the gloom, the harsh black stitches that darted in and out of the pale silk made it look like someone had stitched through her skin. Plus, her hair had been scraped back so tightly it made her skin hurt, and her dark brown eyes almost bulged with the pain of it. And, Minnie had to admit, without a few tendrils framing her features, there was no getting away from it: her nose really did look a touch on the large side.

Everything about me, she thought with a sigh, *is either too small or too big.* The only thing that was a proper fit was her name: Minnie. She was the smallest in her classroom, the shortest child on the street. *You think I look perfect?* thought Minnie. *Perfect for what?*

'Do you think maybe we could take my hair down?' she asked.

'Absolutely not,' said Mama, firmly. 'Now go and have a rest, so you're able to enjoy the ceremony. There's dancing, you know, and you must take part in that. Hurry along. And don't open your bedroom window. Did you hear about that poor boy, Milton? Can't have that happening to you.'

'But they caught the giant who did it.'

'There'll be ten more like him, coming down the mountain path, you mark my words. Window shut. Off you go, love.'

Minnie limped away slowly, and lay down on top of the sheets on her bed. As she drifted in and out of a fitful doze, she thought she could hear, underneath the faint scratching of Papa's pen coming up through her floorboards, the sound of the jackals crying again.

- 7 -
RED BRIDGE

THEY *HAD* PLANNED to go to the ceremony by carriage, but the wobbly wreck that Speck pulled out of the carriage house clearly wasn't going anywhere. Mice had nibbled away at the seats. It had a bad case of wood-rot and one of its wheels was rotten and damp. Like almost everything the Wadlows owned, it was on its last legs. Their horse looked at them glumly.

'We'll walk,' said Papa.

Mama glanced down at her high heels and Minnie's cream dress. 'Our clothes will be ruined. What will the Athelstans think of us?'

But there was nothing else to be done. The four of them set off down the potholed drive; Minnie between her parents, Speck behind, as usual.

Despite it all, Minnie was still excited about their destination. Florin Athelstan hadn't stopped bragging about his ceremony for *a whole year*. She'd heard him boast about the food so much she could have recited the menu in her sleep. But it wasn't just the feast she was excited about. It was the location. The ceremony was going to be held somewhere entirely new. She was going to go from west to east. She was going to cross the river for the first time in her entire life.

In the Old Town, the moans of pain from within the dungeon had stopped completely. A single screecher bird perched on the castle's battlements, a lethal patience in its eyes as it stared down into the dungeon, watching whatever was happening inside. Screechers liked death throes.

The Wadlows moved out of the city gates and took the river path along the sluggish Five Bridges river, which was brown with waste from the jackal-meat factory and burbled, quite disgustingly, next to them the entire way. By the time they reached Red Bridge, all four were covered in a fine layer of grit thrown up by the carriages that went past them. As her parents checked their pockets for the invitation and tried to wipe the worst of the dust off, Minnie studied Red Bridge. It was the only surviving bridge of the original five that had given the river its name. Its blood-red masonry was crumbling. One of the statues that propped up its mid-section looked as if it was about to lose an arm. Yet as the sun set over the filthy river, Red Bridge took on a certain glamour. Covered in ribbons, adorned with flowers for the ceremony, it stretched before them like a path to another world. On either side of the bridge, large jackal-skin torches had been lit, from which flames roared and snapped at the oncoming dusk. Sounds of celebration reached them from the other side of the river; excited chatter, crystal glasses being clinked.

The fragrance of the flowers cut through the stench of the petrol-soaked torches. As they walked over, Minnie began to flicker with excitement. She'd grown up hearing about ceremonies. Now, finally, she was going to attend one.

HOW SHOULD I BEHAVE AT CEREMONIES?

Everyone is meant to be happy at a Goodbye ceremony. Sadness is not permitted. If you look unhappy, you will be sent home before your mood infects that of your classmates.

There is absolutely nothing to be sorry about, anyway. Everybody knows that giants and children can't stay together for ever. Wipe your eyes and don't be foolish. Now go and enjoy yourself.

- 8 -
THE RUBBLER DISTRICT

ONCE OVER RED BRIDGE, Mama and Papa rapidly disappeared into the group of guests that had gathered on the rough dirt square. But Minnie stayed where she was, and stared.

The Rubbler district was so different from Quake Avenue and the Old Town that it was hard to believe it was part of her island. She'd never been anywhere so full of nothing.

Well, nothing but rubble. Even the air was full of it; a dusty quality that made her eyes itch. *Everything* here was built from it. From the small cottages to the humble shops, the tiny tavern with its swinging rusty sign saying THE BROKEN BACK, and the stony paths that snaked between all these things, *all* were made from rubble – broken bricks and broken stones, jagged and rough.

She'd grown up catching glimpses of the rubblers – those hunched adults and stooped children – as they cleared away broken bricks after a quake. But she'd never stopped to wonder *where* they took the rubble. Now she could see it had been squirrelled away over here.

She looked away, towards the horizon, then instantly wished she hadn't. That sharp line of peaked mountains she'd seen from the other side of the Five Bridges river was now much closer. They were dark grey in the dusk and topped with bleached white trees, like teeth. For a moment she was sure the mountains were waiting to eat her alive.

The No-Go Mountains. Where the bad giants lived.

She took a tiny step closer to Speck, who seemed in no rush to leave her side either. When they were almost touching, she risked another look. The air that rolled off the mountains felt icy cold as it wound its way down the paths and puddled at Minnie's feet like a fog. Her heart began to hammer inside her chest. Because even though she was scared of the mountains, she felt a strange pull towards them, too, and that was the most terrifying thing of all.

On the other side of those forbidding peaks, she thought with a shiver, *are the dastardly child-stealing runaways of the island.* The reason every child's bedroom in Quake Quarter came with the strongest shutters. Why every family she knew had hired guards, and gave guns to those guards. Without them, the children would be stolen from their bedrooms as easily as apples were plucked from a tree.

Minnie felt the cold breath of the mountains against her face, and she shuddered again. 'Where are their sentries?' she wondered, almost to herself.

'Rubblers can barely afford to eat, let alone pay for guards,' muttered Speck. 'That's a privilege only Quake Quarter residents have.'

'But . . .' Minnie stammered, horrified, 'how do they stay *safe*?'

'Squash, madam?' A waiter had appeared at her side. Minnie took a glass of juice, then turned her attention to the party: a noisy group of adults and children, and around them, the giants. The good ones. Twenty-nine of them, silently waiting in a perfect square on the fringes of the gathering. Each giant was the property of a Quake society family, and Minnie knew them all by sight and name, for she had grown up with them, just as she had grown up with the children they cared for. Between each giant burned a flaming jackal-skin torch.

Walking around the servants were two officials from the Giant Management Company. In the dusk, their black uniforms and black caps made them look like shadows. Each held a long, leather whip and a snarling dog on a leash. As the officials walked between the servants, the giants straightened his or her back, or looked at the ground, depending on what they were told to do.

One official glared at Speck; his meaning was clear.

'See you in a bit,' said Speck, and she walked away quietly to join the others.

'What took you so long?' cried a voice in the crowd.

Hester looked dazzling in a shimmering coral gown Minnie hadn't seen before.

'Our carriage broke,' Minnie said. 'We walked. You look nice.'

'Three hours they spent on my hair,' grumbled Hester. 'Then they did my nails. It was so boring!' Even so, Minnie's classmate shone with prettiness, and next to her Minnie felt as badly stitched together as her dress.

'Florin seems happy,' said Minnie after an awkward pause, anxious to change the subject, and pointing at the boy who was the reason they were all there.

Through the bustling crowd came Florin Athelstan, swaggering and smirking, accepting the shoulder claps and arm punches his friends flung at him as he made his way towards the ceremonial table. This table was almost the same height as Minnie's house, and had been used for every ceremony since ceremonies began. When it wasn't being used, it was stored in a specially made hangar behind the jackal-meat factory. It took three giants to carry it.

Seated at the ceremonial table, as tradition dictated, was Florin's giant. His name was Sandborn, and he was currently the most impressive giant in society, the tallest, at nineteen feet, and without a doubt the strongest. The one every family in Quake Avenue had wanted for their own, until the Athelstans had made the highest bid at his auction and won him for their son's pairing. Sandborn the Mighty, they called him in Quake Quarter.

The closer Florin got to the table, the more his swagger left him. By the time he reached the legs of his enormous chair he wasn't smiling at all, and his handsome brown face was tense and pale. Nevertheless, he climbed the rungs.

When he took his seat opposite Sandborn a gong was sounded. The crowd fell silent.

'Dinner will now be served,' somebody called, and Minnie felt a thrill run through her entire body. The ceremony was well underway.

- 9 -
ROBIN SCRAGG

AT THE SOUND of the gong, Hester skipped off to find her parents.

Once Mama, Papa and Minnie found each other again, they walked to their places at a table on one of the furthest edges of the square, and Minnie eyed her fellow diners before she sat down. Mr Straw, who sold them Minnie's medicine, gave Minnie a tight nod then stared deep into her eyes, which was what he always did when they met. She looked quickly away, squirming. Also at the table were some shopkeepers Minnie recognised, and one or two adults she didn't. The boy at the foot of the table was so small and so still she almost didn't notice him at all: he was thin and grubby and solemn, in a yellow short-sleeved shirt with a few buttons missing. He barely glanced up at her, as he was busy staring at the food on the table instead.

Mama took her chair quickly, clearly glad of a chance to sit down after walking in heels, but Papa seemed to hesitate at the sight of the boy, who took this in with a quick, clever look; underneath his sunburned brown skin he flushed.

'I might be a rubbler but it's not catching,' he said wearily. 'You're safe with me.' Then he went back to staring at the bread rolls, as if to say, *The bread, on the other hand, is not.* Papa had the grace to look ashamed, before pulling out the chair next to the boy and indicating that Minnie should take it. Minnie sat down awkwardly, her badly made dress making it even harder than usual to move gracefully.

'Robin Scragg,' the boy said.

'Minnie Wadlow,' said Minnie, politely. Robin reached a calloused hand out, and she tried to take it, but he reached for the bread basket instead. Her cheeks flushed. He wasn't going to shake her hand, after all.

Minnie sensed, rather than saw, that Papa had gone very watchful on her left. *Not this again.* The way her parents acted so protectively around boys was hugely embarrassing. If only they knew how much boys always teased or ignored her, and how little she cared for them in return.

She turned her back very deliberately on Papa and studied the rubbler next to her.

She had never seen one so close-up, let alone sat

next to one. He was not like the boys in her class, who lived in the huge mansions of her avenue and had the soft skin, washed curls and pampered faces to prove it. Robin's head was closely shaved, and even though he was sitting down Minnie could see that his back seemed stooped and stiff: the typical posture of someone who had spent his life carrying buckets of broken bricks. And his hands . . .

Robin saw her staring at them. Then he very carefully laid them on the table. It was an unexpected gesture, and there was something graceful about it, even though his fingers were twisted and swollen.

'Is this your first ceremony?' she said quietly.

Robin coughed. 'Yeah. And hopefully the last.'

'How come?'

He jerked his head in the direction of the ceremonial table. 'I don't like eating around monsters.'

'*Monsters?*' Minnie gasped. 'You mean Sandborn? He's the most impressive giant of all—'

'He's a monster. They all are.' He hastily swallowed down some bread and reached for another roll. 'They're the reason I lost my—' He'd clammed up. Minnie glanced around the table. *Where are his family?*

'Smoked jackal?' A waiter hovered between them, handing out thick red slabs of meat. Minnie had no appetite, but she took some anyway.

'Look, I can see how, if you've never had your own, you might think of giants as monsters,' she said, gently. 'But they're really *not*. My giant looks after me. Which means my parents are able to devote themselves more to serving the island. My giant's a time-saver.'

'Oh, they serve the island, do they, your parents? Bully for them. How do they do that?'

'Well, if you must know, Mama helps those less fortunate than we are. She does very important charity work.'

'Oh, she's one of those do-gooders who comes here with hand-me-downs once in a while? Makes sure not to touch us while handing out ragged clothes and tins of jackal meat past their expiry date?' He shook his head mockingly.

Minnie ignored this. 'And Papa is an earthquake engineer.'

'What's one of those then?'

'He designs machines to detect and prevent the quakes.'

'They're working well,' came the sarcastic reply.

'Anyway, until his designs are approved, we need the giants, Robin. They help us fix things. They're very important, and you mustn't call them monsters, as it's not true and not nice.'

Robin chewed something without any obvious pleasure, then said, 'Stone's breath, you've been properly brainwashed, haven't you?' He began to mimic her. '*Not true and not nice . . . Very important . . .* These are lies you've been fed.' He wiped the jackal grease off his mouth with the back of his hand. 'The truth is, Minnie, they're monsters. Giants *invaded* our island, caused the war and brought the earthquakes with them.'

'Well, yes, technically that's correct . . .'

Robin, Minnie realised with a sinking heart, clearly knew his history.

'We wouldn't even *have* earthquakes if they hadn't invaded us,' he went on. 'The quakes started during the Great War and they've never stopped. The only reason I'm a rubbler in the first place is because of the quakes – and therefore them.' He jerked a fork in the direction of the giants standing around them, quietly, in the dark. 'You can put them in a uniform and call them servants if you must, but they're monsters. Ogres. They *all* belong in the dungeon, not just the ones who try to steal kids.'

Minnie's cheeks burned with anger. But in the next breath, Robin fixed her with hollow eyes and said,

'If it wasn't for them, and we hadn't been rubblers, my parents and brothers wouldn't have . . .'

Minnie finally guessed the final word.

'When?' she whispered.

'Remember that really bad quake a few months ago?'

Minnie nodded.

'We got sent down to a site too early. We should have waited it out, but we got told to hurry. It was an office block. I was getting a wheelbarrow; they went on ahead. An aftershock came along, the block collapsed with them inside. Never saw them again.' He looked, briefly, as if he was going to cry, then he blinked rapidly with the determined air of someone winding up an argument. 'I call them monsters because that's what they are.' He glared in the direction of Sandborn. 'And he's the biggest monster yet.'

Minnie felt pity for the orphaned rubbler boy, but she still needed to correct him. 'He's being *donated* to you. It's an act of kindness.'

'Kindness?' Robin's laugh was as broken as the rocks around them and turned into a ragged cough at the end, which went on for nearly a minute. 'If your lot really wanted to be kind, they could donate something that lasted.'

'What do you mean?'

'If the Giant Management Company wanted to be generous, they'd give us schoolbooks. Or, better yet, make the quake excavation sites safer so we can go down into the rubbler tunnels and not get crushed. Who knows? Maybe they could even help your dad build a machine that actually works.'

This boy, Minnie realised, hated not just the giants, but *everyone*. Angry resentment blazed off him like a force field. He spoke of humans with the same loathing as he spoke of the giants.

'Everyone's a monster to you, aren't they?' she muttered, annoyed.

Robin yawned. 'Oh, what's the point of telling *you*? A rich girl from Quake Quarter? You're *part of it*. You're born into it. You'll carry it all on, I expect. Your kids will have monsters and so will their children, and you'll be at all their ceremonies too, and this . . . this rotten way of life will carry on for ever. Giants and feasts and rubbling. On and on and on.' He put one of his twisted hands up on his scalp and rubbed at it, tiredly.

'You think everything and everyone is terrible, basically,' said Minnie, annoyed. In the space of five minutes, Robin had insulted everyone in her entire life – including her.

He gave a tiny grin then. 'Not everyone. I like my chickens.'

While she struggled to think of a response, Robin glanced at the untouched jackal meat on her plate. 'Aren't you eating that? Can I take it for later?'

'Go ahead,' she said, curtly, as he stuffed it into his pockets. Any pity she had felt for him had vanished. How dare *he* call Sandborn a monster! Why, that meant he thought that *Speck* was a monster. Her giant was worth a hundred dirty rubbler boys, she thought, brushing her eyes roughly. If he thought giants were monsters, and that the work her parents did was useless, that was because *he was stupid*. When it was *her* turn to donate her giant, she decided suddenly with conviction, she'd make sure the rubblers didn't get Speck at all.

She gave him a flash of contempt from her dark brown eyes, and Robin saw it, and for a moment he looked puzzled as he stared back at her, and then he shook his head and went back to his food.

And that was the end of their conversation. Minnie and Robin ignored each other for the rest of the meal.

ON TABLE MANNERS AT CEREMONIES

All island children above the age of eleven must attend Goodbye ceremonies, whichever neighbourhood or background they come from.

Dining with your fellow islanders is a wonderful way for children from all walks of life to build mutual respect. In that way, we can continue to uphold our traditions.

(Don't worry, there's no need to invite rubbler children to any of your birthday parties. We know this might make you feel uncomfortable.)

- 10 -
LOSS OF APPETITE

MINNIE COULDN'T TAKE her eyes off Florin. It looked like he had gone off his food completely. Even though he could have his pick of the silver platters in front of him with the finest, richest food, he wasn't eating any of it. Not a dumpling. Not even the tiniest of sips from the golden goblet in front of him.

What a waste, thought Minnie crossly. He should have been tucking in with gusto. That was the whole point of this final feast: it was traditional to gorge yourself at your ceremony.

Minnie had *never* seen Florin sit at a table of food and not hoover it up. But now, sitting high up at the ceremonial table, pale and clammy, he could only half-heartedly dip his spoon in and out of his bowl. Despite the merriment beneath his table, the flowers and the torches, the boy who'd spent the last twelve months boasting about this very night looked like the most miserable boy on earth.

In spite of her pity, Minnie was infuriated. As the first child in their class to turn twelve, Florin was also the first to have a ceremony. Shouldn't he be making it look easy for them all? They'd all be sitting at the ceremonial table sooner or later.

Sandborn, however, had been eating steadily since everyone had sat down. While he took nothing from the plate of jackal meat, he had no problem with the fruit, his jaw munching through the apples and berries like farming equipment ploughing up a field. But he ate with no enjoyment. It was his eyes that seemed more alive.

If he wasn't looking at Florin, he was gazing, one by one, at the other giants standing around him. They, too, returned his look in a quiet sort of way, as though they were full of emotion that couldn't be put into words. The officials from the Giant Management Company couldn't seem to stop Sandborn and the giants saying their goodbyes like this, even though they seemed furious about it and snapped and flicked their whips at the backs of the giants' legs repeatedly.

Minnie shifted uncomfortably. Her afternoon medication had worn off, the walk had exhausted her, and now her muscles and bones were cramping up. The sight of the whips and the guards made her feel a tiny bit sick.

She glanced at Mr Straw, the doctor, without meaning to. The healer was a scrawny man, who carried a cloying, sickly fragrance about him that spoke of many hours hunched in his laboratory. And even though he lived in one of the larger mansions on Quake Quarter, his tie had flecks of dried egg on it and his glasses were always smeared. Minnie couldn't look at him without thinking of the needles she had to stick into herself every day. Even though his medicine healed her, she felt ill at the sight of him.

It was actually a relief when the gong sounded for a second time. The guests sat up straighter, nudged each other, seemed to come to life. The older islanders were shaken awake from their naps.

Everybody fell silent. Even the guard dogs prowling the perimeter went quiet. An electric atmosphere spread through the crowd. The only things that moved were the flames of the torches as they twisted in the dark. Chairs were scraped back as everybody stood up. Only Robin Scragg stayed seated, ignoring every pointed look from the people around him.

Minnie got up too, placing both hands on the table for balance.

Then Sandborn got down from his chair. He uncurled all nineteen feet of himself. When standing, he was as tall as the waterslide at the lagoon. Quite a few people gasped. One of the dogs growled, but was silenced by a kick.

Then Florin got down from his chair. Together, the boy and his giant walked away from the ceremonial table towards the shrouded building a few feet away, the ground shaking a little with each step.

The guests, the guards and their snarling dogs, and finally the servants followed quietly, towards the final part of the ceremony.

NOTE TO PARENTS

Children will be paired with their giants until the child turns twelve, when the child will give their giant back to the island and kiss them goodbye. This will be known as the Goodbye ceremony, and it is obligatory for every family in Quake Quarter to attend.

Ceremony festivities must be funded by the family.

You must provide dinner for your guests, as well as security in case the servants choose to rebel. (Who can forget the bloody mutiny at Ivy Coles's ceremony back in 1912? A terrible business.)

For affordable loans for your child's Goodbye ceremony, contact our Finance Team at your earliest convenience.

- 11 -
SANDBORN IS STILLED

EVERYONE GATHERED IN a semicircle around the rubblers' broken school.

If I'd had Sandborn for my servant, Minnie caught herself thinking, *I'd have made the most of it.*

I'd have asked him to pick me up and hold me above his head with straight arms, so I could see right across the island, and I would have pretended I was flying.

Most of all, she thought with a ferocity that surprised her, *I'd have asked him to try to squeeze all the pain out of my bones.*

Night was falling now, but the faces around her were alert and awake. Some guests were looking a bit wistful, as if remembering their own long-gone ceremonies. One or two even dabbed their eyes with tissues. Minnie felt sick . . . and then guilty, aware she wasn't experiencing the excitement and pride that was expected of her. She glanced at Hester, who was standing on tiptoes to get a better view. *What's wrong with me this evening?* Minnie scolded herself. *I need to get a grip. It's a beautiful tradition.* Everyone said so.

She saw Mrs Primrose's eyes resting on her for a moment. The elegant old woman frowned. So she copied Hester's beaming smile and hoped it looked convincing.

Then a man walked through the crowd – a tall, elegant figure in a blood-red suit.

'It's only Melchior de Wit!' gasped Hester, craning her neck to see him. 'The most famous giant arranger on the entire island. Of course Florin would have him. *Everyone* wants him for their ceremonies. My parents are saving to book him for mine. Who are you having for yours?'

'Oh – we're just mulling that over,' said Minnie. But the truth was, they had no one booked at all. For whenever her parents tried to discuss her ceremony with her, Minnie would say her pains were bad, so she could be sent to bed and put the conversation off for another day.

Melchior's red suit reminded Minnie of the flames leaping around them in the dark. He nodded at Florin. 'Time for your speech.'

Florin gulped, but then turned to his giant. In a voice that shook, he said: 'Sandborn, you have protected me, raised me and cared for me well. You have served me properly, and I will . . .'

Everyone held their breath. Florin forced the rest of the sentence out: ' . . . always be grateful.'

Sandborn gave a small nod, then smiled at Florin with

his lips closed. For a terrible moment, Minnie thought Florin was going to burst into tears.

He can't cry, he'll disgrace himself, thought Minnie, crossly. But the truth was, she was scared that if he cried, so would she.

'Let's get you in your final position, shall we?' said Melchior.

At a nod from Melchior, the drapes surrounding the rubbler school were pulled down. Everyone could now see how broken the building was: one wall had fallen completely away, the upper floor sagged dangerously. Right in the middle of the school was a vertical hollow in which a metal joist had snapped in half.

'Walk into the cavity now, Sandborn,' said Melchior, 'if you would be so kind.'

Sandborn slowly manoeuvred himself into the space. Everyone watched with bated breath. But as the giant squeezed in, it was clear he was a perfect fit. Melchior the arranger was clearly a genius.

'One final thing,' he said, smiling widely. With a theatrical flourish, he beckoned to three assistants, who, huffing and straining, approached carrying a large stone carving. It was as wide as the three of them put together, and in the shape of a large open book.

'Pick this up,' said Melchior.

The giant picked up the stone book.

'Now, hold it just so,' said Melchior, indicating with his hands what he wanted the giant to do.

Sandborn held the stone book in his hands.

'Finest giant stone,' Melchior told the crowd. 'Made from a surplus of supply. Rather fitting.'

'Marvellous,' said Mr Athelstan.

'Now,' the arranger said to the giant in front of them. 'Look down at the book.'

Sandborn did as he was told.

'Try to look a bit less sad, Sandborn.'

Sandborn rearranged his features.

'Oh, wonderful!' gasped the crowd. For now Sandborn looked as if he was reading the book, within the cavity of the school, and appeared to be perfectly delighted about it too. What's more, now he was in position, the broken building stood straight.

'A monument to education,' said Melchior, proudly. 'And now he is in place, Florin, you may perform the final rite.'

At a push from his father, Florin climbed the scaffolding around Sandborn until he reached a wooden platform that was level with Sandborn's face.

'Eyes down, Sandborn. Keep them fixed on the book,' said Melchior. 'Don't look at Florin any more.'

Minnie's ears began to ring. Her stomach churned.

The air around her seemed too still, too heavy. Was this *really* for the good of the island?

She blushed at the disloyalty inside her, and plastered that big smile back on her face.

'I now call upon you to perform the Last Goodbye,' said Melchior softly. The crowd went extremely quiet. The older ones remembered their own ceremonies, and the giants they had done this to, and a few wiped away bitter-sweet tears.

Florin stepped forward. For a moment, he rested his face on the giant's cheek. Florin and Sandborn both closed their eyes.

And then Florin pushed his mouth forward and kissed his giant.

By the time he pulled his lips away, the process had already begun. It started at Sandborn's feet. Like a slow, winter tide, the cold grey colour swept up his legs and then his torso, turning his clothes and flesh to stone. The sound of his flesh hardening and thickening, splintering a little in places, filled the air – an eerie, strange sound that Minnie didn't much like, like twigs cracking as you walked over them.

Florin glanced away from the scaffolding, down towards his mother. But his mother firmly shook her head at him, and then Melchior seized his left hand and whispered something to him.

'You must believe,' Melchior whispered dramatically, and, in the hush of the night, everyone heard him. 'Tend to the process. Watch and have faith.'

Florin gave a tiny, miserable nod. Then he straightened his back and watched his giant, as the grey wash of stone reached Sandborn's throat. It crept upwards and, at the same time, inwards from his cheeks. Everyone looking on was completely transfixed – even those who had seen it many times before. It was a sort of magic, in a way. To watch something so huge and so alive become so still.

This is how it's always been, Minnie thought to herself, desperately. *He's helping rebuild the island, and making up for the invasion.*

She glanced at Speck, imagined it happening to her, knowing they only had ten months left together, and felt dizzy.

Sandborn's eyes, still obediently fixed on the book in his hands, were the last to turn to stone. Once they too turned grey, and every last eyelash hardened, there was a moment of silence. Sandborn had been stilled for ever.

Then the guests burst into applause.

Melchior looked at his watch. 'Under two minutes,' he announced. Everyone clapped again. 'Well done, Florin. Your belief was strong.'

'Good lad,' said Mr Athelstan, proudly. 'Let's open another crate of champagne!'

People began to drift away, but Minnie was too confused and upset to move, so she stayed where she was. When she next looked up, Florin had climbed down from the scaffolding and was lingering uncertainly on the ground.

Their eyes met.

The flickering shadows did not conceal the awful clamminess of Florin's face. He looked at Minnie, and blinked several times. Then he shoved his hands in his pockets and walked away quickly.

How strange, she thought in a daze. Technically, Florin had come down from that scaffolding a man. The minute you turned your giant to stone, that was the minute your childhood ended. But on the ground, in the shadow of the statue he'd just made, Florin Athelstan looked smaller than ever.

- 12 -
TIME FOR BED

THE CEREMONY WASN'T over yet. Tables were cleared and
the musicians began to play. Mrs Primrose began to move
through the crowd, pairing boys and girls and telling them
to dance together: another tradition. Minnie huddled
in the shadows for as long as she could; she hated the
thought of dancing with *anyone*.

She caught sight of Robin Scragg, scowling in her general
direction. She scowled back at him then looked the other
way. A few seconds later, Mrs Primrose reached her.

'Minnie Wadlow,' she said, her weather-lined face
strange in the shadows, although she spoke with her usual
gentleness. 'I'd like you to dance with that rubbler boy
from your table.'

As the other boys and girls began to dance with prim,
sedate movements they had learned in dance classes,
Robin scowled as he held his hands out. 'How do you
dance to this then?'

Minnie shrugged as she took his hands. He winced
a little.

'What's wrong with them?'

'Years of carrying buckets and digging out large stones is what's wrong with them,' he said, matter-of-factly. 'Let's just do one waltz?'

'Fine by me.'

After a few seconds, however, the music played by the violinists began to change and got quicker. A spark of enthusiasm flared deep inside Minnie, and she broke away from their position, threw her arms above her head and began to clap, much to the surprise of Robin, who took a step back and looked at her uncertainly.

The children around her were moving too slowly. The music demanded a faster movement; she knew this, completely. She shot a look of frustration at Robin – did he not feel it too?

She lifted one foot and then stamped it so hard on the ground that a little puff of dust came up. When she next looked for Robin, he had disappeared. Someone grabbed her hand, tightly. Her eyes flew open, delighted. *Maybe someone wanted to dance with her?*

But it was only Speck.

'You seem tired,' she said quickly. 'Time for bed. Come on.'

'But I don't want to go home!' Then she lowered her voice to add: 'I've only just started enjoying this ceremony.'

To her surprise, Speck tugged, hard, on her hand.

'Please,' she said, in a low voice. 'Come with me. I'll – I'll make you a hot chocolate when we get home, how about that? With proper chocolate flakes?'

Minnie rolled her eyes. 'We haven't got any cocoa,' she reminded Speck. 'And you broke the last mug yesterday.'

'I – I'll put it in a beaker, or a bowl,' said Speck, and she sounded so desperate that Minnie forgot all about the dancing. She felt a stab of sympathy for Speck. Maybe she was upset about seeing what had happened to Sandborn, a fellow servant, and couldn't bear to be around him any more? The next time Speck tugged Minnie's hand, Minnie followed her away from the dance floor, and back over the bridge towards the river path, leaving the party behind them. And under Sandborn's stone eyes, the people of the island celebrated another successful ceremony.

- 13 -
'I'VE HEARD IT WAS WONDERFUL.'

Now NIGHT HAD fallen, and Red Bridge was behind them, the air was a tiny bit cooler. Pools of yellow cast by the streetlights lay ahead of them. They followed them along the path as if they were stepping stones.

Minnie bit her lip. Why had Speck dragged her off the dance floor? Had she looked foolish? Was her servant trying to stop her from embarrassing herself? As they walked under a flickering lamp, Minnie looked up into Speck's face, and just as the bulb was at its brightest, temporarily blinding her, she saw Speck's face twist with concern.

'What's wrong?' Minnie said, blinking and stumbling as they walked back into the dark.

'Oh, nothing,' said Speck, but her voice sounded hollow. And then, as if to fill the silence, the giant added: 'You know, Minnie, in just under ten months, it will be us sitting at that table.'

'I don't want to talk about it.'

Speck said, softly, 'Did you not enjoy Florin's ceremony

then?' and there was a strange note in her voice, bubbling away like a secret in a pot.

'Not really,' whispered Minnie, after a while, as she thought of Robin, and Sandborn and Florin. 'It was strange. And sadder – sadder than I thought it would be.'

Speck said nothing, but, after looking over her shoulder, gave a small nod.

Minnie grew restless. 'Tell me about the island your ancestors came from, before they invaded this one. Do you know much about it?'

'I have heard that it was wonderful, from those who hand the knowledge down,' said Speck. 'There were sacred spaces where we sat in peace. There were wild spaces where we played. We had everything we could ever want.'

'You must be sad,' Minnie said, 'that you never saw it.'

'Very,' said Speck.

'If it was so wonderful, though,' said Minnie, growing thoughtful, 'why did you giants even bother invading us? Why did they come here?'

Speck said, 'I'm not sure.'

Minnie went on, the dark and the quiet working on her imagination. 'But . . . why would giants leave a place they loved to invade this island instead?'

But they had reached the city gates, and Speck clammed up like a shell, not wanting to be overheard by anyone. In the dark, the statues in the Old Town looked as if they were still alive, but sleeping. Minnie winced a little as she walked past her favourites, remembering how Sandborn had been stilled.

Would future children of the island shudder a little too, when they passed Speck's statue? Would they look up into her stone face and know, or care, that she had once looked after Minnie Wadlow, and swum in a lagoon for forty-five glorious stolen minutes? Or would they not even *see* her, would she just fade into the background, as so many of the statues did after a while? How would they ever know that Speck liked watermelon slices, and broke a plate every day, and had a specially soft voice if Minnie ever cried?

They reached Minnie's house by midnight. Their guard, Magnus, woke up with a snore from his sentry post, a plastic chair on the front porch. 'We're back,' said Minnie, softly. She quite liked Magnus, although she wasn't sure he'd be much of a match against any marauding, stealing giant from No-Go. By the time he'd stumbled to his feet and burped himself awake, the marauding giant would be long gone, no doubt with Minnie clutched tightly in their fist.

'Good ceremony?' yawned Magnus, opening one eye and fixing it blearily on Minnie.

'Yes, thank you.'

'Was the belief strong?'

'Under two minutes,' muttered Minnie.

'Very impressive. Hope he had a good send-off. Always did like Sandborn as a giant – respectful, obedient . . .' but Magnus had fallen asleep again.

They parted ways – Minnie to her bedroom, and Speck to the pile of hay that she slept on in the carriage house. Once inside her room, Minnie peeled off her ripped cream dress and let it fall to the floor with a grimace. It would always smell of jackal fat and torch smoke, she realised. *I never want to wear it again.*

- 14 -
GET-TO-THE-CASTLE

MINNIE COULD TELL it was late morning by the rich golden light that came in through the slats. She pushed down her tangled sheets and glanced down at her legs, wincing. Her skin looked like a glass of milk filled with angry red jellyfish – white and red and mottled.

She stumbled to the bathroom for her morning injection, then began to make her way downstairs. Even halfway down, she could hear Mama and Papa snoring. She walked slowly to the kitchen, thinking about last night's ceremony. Florin would be waking up to his first morning without Sandborn: what would that feel like?

'What's for breakfast?' Minnie's words were a bit slurred. When the pain in her body was at its worse, before the medicine began to work, walking was not the only thing that was difficult. At times like this she felt like a rubbler herself, hauling up words like heavy rocks from her throat. A memory of Robin Scragg hung in her mind for a minute, before she pushed the rude boy out of her thoughts.

'Breakfast?' said Speck, looking up from her coffee with a funny look on her face. 'You can have it later. How about we play a game of Get-to-the-Castle first?'

Minnie thought her giant looked exhausted; her bonnet was limp and there were dark shadows under her eyes, as if she'd been up all night. 'Speck, have you been to bed?'

'Ah, no,' said Speck. 'I was thinking.' Then she gave Minnie a bright, odd smile. 'Shall we play outside?'

This was all very strange. Speck never had trouble sleeping. Mama often grumbled that sometimes she had to bang a bell outside the carriage house to wake her up. Even her suggesting the board game was a surprise. Minnie loved Get-to-the-Castle, but normally she had to work hard to persuade Speck to play with her. Speck wasn't very good at board games, because all the pieces were too small for her hands.

Speck turned abruptly and walked out into the back garden.

Minnie limped after her, too surprised to do anything but follow, and her legs were immediately attacked by the tall, harsh grass that had sprouted up in the neglected yard. As Minnie had guessed, the day was hot and muggy. Yellow and grey clouds mushroomed across the sky. It was hard to understand Speck's excitement about being outdoors.

Because she *was* excited – or restless. She was *something*. She was bunching her apron up into her hands. The way she bustled off into the carriage house was quicker than usual. Moments later, she was out again, an old sunlounger balanced in one hand. Hurriedly, she swept the mouse droppings off it, then put down some cushions.

Slowly, Minnie tried to make herself comfortable on the sunlounger, and they began to play. The aim of the game was simple: each player needed to put all their opponents inside the dungeon, right in the middle of the board, before they themselves were captured. Whoever won had to shout, very loudly: *Get to the Castle!*

Usually, Minnie liked the shouting. But she also liked it for another reason. Unlike her, her counters never limped. She liked watching them as they moved, imagining they were her racing around the island. Because it was Minnie's world on the board. Painted on to the board game was the island itself. Most of the colours had faded, but all the lines were still visible.

It didn't take long for Minnie to take the winning lead. Speck was extremely distracted – she was almost giving the game away, and even though she stared at the board intently, she didn't seem to care if Minnie took all her counters or not. After Speck had miscounted her counters five times, Minnie put down her dice and stared at her.

'Can you make a bit of an effort, please? It's no fun if you just let me win.'

In reply, Speck heaved a huge sigh, rubbed her eyes, and then looked down into Minnie's face.

'Minerva,' said Speck, 'I need to tell you something important, and I need you to listen.'

Well, that had Minnie listening all right. Speck *never* called her Minerva.

'Now look. Please. We don't have much time, and this is important.'

'Look where?' Minnie asked, glancing around. 'Speck, you *really* need an early night—'

'Look here.' Speck jabbed a huge finger on the board, scattering all the counters, much to Minnie's disgust. 'I was about to win that,' she protested.

'The game isn't important. But the board is.' Speck's pale-yellow eyes burned into hers.

'Has anyone ever told you, Minerva, that there are caves behind the lagoon?'

Minnie shook her head.

'Well, there are.' The giant's words might as well have

been ringed with fire; they flew like meteors. Minnie wanted to dart between them to avoid getting burned. 'Take the track to the right of the lagoon and carry on walking down it. It will skirt the back of the lagoon, into what looks like a solid wall of bramble, where no one ever goes,' urged Speck. 'Then you'll see a cave mouth that leads to a network of caves and tunnels. Walk through the largest tunnel, right in the middle.' Speck pointed to the middle of the board. *Jab jab jab.*

But the morning injection was finally working and Minnie was growing drowsy. Everything was very confusing. 'Can I have a tiny nap for a minute?' she muttered.

'I'm sorry, but you have to listen. This is very important. Minerva, *please*.' Speck clicked her fingers in front of Minnie's fluttering eyelids.

Reluctantly, Minnie forced her eyes open. Those huge fingers that had soothed her brow when she was ill, taught her how to lace her first shoes, turned the pages of picture books – they were now tracing a route through two squares on her favourite board game, which seemed to have turned into a map.

Speck put the tip of her finger next to the painted lagoon on the board. 'The only thing you need to watch out for are the screechers. The cave mouth is very near one of their main lairs. You might find . . . rather a lot of them.'

'Screechers?' stammered Minnie, shuddering at the very thought of them. 'Can we just go back to playing the game, Speck?'

'If you make it through into the cave, you'll see three tunnels. Take the middle one.'

'*If* I make it through the cave?' shrieked Minnie.

'In the middle of this tunnel,' Speck went on urgently, 'you'll find a clearing. It's a safe place. There's a spring of natural water. You can sleep there, hide there, if you ever need to. None of the islanders know it exists.'

'Why not?' said Minnie.

'Because of the screechers' lair,' said Speck, quietly. 'They frighten them away. That's why you'll be safe there.'

Minnie stared, confused, at the face she'd known almost all her life. Confusion raced through her as she looked at the smattering of freckles on the bridge of Speck's nose, that one slightly wonky front tooth she had. She'd looked at that face every single day of her life since she was three. Everything about it was familiar apart from the words coming out of her mouth.

'I don't understand,' said Minnie. 'Why would I need a safe place? Why would I want to sleep anywhere that isn't my bed?'

'You just *might*. And if that's the case, you know where to go now, don't you?'

Then, to Minnie's surprise, Speck stood up, brushing her apron down.

'You remember that place, Minerva,' was the final thing she said to her that morning. 'And go there, if you need to. Tell *no one* else about it.'

'No one?' stammered Minnie. 'Not even my parents?'

At the mention of her parents, Speck made a tiny but distinct frown, which was *very* confusing.

'Definitely not them,' said Speck. 'No one. This is our secret.'

Minnie gasped.

Speck had the grace to look ashamed, but kept her eyes fixed on Minnie's. Neither of them spoke: Minnie because she couldn't, Speck because it seemed she had said all she wanted to. After a second or two, the giant touched her bonnet absent-mindedly, straightened it badly, and then went back to the kitchen. But Minnie stayed out in the garden, shaking a little from fear.

Because Speck had just asked her to keep a secret.

And that, according to the manual, was the worst rule to break of all.

WHAT SHOULD I DO IF MY GIANT BREAKS A RULE?

A bad giant must be pulled out of your household like a rotten tooth. If your giant breaks any of the rules within this handbook, inform your parents at once. Ask them to call our emergency 24-hour Bad Giant Helpline for affordable and prompt giant removal. Do not delay, dawdle or doubt. Do not, under any circumstances, hide your bad giant away and hope for the best. IT WILL NEVER BE FOR THE BEST.

Once the rot sets in, the rot will spread and that one bad giant will destroy you, and your family, and our way of life.

AND REMEMBER: if you do not inform us, we will sniff them out.

And then we will punish you both.

Have a wonderful day!

- 15 -
NOT THE BEST GIANT

MINNIE WASN'T SURE how long she stayed out in the garden after that. She glanced at the board game, now abandoned on the table like a discarded map. *Safe place. Tell no one.* All of that was wrong and, by the look of guilt on Speck's face, she knew it too.

Minnie hauled herself up and limped to the kitchen. She could hear Speck clattering around in the hall, possibly getting the vacuum cleaner out, and she was relieved to have the kitchen to herself. The manual was in its usual place, hanging from a rusty nail near the telephone. Even though she knew its contents inside out, she still wanted to check. Her heart beat a little too fast as she read:

ON THE QUESTION OF SECRETS

Giants must never ask any children to keep secrets, and children must never keep a secret told by a giant. Secrets

told by giants are usually lies and are almost certainly extremely dangerous to life and limb.

Any giant who suggests keeping secrets must be reported by you IMMEDIATELY. You will not be punished if you report them promptly. Your giant will be banished to the Forgetter. And then you must forget about them.

(You will be sent a replacement giant when stocks allow.)

Minnie felt sick at that phrase. *Banished to the Forgetter.* The dirt-lined dungeon right in the middle of the castle.

Her eyes filled with tears.

She had to tell Mama and Papa straight away. She knew that. Every child in Quake Quarter was drilled on that, from the moment you could walk; if your giant broke any sort of rule, you had to report them right away.

Speck would be marched out of the house immediately and thrown into the dungeon within the hour. Minnie would never see her again. But she'd hear her all right. She'd hear her getting weaker, every time she walked through the Old Town. And then she'd hear her silence too. And she'd see the screecher birds, circling around the castle, waiting to feast.

The vacuum cleaner spluttered into life out in the hallway, and she caught a glimpse of Speck pushing the machine up and down the old carpet, bending awkwardly over the contraption, which looked tiny in her hands. There was a funny, faraway look in the giant's eyes, as if she was busy thinking of something else.

Probably busy thinking of other ways to break rules, thought Minnie bitterly.

How had it come to this? She remembered, guiltily, the day before, and how she'd encouraged Speck to swim in the lagoon. Was that when the rot had set in? Or had it happened even earlier? From the off, hadn't they all been warned that Speck wasn't perfect? When Minnie had turned three, the official age at which families in Quake Quarter were given their servants, there'd been a fairly honest discussion about her giant's faults.

'She's not the *best* physical specimen on our books, I'm afraid,' said an official from the Giant Management Company. 'Look at her. Rather stunted, for a giant. Clumsy. But she's available and in line with your budget, and she'll do.'

'Only bad families make bad giants,' Mama had muttered, staring uncertainly up at the brown-haired giant standing shyly in their hallway.

'Exactly,' said the official, approvingly, taking in

Mama's beauty and blushing a little. 'Keep her on a tight leash, don't give her any slack, and she'll be fine.'

The Wadlow family had, as one, looked at Speck. What had they seen? Well, they'd seen a standard female giant, a bit shorter than they'd like, dressed in the customary Giant Management Company uniform.

'Her features are acceptable,' stated Papa. Speck's large yellow eyes had blinked a little, out of nerves. 'Show us your teeth.'

Speck had looked nervously at the official, who had nodded his permission. Speck had bared her teeth obediently. Minnie, who had just turned three and was easily scared, had cried.

'Nice and strong,' said the official. 'She'll make a great childminder, I assure you. Capable. Freeing you both up to do your work.'

Their eyes had lit up then, with dreams of making the island a better place. 'She does look strong enough,' said Papa. 'And Minnie . . . well, she'll get used to her.'

And what had Speck noticed? The small girl peering up at her, a weak-looking child with a big nose? Did she notice Minnie's dark brown eyes first, or the way she stumbled a bit as she walked? Or did she look at Mr and Mrs Wadlow first, and see their ambition and yearning? If she'd looked really hard – which she shouldn't have done, because staring at humans was not permitted – she might even have seen, in the eyes of the parents, a secret they didn't want anyone to find. But most adults had those. Besides, what Speck noticed was not of any importance. She was their servant now, and private thoughts were not to be encouraged.

Mama, who had just seen Sandborn being delivered to the Athelstans over the road, said, 'And you're sure there were no other options? No one more . . . impressive?'

'You *do* have the smallest house on the Avenue, if I may be so bold,' said the official. (Now it was Mama's turn to blush.) 'To be honest, I think you're lucky; none of our other giants would have fitted inside this hall. She's not been the quickest to pick up the training, but she passed all the tests, eventually. And a twelve-foot giant is the best one for your money, and your ceiling height.'

'Well,' sighed Mama. The mention of money sealed the deal. Even then, Minnie's medication was costing them all dear.

'If she gives you any trouble,' said the official, hurrying towards the door, for he had five more giants to deliver to families that day, 'give us a bell and we'll throw her in the dungeon and start again.'

And after that, the Wadlows had grown used to their giant's funny ways, in the same way they were used to their front door sticking on its hinges. It was just the way things were. Besides, privately, they all realised that Speck and Minnie had really quite a lot in common. Speck was short for her breed, and so was Minnie – the shortest of all her classmates. They were a good match. They understood each other.

After eight years together, they felt as comfortable around each other as it was possible to be.

So why had Speck ruined everything?

- 16 -
'DON'T LEAVE ME'

MINNIE WANDERED UPSTAIRS to get dressed, lost in unwelcome thought. Perhaps Speck had just been pulling her leg? Perhaps Minnie could forget it had ever happened? She imagined listening to the sound of Speck's cries filling the air in the Old Town, and shuddered.

But all her life Minnie had been taught that her loyalty was to the island, and not to her giant. She had to tell Mama and Papa. If she *didn't* tell, that would mean that she was protecting a bad giant. And putting the island in danger. Besides, they'd all be punished if it was ever discovered.

Speck stopped hoovering the carpet, and the house was deathly silent. Minnie had a sudden premonition of something dreadful coming their way. With tears in her eyes, she raised her hand to her parents' bedroom door.

And it rattled.

At first, she thought Speck might have just shut the cupboard door a little too violently when putting the vacuum cleaner away. But then it happened again.

This time, the entire door shook in its frame.

A *tremor*.

She knew what that meant. A quake was on its way. They always sent these little messengers on ahead. She'd been through enough to know that.

'Minnie,' said Speck, loudly. 'Wake your parents then come down here. It's a big one. I can feel it.'

And the odd thing was, so could Minnie. The air seemed to flex with the threat of it. She knocked loudly on the door, and shouted: 'Earthquake!'

The sound of snoring stopped abruptly and her parents' door flew open. Papa, wild-eyed, raced down the stairs towards the ballroom, followed by Mama, hair in dishevelled curls.

'Come on, Minnie,' said Speck urgently. 'We haven't got much time.'

All thoughts of what she'd been about to do, the secret she was going to reveal, were forgotten, and on shaky legs Minnie went down the staircase as quickly as she could, where Speck was waiting for her, looking worried but calm. Once Minnie reached her, Speck glanced at the front door, but when Minnie hobbled to the ballroom, Speck followed obediently.

The ballroom had once been a beautiful space with a polished floor, fitting surroundings for all the parties

Mama had hoped to throw. Now it was a dusty study where Papa kept his inventions and equipment.

Minnie stood in the doorway, waiting to be told what to do. This was the first time in her life that she'd seen her house shake so badly.

'Papa?' she whispered, but he was too busy staring at the broken seismograph with a stricken look on his face.

'If I'd fixed it in time – or had a new one – I could have warned everyone and—'

The glass in the window frames began to rattle so fast it drowned out whatever he'd been about to say next. Mama and Papa looked at the windows, then turned to Minnie, still standing in the doorway. 'Get under the table,' said Mama. 'Now!'

But Minnie couldn't run and she couldn't reach Papa's table in time. When she was halfway across the floor, a huge tremor threw her to the ground.

She heard the roof above her groan. She knew that only one more tremor lay between her and the entire contents of her bedroom falling on her. She braced herself for what she knew was coming next, and closed her eyes tightly. *Just let it be quick*, she thought.

But even as another shock rippled towards the house, and plaster and bricks began to thud on to the floor all around her, she remained untouched.

She opened her eyes and looked right into the upside-down yellow eyes of her giant.

'Speck?' Minnie muttered.

'The first rule of all rules, Minnie,' said Speck, smiling slightly, then wincing the next second as tiles and plaster began to thud on her back. Minnie realised that Speck was shielding her, crouched over her like a table. Tiles and plaster and bricks fell down around them, but Speck took the blows, and Minnie was safe underneath her. She wanted to cry with gratitude.

As the most violent earthquake the island had ever seen finally arrived, everything around and beneath them shook and tore and pulled, as if the muscles of a huge body were at war. Their dusty old house, in its defence, did put up a fight – Minnie could almost feel every brick and plank try to push against the forthcoming destruction.

'Speck . . .' she began, 'I'm scared.'

'Close your eyes, Minnie,' said Speck. 'I'm right here.'

'Don't leave me,' Minnie whimpered quietly, and there was a catch in Speck's voice when she said, 'Never.'

A terrible rain of bricks and planks began to fall all around them. Minnie curled up into a tiny ball near Speck's right arm, reached out an arm so she could touch Speck's wrist, and sent out a prayer that the quake wouldn't last too long. Then the world went black.

*

A woman coated with a layer of white dust appeared between Speck's forearms and leaned next to Minnie's head. Mama's mouth was moving, but Minnie heard nothing. Mama reached for her hand and squeezed it lightly. This time, Minnie heard something. 'Over. It's over.'

Speck slowly got to her feet, and Minnie followed. The ballroom looked as if it had been in the middle of a snow blizzard – an unfamiliar terrain of broken, splintered furniture covered in white plaster dust. Her ears rang. As she followed her mother and her servant out into the hallway, she saw the cuts and blood on Speck's back from falling masonry. Speck staggered a bit as they walked out on to the Avenue, where other families were gathering, shocked and pallid and covered in plaster and dust too. Whole pavements stuck up in jagged lumps, and trees lay across the road with broken carriages underneath them.

Those whose houses had not been affected as badly were beginning to shift into another gear: carrying blankets, boiling hot water on cookers for sweet tea. Minnie sat in a camping chair and drank and ate things that were put into her hand. People milled about or gathered in loose groups, muttering in shock. Through it all, Speck stayed nearby. Despite the cuts on her back and the plaster dust she was coated in, there was a strange sort of detachment to her, as if the earthquake was the least of her concerns. Whenever Minnie glanced in her direction, she would catch the giant staring down at her, as if seeing her for the first time.

It didn't take long for the oiled cogs of the Giant Management Company machine to begin to turn. Under the command of the Athelstans and Mrs Primrose, all the servants on the Avenue were organised into two long rows to begin to clear up the immediate debris from the quake.

With Sandborn missing and many of the giants bearing similar injuries to Speck's, the clean-up operation was a less-than-impressive sight, as the bedraggled giants began to pick up overturned carriages and straighten lampposts, wincing from their wounds and moving more slowly than usual. Even so, it wasn't hard to spot that, of all the giants, Speck was in the worst way. She shuffled between the houses in a daze, as if she was dreaming or lost in thought, periodically stopping to look back at Minnie, and only moving again when someone shouted at her or threatened her with a lashing.

Ordinarily, Mr and Mrs Wadlow would have rushed up to their servant to tell her to pull her socks up and stop embarrassing them, but they were far too busy having an intense discussion in the middle of the road to notice.

The ringing in Minnie's ears was still bad, but it had improved enough for her to be able to hear Mama mention the words 'Minnie's medication' several times. Her parents glanced at her, looking anxious, and then Mama said, 'Can you imagine the pain she will be in if she can't have her medicine?' She gave Papa a firm look. 'And don't forget her sun cream, either.'

Papa disappeared into the ruins of their house and reappeared with a few bottles. Even so, Minnie was slightly taken aback when Mama insisted she inject herself immediately.

'I'm feeling okay, Mama,' Minnie protested, mortified at the idea of doing it in front of everyone.

'Don't argue, Minnie,' said Mama. 'You don't want to have the complication of a seizure from not having enough medicine in your bloodstream. Not on top of everything else that's happened today.' And so Minnie injected herself with some more of Mr Straw's muscle-building medicine.

As dusk fell, the Athelstans invited those who couldn't return to their homes to spend the night in their garden.

Lots of Minnie's classmates began to pour on to the lawn, where large tents and camp beds had been put up by the servants, by now staggering with exhaustion. Florin, who looked pale and somehow aimless, seemed grateful for the distraction, and within moments he and some of the children were starting a game of tag around the lawn.

By evening Minnie's eyes were heavy, and she longed to sleep. The residents of Quake Avenue sat around a makeshift campfire eating canned jackal casserole. The servants were organised into sentry duty on the Athelstans' drive, to keep an eye out for No-Go giants while the children got ready for bed.

Minnie and Hester put their camp beds as close to each other as possible. Then they turned and, under the night sky, faced each other.

'Have you heard what the grown-ups are saying? Around the fire?' Hester whispered, eyes glowing with the satisfaction of having the gossip, as usual.

'No?'

'This is the worst quake on record.'

There was a pause. 'Shame your Papa wasn't able to spot the quake coming,' said Hester, casually. 'That's his job, right?'

Minnie felt a spark of embarrassment and fury on his behalf. 'He probably would have been able to, if *your*

Papa had given him a tiny bit more money for the latest equipment.'

The two girls glared at each other for a minute. Hester sighed, then turned on her back and stared up into the dark sky.

'Minnie?' she said eventually. 'Do you know what a fast-track ceremony is?'

'No. Why?'

Hester shrugged, then closed her eyes. 'It's just another thing they've been saying a lot.' She yawned. 'I *really* hope there aren't any raids by the No-Go giants tonight.'

'The servants will protect us,' said Minnie loyally, thinking of Speck, even now standing out there and keeping her safe.

'My mama doesn't seem to think that every servant is as frightened of the bad giants as they should be. She says she's even intercepted a few notes, here and there, written by the No-Go giants for the servants.'

'What?' gasped Minnie. 'Notes?'

'Two notes in fifty years, apparently.'

'What did they say?' Minnie gasped.

'No one knows, because they were written in Giant.'

Minnie's mind swam. She refused to believe that giants like Speck – kind, dutiful Speck, who had just saved her life – would ever communicate with the most evil beings on the island. 'But our servants are – good giants.'

Hester snorted. 'The only really good giant is a stone giant, Minnie, and don't ever forget it.'

A few minutes later Hester was snoring.

Minnie closed her eyes and rolled over too, desperately tired. Yet despite her fatigue, what Hester had just told her kept her awake for a few hours more. *Were* there notes flying back and forth between the bad and the good giants, and, if so, why? And why had Speck behaved so oddly all day – both before and after the earthquake, even risking a whipping because of it?

And – as if all that wasn't enough – what *was* a fast-track ceremony, and why did it sound so bad?

- 17 -
MRS PRIMROSE'S REQUEST

It didn't take long for Minnie and Hester to find out. After a makeshift breakfast of crackers and jam the next morning, Mrs Primrose appeared on the lawn. She delicately clapped her hands together, and said: 'Can all the children follow me, please.'

Like obedient ducklings, Minnie and Hester and all the other children in the dew-dropped garden followed the sweet old lady to a semicircle of rugs and blankets. 'Sit here, my darlings,' said Mrs Primrose. The children sat. They knew Mrs Primrose well, and loved her. She had weathered, lined skin that reminded the children of all the long lazy afternoons they had spent in her garden, eating cake and singing songs about the island, songs about community and sacrifice and pulling together. She was like family.

Now, she adjusted her green silk turban, then smiled round the gathering with affection, and all the children smiled back and felt happy.

But then Mrs Primrose's smile faded. 'Yesterday's quake

was the worst in our history. The level of destruction it left has never been seen before. There's not a part of the island that hasn't been affected.'

The children nodded, hypnotised by Mrs Primrose's soft brown eyes. 'We have all suffered. We have lost homes. We're frightened. And there's no shame in that.'

One or two of the younger children, not even ten yet, cried a little, almost in relief, and she watched them and nodded. 'The good news is, little ones, there have been no casualties. Not one death. *But –* and here, her eyes seemed to glisten with tears. Watching her, the children suddenly wanted, very much, to do anything to stop her tears. No one could bear for Mrs Primrose to be sad.

Mrs Primrose dabbed at her face with a pretty little hankie. ' . . . But our much-loved island has been very badly hurt indeed.'

A collective sigh came from the children at the thought of their island being hurt, and that poor Mrs Primrose had had to witness it.

'I've never seen such destruction. Almost all the roads are smashed. Your school has been broken; every shop, café and ice-cream parlour; barely one single building has survived. Even the cages down at the jackal-meat factory have broken, and the jackals that didn't die are on the run.'

Minnie shivered. *Jackals on the loose?*

And here Mrs Primrose reached for her tissue and had a tiny little weep herself. This was more than the children could bear.

'What can we do to help, Mrs Primrose?' said Hester, quietly.

'Well, Hester, I'm very glad, and very proud of you, that you asked me that. Because you can help us. All of you can help us. We need you to give us something sacred, earlier than you ever thought you were going to do it.'

Minnie's stomach churned with a terrible sense of doom.

'Our island needs us to come together. The only possible way that we can rebuild it, and carry on with our happy lives here, is if we are prepared to make difficult sacrifices.'

And Minnie suddenly understood what a fast-track ceremony was.

*

Mrs Primrose put her hankie away in a very expensive-looking handbag, then regarded the children gently. 'Normally, my darlings, when it comes to . . . your ceremonies, you are given a whole six months to prepare. We believe it's important to have that time so that you are ready, emotionally, for turning your giant to stone and taking a step into adulthood.'

Minnie dared to hope.

'Usually,' said Mrs Primrose.

Minnie gulped.

'But this is not a usual situation. We need giants to be donated *tomorrow*. If we wait six months, there's a chance that all the damaged buildings will continue to collapse, and that could be very dangerous indeed. To put it simply, these are desperate times. We need brave children, and we need giant stone.'

Mrs Primrose regarded the children solemnly. 'I think you know what I'm asking of you all, don't you?'

Hester put her hand up again. 'I do!' Minnie wanted, just for a second, to throw a cushion at Hester's face. 'You want us to donate our giants straight away, don't you?' said Hester. 'You want us to turn them to stone as quickly as we can, to fix all the broken buildings.'

There was a gasp from the children who hadn't worked it out yet. Mrs Primrose nodded. 'That's exactly right, Hester. Clever girl! It's not what I want – but it's what the island *needs*. We need to skip the preparations and go straight to donations. Starting tomorrow.'

Everybody sitting down realised what that meant. They'd all be turning their giants to stone within the week. They'd all be giant-less. A ripple of shock and sadness ran through the children, but looking at Mrs Primrose's much-loved face, they understood that this was the only thing to do, if they wanted to save their island from destruction.

In the gentlest voice they had ever heard, Mrs Primrose said, 'Is that all right, children? Do I have your co-operation? Will you give your giants back to the island, and help us save one another?'

Next to Minnie, Hester nodded so hard Minnie was surprised her head didn't fall clean off. And all the others nodded too, and so did Minnie, but only because everyone else was nodding.

Mrs Primrose began to tell them all where their giants were being donated, and when. It took a while for her to work her way through the alphabet. Minnie Wadlow was almost gnawing off her fingers by the time it got to her turn. By then, almost all the children had been told where their giants were going, and they had begun talking softly among themselves. A few had even wandered off.

The sweet old lady fixed her brown eyes on Minnie. Minnie looked back at her, churning with despair and a flicker of suppressed rage. Mrs Primrose looked right into her eyes and gave a startled blink. Then she shook her head and consulted her paperwork again.

'We've decided to use Speck to fix the eastern side of the city walls,' Mrs Primrose announced. 'Congratulations, dear. That will be nice for you – you'll see her every time you go through the Old Town.'

Minnie smiled automatically, unable to reply. It took all her effort not to burst into sobs. Mrs Primrose's indulgent look vanished, and she gave Minnie a slightly pointed stare. 'Well?' she said. 'Don't you want to know when your ceremony has been scheduled for?'

'Yes, Mrs Primrose,' said Minnie meekly, slightly ashamed of herself.

'Tomorrow.'

'T-tomorrow?'

'Indeed,' said Mrs Primrose. 'I know it seems soon, but perhaps it's best to get it over with. The quicker the better.' Then she gave Minnie a funny sort of smile. 'It might even be a relief for you, one might say.'

'A . . . relief?' Minnie wondered if her ears were still ringing.

'She was rather substandard in the height department, wouldn't you say? Let's hope she makes a better statue than she did a giant. Now, why don't you go and see if you can borrow a hairbrush, Minnie?'

And with that helpful bit of advice from Mrs Primrose, the conversation was over.

ON THE ISSUE OF 'LOVE'

You must learn to live with your giant in a PROPER
and SENSIBLE way. It's very, very easy for children
and giants to develop a bond over the years; after all,
you will spend every day together, and your giant will
teach you some important things.

You will feel fondness for your giant.

But you must not mistake that for love.

Remember: they are your servants. They are <u>not</u> your
family. And they do not belong to you, nor you to them,
for they belong to the island.

You must NEVER think of your giant as anything
more than a servant who you respect.

IF YOU FIND YOURSELF FEELING AFFECTION FOR YOUR GIANT
THAT IS STRONGER THAN THAT FOR YOUR MAMA AND PAPA, WE
STRONGLY SUGGEST YOU IGNORE THOSE FEELINGS, BURY THEM
DEEP INSIDE YOU, AND NEVER FEEL THEM AGAIN.

- 18 -
THE LAST CONVERSATION

MINNIE STAGGERED AWAY from Mrs Primrose, blinking back tears. Everyone was milling about, discussing plans, organising themselves. The islanders, she realised, were happy now that they had something to focus on.

But all she could think about was finding Speck. If she could see her, talk to her and listen to her voice, she might be able to breathe a bit better. Did Speck know she'd be turned to stone tomorrow? Or was Minnie meant to break the news to her herself?

She got as far as the pavement when she felt a hand on her shoulder. 'Found you,' said Hester, panting slightly. 'What are you doing out here? Why did you leave the garden?

'I'm l-looking for Speck.' Minnie was uncomfortably aware of how wobbly her voice was, and apparently Hester noticed it too, because she raised an eyebrow.

'You're not upset about the fast-tracking, are you, Minnie?' There was a small bite to Hester's voice. 'Because if you are, it would seem like you might have a . . . an inappropriate level of fondness for your servant.'

'Upset? Me? No. I just . . . um . . . wanted to check that she'd cleaned her bonnet. She looked a bit bedraggled yesterday,' said Minnie, as casually as she could.

'Oh, I wouldn't worry about that. I'm sure the Giant Management Company will spruce her up for your ceremony. Anyway, I've been told to come and get you.'

'Why?'

Hester flinched at the impatience in Minnie's voice. 'B-because it's school time. There's lessons on the lawn, now.'

Minnie looked yearningly over Hester's shoulder, where she could just make out a line of giants, right at the end of the Avenue, going into Mr Straw's house. It was easy to spot Speck – she was the shortest and she was nearly drooping from tiredness.

'Minnie Wadlow,' said Hester, warningly, 'don't make a fool of yourself. If you start calling her name now and crying, you know that your family will be *fined*, don't you? And Mrs Primrose will say that your parents didn't bring you up properly. And then your dad will lose his job. And then you'll all probably end up working as rubblers. Do you want that to happen, Minnie?' Her eyes bored into Minnie's. 'Do you?'

Minnie shook her head slowly, and reluctantly allowed herself to be led back to the lawn.

*

The rest of the morning and afternoon passed in a blur of shock. The children were kept occupied with back-to-back outdoor lessons, which focused mostly on the events of the Great War and the names of the islanders who had died in glorious battle. Minnie could barely concentrate, but managed to nod in the right places. All she could think was: *tomorrow*. When the lessons finally ended, it was nearly dusk, and Hester and some of her classmates went to the bottom of the garden to build a den.

Minnie was about to follow them listlessly, for want of anything better to do, when she glanced up the lawn and saw Speck standing shyly by the side of the Athelstans' house. She looked dusty, and was swaying on her feet from tiredness, but the minute she saw Minnie, she smiled and waved.

Minnie went to her as quickly as she could.

'Hello,' said Speck quietly.

'How – how did you get away?' said Minnie, after a moment.

'I said I needed to use the bathroom. Then I just kept walking.' Speck sounded weary. 'I wanted to see you.'

'Me too,' said Minnie, and then she couldn't say any more, because she was worried she would cry, right there and then. Instead, she just looked up at her giant, taking in every last freckle on her face. Up close, Speck looked awful. Her uniform was ripped and covered in grime. Under her eyes were huge shadows.

'How are you feeling?' asked Speck. 'In yourself?' That funny look was in Speck's eyes again.

'I feel – I feel all right, thank you,' said Minnie, uncertainly, too aware that her heart was full of emotions that she wasn't allowed to feel, let alone put into words.

'Do you feel – different, Minnie?'

Minnie frowned, then nodded. 'Yeah,' she said. 'Obviously. Everything's changing.' Speck's eyes widened.

Minnie felt a pang of remorse then. Speck didn't even know. 'Do you . . . know? About the—' She forced herself to say it. 'About the fast-track? Our ceremony?'

Grief flew over Speck's freckled face and then disappeared as quickly. 'I do know,' whispered the giant. 'Tomorrow, they said.' There was a pause. 'Is it . . . true?' whispered Speck.

Minnie hung her head. 'That's what they told me, too.' One tear rolled down her nose.

Speck started to speak, stopped, and then started again. Her voice was gentle. 'Don't cry, Minnie. It was always going to happen, wasn't it? We knew this day would come eventually.'

Minnie took a deep, shuddering breath and whispered: 'I know. But . . . not just yet. We were meant to have more time.'

'There you are!' a voice shouted. Speck's head whipped round, and she went instantly still. For an official from the Giant Management Company had reached the top of the drive. The woman frowned and began to hurry towards them.

'They found me,' said Speck, sounding disappointed but not surprised.

Minnie estimated they had thirty seconds left with each other before the official reached them. She had so much she yearned to say. Speck also seemed agitated, and at the sight of the woman approaching them, she looked down into Minnie's face and said, urgently: 'Minnie, I need to tell you something. Ever since I can remember, I've heard rumours about a child—'

The Giant Management Company official reached them, a woman with long black hair tied back in a tight ponytail. 'That was a long bathroom break, Giant 581.'

'Her name's Speck,' muttered Minnie.

The woman frowned at her. 'She has no legal name once she's assigned a ceremony date. Anyway, is she bothering you, Miss Wadlow?'

'I-I asked her to stay and talk to me,' stammered Minnie. 'To run over some details for our . . . um . . . fast-track ceremony.'

'Ah, good idea. Well, don't let me stop you.' But the official stayed right where she was, idly cleaning her fingernails. 'You have one more minute.'

Minnie's heart sank. This was their last chance to speak, and this woman had robbed her of the chance to say anything else.

Minnie looked up at Speck and tried to stop her mouth from trembling so much. 'Did – did you want to finish telling me something? Something about a child?' she asked.

But Speck shook her head quickly, a flash of warning in her eyes. Then, in a strangely formal voice, her servant said: 'I look forward to our ceremony tomorrow, Miss Wadlow. It will be an honour to serve the island earlier than I thought.'

'Quite,' said the woman in the uniform.

Speck's eyes burned into Minnie's with an earnestness that would have pleased the official. Only Minnie could detect the hidden urgency burning bright within her pupils.

'And, if I may say so,' Speck said, a curious, almost calculating look on her face, 'I look forward to making this island a *safe place*.'

Minnie frowned as something began to ring in her mind. 'A safe place?'

'Exactly, Miss Wadlow. A *safe place*. Like the one I showed you yesterday morning. Remember?'

'Oh!' said Minnie suddenly, looking into Speck's grimy face. 'Yes! I do.' The memory of the board game, of Speck's insistence, hung between them for a moment.

The Giant Management Company official checked her watch, and then cleared her throat. 'Now I must relieve you of your servant, Miss Wadlow, for we're going to the Old Town. We need as many giants as we can to help with the broken drainage system underground. Come along,' she said, addressing Speck. The woman flicked a whip idly.

For an entire second, Minnie and Speck looked at each other.

'Goodbye,' whispered Minnie.

'See you tomorrow,' said Speck. And then, with one more look from those yellow eyes, full of a message Minnie couldn't decode, her giant trudged away.

Minnie was left shivering in her wake, as grief and misery tumbled through her. That was the final conversation they'd ever have, and it had been frustratingly confusing, full of unfinished sentences and strange hints.

In a daze, she returned to the Athelstans' garden, where people, she saw with a burning outrage, were still wandering around, acting as if everything was fine, laughing gently, discussing what they might make for dinner.

Stupid. They're all so stupid.

She stared at them all from the middle of the lawn, and felt her breath begin to come in quick gasps. If she didn't escape for a while, she would burst into confused, exhausted tears right in the middle of everyone, and then she'd have to lie about why she was sad, and she wasn't convinced she'd do a good job. What if everyone guessed the truth? That she didn't want her ceremony to happen so soon? That would get her family into a whole heap of trouble. Hester's troubling words replayed in her head: '*Mrs Primrose will say that your parents didn't bring you up properly. And then your dad will lose his job. And then you'll all probably end up working as rubblers . . .*'

I need to be alone, she thought. *Just for a bit.*

She needed somewhere to hide out until she could get a grip on her emotions. But where? The Athelstans' garden was full of people.

Home. It was quake-damaged, but empty, and that was exactly what she needed. She glanced around the lawn. Everyone was busy. Mama was in a little huddle of women, drinking tea. Papa was nowhere to be seen. Most of the children were playing. No one would notice if she went missing, just for a little while, in the dusk.

She slipped away and hurried home. Turning up her drive, she was dismayed to see Magnus stationed outside the front door of their house. 'What are *you* doing here?' she stammered.

He pointed to the front door, hanging by a thread in its frame. 'Guarding your house.'

'Why?'

'Thieves. You'd be surprised. If there's no lock on an empty house, they'll come. Usually at night, but the bolder ones might try their luck in daylight.'

'Who?' said Minnie.

Magnus shrugged. 'Some say the rubblers are quite light-fingered.'

Minnie thought, suddenly, of Robin Scragg and his calloused hands.

'Well,' she said quickly, trying to step round him into the hallway. Magnus put a firm hand on her shoulder, and she had to fight the urge to flinch.

Magnus said, 'You shouldn't be going in there by yourself. It's not safe.'

'But Mama sent me,' said Minnie, surprising herself

by how easily the lie came out. 'To fetch a pan from the kitchen. For the volunteers. They're making coffee and, um, ran out of milk pans. I won't be long. I won't step on any loose floorboards. I know the drill.' She felt her mouth tug downwards, a sure sign she was going to cry. 'Please.'

He glanced at his watch. 'Fifteen minutes and that's *all*.'

Once she was inside the hallway she breathed out heavily and closed her eyes. Finally. A dark, familiar place. Space to think. Her tears came, and she let them. She had to turn Speck to stone tomorrow? It felt impossible. Even *Florin* had visibly struggled at times, and he'd had six months of lessons beforehand. How would she manage with so little warning?

And what if she didn't do it properly? Shuddering, she thought of the blinking statue outside the lagoon, whose eyes were always searching the path for the child she'd once cared for. She couldn't do that to Speck.

Or Mama and Papa.

At the thought of her parents, she bit her lip. Unease twisted through her, at the memory of the table they'd been placed on at Florin's ceremony, how far away it had been from everyone else. In her mind's eye she saw the furrows on Papa's forehead, all his beautifully detailed designs fading away to nothing on his desk in the cluttered ballroom.

If she messed up her ceremony, the Wadlow name would be a joke, for ever, and they'd never fit in. *Papa might even lose his job. They'd struggle to feed themselves. Hester was right. We're on thin ice as it is.*

One thought bubbled up, sudden and sure.

I can't do it.

The best thing Minnie could do for *everyone* was to delay the ceremony until she could perform it properly. Until she was able to stand on the platform like Florin, and tend to the process, until it was done. For if her faith was sprinkled with doubt and resentment, they'd all be left with a faulty statue on their hands.

But how can I delay the ceremony? Minnie asked herself in desperation.

It was as though there was a whole other Minnie inside her, and this version had been waiting for the right time to take over, and that time was now. It was this other Minnie that replied, calmly, *The ceremony can't take place if I'm not there to perform the final rite.*

Minnie gasped, examined the thought, and realised it was true. Giants only turned to stone properly when kissed by the child they had looked after. If she wasn't there to kiss Speck, then . . . the ceremony couldn't go ahead. She wouldn't bungle it. She wouldn't doom her giant to a terrible existence like the statue by the lagoon; still alive but not able to move an inch.

Her eyes fell on an old canvas rucksack of Papa's, hanging on a coat hook in the darkened hallway. The other Minnie said, as calmly as if she'd decided it a while ago: *I have to run away.*

- 19 -
MINNIE'S PLAN

EVEN THOUGH IT was her idea, she trembled all over from fear. Yet that other Minnie began to reassure her. *We're not talking for ever. Just till it's safe to have a giant again.* Perhaps she could hide away until all the buildings had been restored, and the emergency was over. That might only be a week.

Maybe two.

Maybe three.

Maybe longer. But we can play that by ear.

'Seems like a plan,' one version of herself whispered to the other.

In the safety of her house, almost anything seemed a better idea than taking part in a fast-track ceremony that she was in no way prepared for.

She was doing this for her family's honour. It was actually a noble thing to do.

Now for the most important bit. Where would she run away *to*?

Beyond the lagoon and, most recently, the rubbler

district, she knew the island very little. Like most Quake Quarter children, Minnie left the city gates rarely, and *never* without her giant a few steps behind her.

She glanced around the dark hallway. Where could she *go*? She closed her eyes, trying to imagine a way out, and in her mind's eye saw the walls of Quake Quarter closing in on her like a straitjacket.

Remember. There is somewhere you can go.

With a sudden burst of realisation, Minnie had the answer. Speck had told her, hadn't she? She had shown her, on the board game. She had even hinted at it again, out on the Avenue, just now. *A safe place.*

Had Speck known the quake was coming all along? How was that even possible? Or had there been another reason she'd told her about the safe place? Either way, Minnie was incredibly grateful now.

She forced herself to concentrate. *Where was it?* She tried to remember the route Speck had shown her on the board. The dirt track by the lagoon that led to the caves, hidden by bramble.

That's where I'll go, she thought.

She'd never ever run away before.

How did you do it?

She'd have to get some things, and she didn't have long. There were only about nine minutes left before

Magnus came looking for her, and if he found her packing a rucksack with clothes, the game would be up.

We'd better be quick then.

That stealthy part of her, the *other Minnie*, took over. With laser focus, that cannier, more composed Minnie began to plan.

I'll need food. Clothes. Torch. Bedding. Stay warm, stay fed, stay hidden.

She quietly eased Papa's bag off its peg and trod carefully up the middle of the damaged staircase and towards her room.

Part of its floor had fallen through. Through the hole she saw the remains of her bed, splintered on the ballroom floor. She felt a twinge at the sight of it: *it broke over Speck's back. She saved me.* In the room itself, the contents of her chest of drawers were spilling out. She eased out what she could from the tangle, careful not to get too close to the perilous hole. Comfortable trousers, long-sleeved tops – these went into the bag. She bent down and retrieved her torch, and that too went into the bag. She tried to get to the bathroom to find her toothbrush and toothpaste, but the way was blocked by a massive pile of roof tiles. She'd just have to go without.

A voice inside her said: *Now food.*

She tiptoed back down the stairs and walked as quietly

as she could into the kitchen. The quake had thrown cupboards off the walls, scattering cans and packets of food all over the floor. *Hurry.* She crammed the rucksack with whatever came to hand: tinned jackal meat, canned peaches, packets of biscuits, matches, a can opener. The bag was much heavier now, and made her limp more pronounced.

She went back into the hallway.

And then she remembered. The most important thing of all.

Her special pain-numbing, muscle-building medication.

She couldn't bear to think of how she'd suffer if she forgot to take it.

In the bathroom, many of the glass bottles had smashed across the tiles, but right at the back of the cabinet she spied a box with at least a week's worth of bottles and needles. She tiptoed her way carefully over the shards and grabbed them.

And that was that. No more room in her bag, no more time, nothing else to do now but flee.

She glanced out through the doorway at the evening's shadows and her heart thudded. The fact it was dark could make it easier for her to slip away, but it also meant people would be looking for her, right now, for dinner. She'd have to move quickly if she was going to do it.

- 20 -
WHERE ARE YOU GOING?

OUT ON THE porch, Magnus gave her a suspicious look.

'Where's your saucepan?'

'Huh?' Minnie blinked.

'For your milk?'

Oh yes! She improvised. 'In my backpack. Thought I'd pack some tea and biscuits too. For the troops!'

Magnus perked up at the mention of biscuits, and Minnie knew she needed to end the conversation before he asked for a brew himself and she found herself trapped.

'Better get going!' She gave him the brightest smile she could, and then stepped away from the porch, hoping he wouldn't look too closely at her suspiciously bulging backpack.

She stopped for a moment and tried to work out her route to the lagoon.

I need to make it down the Avenue without being spotted, then through the Old Town. Then once I get to the river path, I'll be safe. No one walks there when it's dark. Unless . . .

What if the giants from No-Go were walking up the

path on one of their night-time kidnapping attempts? She felt icy-cold at the thought of it. Would she have enough time to get to the place that Speck said was safe, or would she encounter one of them? And what if she did? What would they attempt to do to her? Turn her into a slave? Roast her on a spit? Everyone had different theories about why the No-Go giants kept trying to steal children, and each one was worse than the one before.

Don't think about it or you'll never leave, said the calmer Minnie inside her, and Minnie paid attention.

She hurried down the broken pavement, silently thanking the earthquake for cutting out all the electricity on the Avenue. All the streetlights were broken, and the dark gave her extra space to hide. For a breathless five minutes, the only sound was that of her own breath, and the cans of food clanking against each other in her backpack.

Unfortunately, she hadn't bargained on the Giant Management Company official walking her way. A young man with a ruthless pale face under a severe buzzcut, his dark uniform was clean and immaculate. He stopped sharply at the sight of her.

'You're the Wadlow girl, right?'

Minnie nodded and hoped that would be enough.

'And where are you going in the dark?' said the official, his cold eyes boring into hers.

'Back to the Athelstans',' said Minnie, as calmly as she could, pointing up the road, thankful she hadn't gone very far just yet, hoping the man couldn't hear the words

LIAR LIAR LIAR

booming around in her brain.

'Well, you'd better hurry,' came the reply. The man glanced up and down the shattered road with a practised look. 'Night's coming, and there are all sorts of bad giants out on the loose.' He walked away, laughing softly, and Minnie hurried on.

She walked as slowly as she could, and counted to thirty before checking over her shoulder. When she was sure the official had gone far enough in the opposite direction, she crossed the road and limped on as quickly as possible. Once she'd reached the end of the Avenue without any further encounters, she let out a jagged sigh. Now she understood why she had never run away before. She was pretty sure she had just taken at least twenty years off her life expectancy. It was *exhausting*.

Sticking to the darkness, she entered the remains of the Old Town. Moonlight showed that the once pleasant cobbled streets were broken and full of construction debris. Buildings leaned dangerously. She saw the remains of her favourite bakery, the roof utterly destroyed, all the glass shattered, and felt a twinge of sadness. There was no denying that what Mrs Primrose had said was true. Quake Quarter *was* in pieces – and would take many ceremonies to fix.

Minnie hesitated outside the broken fountain. Her favourite statue – the woman in the fountain, under whose stream she had played as a girl – was totally shattered, lying in pieces within her dry basin. Those broken lumps of stone were all that remained of a giant who would never breathe, walk or live again, Minnie thought suddenly, and she felt the wave of unfathomable grief coming towards her, as grey and overwhelming as the city walls. But this was how things had always been done. Why cry now?

Grief and confusion swirled inside her.

I am not up to this.

But she swallowed hard and forced herself to walk past.

- 21 -
FIRST THE RAT

THE MOON WAS full and the night was warm. Minnie wondered when Mama and Papa would notice her absence, and what they'd do next. Would they go home to try to find her there? Yes. Would Magnus tell them that she had paid the house a visit, just twenty minutes earlier? Yes. Would he remember that she had been carrying a heavy rucksack when she left? It depended how much beer was in his bloodstream, but he might.

And then what? They'd know she'd run away, and they'd guess why. Her heart gave a painful lurch. They'd come looking for her. But they wouldn't know *where* she'd gone. So she just had to get as far as she could before they started their search. She hurried as best she could, and was just congratulating herself on thinking things through so clearly, when she stopped, confused.

She'd reached the city gates – or, at least, where they used to be. But there was no way they'd be opening now to let her out tonight. They were covered in a mountain of rubble, so high it blocked out the moon. It towered over her; it would take two hours to scale, at least, and she didn't have the strength do that, not with her legs . . .

There was no way out. She was stuck within the Old Town. Her plan had failed.

Then she saw something brown and fast shoot past her and climb over the rubble. She watched the rat scamper, deftly and fearlessly, up the rocks, and she thought: *If a mere rat is brave enough to climb, maybe I can too.*

She'd better stop talking to herself and get on with it. Mama and Papa would almost certainly be at home by now. She didn't have long.

She put her hands on the nearest big stone and, panting slowly, pulled herself up and over. It wasn't easy, and her muscles complained, but she gritted her teeth through the agony as she carefully climbed, testing each stone carefully to check it would bear her weight.

Minutes passed, then an hour. Her body ached and all her muscles were moaning in protest. She had to stop often, to catch her breath and ease the burning pain inside her muscles, but, after a sustained effort of climbing, the top of the mound was in sight. Her legs were shaking and she was drenched in sweat, but she'd made it.

She was just about to congratulate herself when she misjudged her next step and slipped down, scraping both legs and palms on the jagged edges of the stones in the process. She cried out, and was horrified to see flashlights below her, darting around the broken courtyard and fountain. Holding her breath, not caring about her injuries, she awkwardly clambered as close to the back of the mound of rubble as she could, and flattened herself behind it, like a child hiding behind a tree in a game of hide-and-seek.

Trying not to make a sound, she watched as the flashlights flew up and down the pile of rubble she had just climbed. Torchlight picked out where she'd been only seconds before. Were they on to her already? A fear she had not thought possible, that seemed too large to contain, bloomed open inside her. 'Whoever they are, they're islanders,' she tried to reassure herself. 'Even if they spot me, the worst they'll do is send me back to the Athelstans' garden.' But a deeper part of her was more frightened than she thought possible.

She held herself in a twisted, uncomfortable position behind a pile of broken roof slates, hunched and bent, and for a few agonising minutes she tried to stay as still as she could. *Please go away*, she silently pleaded with the people below. To ease the pain, she had to shift her weight and move her right foot a tiny, painstaking millimetre, and to her horror the brick she stood on wobbled and made a scrape that was – to her – deafening. It must have given her away – to her, the sound seemed to boom around the entire street.

She held her breath. They must have heard her. They'd know where she was. She even felt an apologetic smile begin to form on her lips as she waited for the torchlight to move towards her.

But as her heartbeat quietened, no beam of light sought her out. Ears straining to detect what was happening, she realised that the people below weren't looking for anything but the chance to talk privately. In the still of the night, their voices carried. Minnie stayed still and listened.

'Did you find anything?' said a woman.

'A few shoes I might be able to flog, from the boutique,' said someone else. 'Leather, I think. You?'

'There was a broken coffee machine under some bricks,' said her companion. 'But I couldn't get at it. Shame.'

'I've heard they're asking for people to go and guard the archives and records centre,' muttered a woman. 'The one in the middle of that boggy old swamp. You don't need any experience, they said. And it's good money. We should go there.'

'They'll want proper guards, though, not cleaners and skivvies like us,' replied her companion, a tired-sounding male.

'Did they say what we'd be guarding, if we got given the work?' asked a third voice.

'Course they didn't. They're all secrets and riddles, that lot. You would think, after a quake, what with all these old, bad giants wandering around stealin' children, they'd step up security on the streets, not send islanders to a toxic old swamp no one passes through. What they got in there that's so valuable, anyway?'

Her companions barked with weary laughter. 'Fancy pencils? A couple of old filing cabinets? Who knows – and who cares? They're paying cash, I heard.'

'Let's head there now, before the others find out,' said someone. 'Can you imagine the rush there, if the rubblers hear of it?

'All right.'

Their searchlights gave one last hasty sweep of the mound of rubble, stopping a few feet short from where Minnie stood, and then, to her intense relief, they walked away, and their footsteps grew quieter.

She was alone again. She stood and stretched as best she could, easing her aching limbs. As she turned to climb unsteadily over the mound, what she had heard played over in her mind. The archives must be important if the Giant Management Company wanted to guard them. A *boggy old swamp*? Where was *that*?

Carefully, Minnie picked her way down the other side of the mound, congratulating herself with every step. Through the bricks poked a stone arm, sticking out of the wreckage. This meant she had passed the stone giant that had marked the city gates. She averted her eyes from the arm of the statue. She was officially out of Quake Quarter!

She stepped off the last broken slab and stood on the solid earth of the river path, breathing heavily. She would not have believed any of this possible – not for little Minnie Wadlow with the wasted muscles. But she had done it! Despite trembling all over, she couldn't stop feeling a bit proud of herself as she looked back at the peaks of rubble she had just scaled.

I did it all by myself, Speck!

She was out of her neighbourhood. She was officially a runaway.

She shifted the backpack on her shoulders and began to walk south, towards the lagoon. And as she walked, a pair of eyes tracked her progress, and soft, deliberate footsteps began to tail her, in the dark.

- 22 -
ANOTHER SET OF FOOTSTEPS

SHE'D *NEVER* BEEN so far away from home before by herself, let alone in the *dark*. To walk anywhere without the sound of Speck's footsteps behind her was like walking without a shadow. She stopped, suddenly. The space behind her felt too empty. There was that grief again.

The night was quiet, bar the sounds of the river moving thickly past the riverbanks, and a few crickets chirping in the undergrowth. There were no shouts of her name, no grown-ups coming up the river path behind her. *They haven't found me yet.*

But she couldn't take her safety for granted. Her eyes darted automatically to the dark night sky, in which she could see – or thought she could – the mountains of No-Go.

Fear and adrenaline made every shadow come alive. Every time a leaf moved across the path, her heart stopped. What if she was seconds away from feeling a huge bad hand grab her around the middle and lift her up into the air?

I have to keep going. I'll be harder to catch if I'm a moving target. Remember where I'm going.

She took a deep, shaky breath, and began to walk.

In the shadows behind her, she thought she heard someone padding softly.

She whirled around and stared, terrified, into the shadows. No one. She shook her head, gulped, and walked on. By her calculations, she had just five more minutes on the path before she could dart up the fern-lined path towards the lagoon, and then she'd be nearly there. At the caves. With the . . . screecher lair. She swallowed. Hopefully they'd be asleep.

Still she heard, occasionally, a stealthy padding behind her. *It must be my imagination. Either that, or I'm mistaking my heartbeat for footsteps. There's no one there. I've checked.*

She reached the lagoon path, the scent of ferns and its cool dark waters already detectable. With a burst of relief, she remembered her torch, and brought it out of her rucksack. The beam shed a comforting ray over the path and brought it back to familiarity. At the sight of the ferns, silver-grey in the dark, she breathed for the first time in what felt like a million years.

I've reached the path, she told Speck, inside her mind. *Like you asked me to.*

She could imagine the small smile Speck might have

made. *I knew you could, Minnie. Now keep going – not much longer!*

Just the thought of Speck made her feel less alone. She put one foot on the path, then the other, and began to walk through the darkness towards the water. Behind her, the ferns seemed to reach towards each other, as if to shield the girl and pull her closer towards the lagoon.

But, a few seconds later, something parted the closed ferns again with insistent legs and made the crickets stop their singing and look around. For these were footsteps they were not used to hearing, and they were startled. *The island*, they said to each other quietly, *is changing*.

- 23 -
PAD, PAD

HALFWAY DOWN THE lagoon path, Minnie could no longer fool herself. There *was* someone behind her. She could hear the *pad, pad, pad* of stealthy footfalls. It *definitely* wasn't her heart.

Itcould only be a giant from the No-Go Mountains.

All I can do is face them, she thought.

She turned, dreading the sight of a large fist reaching towards her, and the face of evil not far behind it. She braced herself. 'I – I know you're there,' she stammered in the dark. 'What do you want?'

But – again – there was no one. She felt foolish and intensely thankful at the same time.

Clicking her tongue against the roof of her mouth, she limped on. Then the noise started again. *Pad, pad, pad.*

She whirled round one more time, looked blindly above her, and saw nothing but the night sky. And then she stopped. Her breath caught in her throat. There *was* someone behind her all right. She'd just been looking in the wrong place. She'd been looking up. But she should have been looking down.

From a spot just a little in front of her knees, two yellow eyes stared at her. Then blinked.

The eyes were so low down that they could not belong to a giant. They could not belong to anything but . . .

An animal?

The small growl that just then rumbled out of the dark spot was full of threat and loathing. An accompanying stench – a musky, pungent smell – made her heart pound in her chest. Then there was a low but distinct howl, a sound she'd grown up hearing, and finally she knew what had followed her down the path.

It was a *jackal*. A wild, feral, stinking jackal. She'd never seen one loose on the island before, but she knew how it had escaped. The earthquake had been so bad, it had destroyed the jackal-meat factory. Mrs Primrose had told them: *The jackals that didn't die are on the run.*

An awful image flashed before her. The picture – the one that was plastered on every can of jackal meat on the island. The one that showed a terrible creature with bared fangs, snarling from a cage, lips curled back in a ferocious grimace. Now there was one standing right in front of her, with no cage between them to keep her safe.

'Easy,' she murmured, taking one step back, then another. The growl got deeper. 'Easy there.'

When she'd been thinking through the dangers, she hadn't even thought about jackals, which she now realised was completely stupid. What a terrible runaway she was! She hadn't even packed a weapon. She was completely defenceless against this beast, who surely would try to kill her before the minute was out!

A tiny, high-pitched whine came from the animal. Some part of Minnie's brain registered this, and she thought: *sounds like a young one*. She caught a whiff of its musk. It must have been on the run for a while; she could hear it panting, felt the heat roll off its body.

Her torch flickered weakly, and she didn't dare shine it in the animal's face. It was too dark for Minnie to see anything but the gleam of the creature's eyes, but her imagination did the rest: the teeth it must surely be baring, the saliva dripping from its chops as it sniffed her flesh. *If it's been on the run since the quake, it won't have eaten.* She was clearly its prey. There was a certain justice to that, she supposed – for years, jackals had been consumed by humans, and now it was her turn . . .

She sensed the jackal come nearer, felt its hot breath through the fabric of her trousers. *No point in running.* Not with her legs, her limp. When it came to speed, it would surely beat her. And, if she ran, wasn't there a risk she could make the attack even more ferocious?

All she could do was hope her death would be swift. Minnie braced herself for the pain of its fangs as it sank them into her flesh. *Time to die*, she thought, thinking of Speck's face. *At least that might mean my giant's safe from a ceremony for ever.*

A small, wet nose nudged her hand. So, that's where it would begin.

Without meaning to, she whimpered, and in reply the jackal gave a tiny whine too, as if mocking her. Then the beast pressed its nose against her hand more firmly, as if to drink in her scent before it began to eat her. And then it seemed to stop itself, and then . . . a small rough tongue gave her hand a tiny lick.

Then another.

She waited for the bite, for the clamping of the jaws, for the blood to come, but just got another lick from a warm wet tongue.

She looked down into those small yellow eyes and in the moonlight she saw that the animal was very small, and very thin, and very young.

The jackal whined again and licked her hand, as if her scent had reassured it somehow.

'Hey,' she murmured, 'aren't you meant to be tearing me from limb to limb?'

In reply, she saw something shake in the dark.

'Did you just wag your tail?' she asked it softly, and the movement got faster.

'Let's get a proper look at you, shall we?' she murmured. The jackal wagged its tail again and took another step towards her, so that it was standing right next to her legs. Forcing herself not to take a step back, she shone the torch around the animal's body, making sure not to point it directly into its eyes.

Pity and revulsion swept through her at what she saw.

He was a young male, his fur a matted mess of blood and dirt. His ribcage was clearly visible, and, as she peered at him, a violent shivering overtook him. There was a large cut on his back leg which was just beginning to heal. His coat was dotted here and there with crusted patches of blood. Yet he had a delicate, pointed face, large triangular ears, comically big for his face, and intelligent eyes that were rimmed with black. Here and there, through the filth and the blood, were patches of golden-brown fur. Tenderness tiptoed into her heart.

'How did you get that cut?' she murmured. He dipped his head wearily. Perhaps he had torn himself on wire when clambering out of a cage. He must have been terrified – and alone. She looked down into his eyes. Even though he was clearly in a bad way, he held her gaze and did not look away. He regarded her, quite deliberately, as if he'd been searching for something and had decided he had found it.

She thought back. When they'd first encountered each other, he had definitely growled. Once he'd sniffed her, he'd decided to trust her. Why? Surely all he would have smelt was her fear? She bit her lip, trying to work out what to do next, while he walked in circles then curled up in an exhausted heap on her foot. Despite everything, this made her smile. She felt his warmth through her shoes, and smiled down at him.

But this was not part of the plan. She gave her head a shake.

'No,' she said, quite gently. 'You have to get up.'

In reply, the jackal took a deep, juddering breath, and then snuggled closer to her ankle. Maybe he had been alone since the earthquake. She imagined his flight from the factory. Perhaps he had looked for his mother, before fleeing alone . . .

'Come on, now,' she said to the exhausted animal curled up on her foot. 'Up you get.'

She moved her leg a little. In return, the jackal squeezed his eyes tighter, and seemed to make his body grow heavier. Minnie did this when she didn't want to go to school, and, for a second, she didn't see him as a jackal at all, but as someone she understood. Impulsively, she wanted to reach out and stroke him.

No, she told herself. *He might be small and have lovely eyes and ridiculously adorable triangular ears, but I know nothing about him. He could be dangerous.* Her hand was still a little damp from when he had licked it so tenderly. *That doesn't mean anything*, she told herself. *He could turn savage any minute. That hand-licking and this foot-snuggling might all be a trick, designed to lull me into a false sense of security. Then he'll pounce. I have to get away.*

She finally eased her foot out from under him and took a step to move away, but when she glanced back he'd gone already. He must have run away. She walked a few more paces down the lagoon path, trying to ignore her feeling of loss, when there was a soft padding sound on her right.

She swung the torch again, and found herself staring straight into his surprisingly delicate, narrow face. He cocked his head and blinked. Both of his ears were completely upright and very jaunty, as if to say, *Come on, Minnie – I'm ready for anything!* He blinked at her slowly. She found herself thinking how different he was to the snarling gargoyles on the meat cans of tinned jackal.

She gave the jackal a stare of wonder and unease, shaking her head. He shook his head too, with a look of total understanding.

'No,' she said. 'Absolutely not. We are *not* doing this together.'

He stared deep into her eyes and gave a tiny whine.

'Look,' she said, as firmly as she could. 'There's no way this can work. I'm *on the run*. I'm a *person*. You're a *jackal*. I can't look after you. Humans and jackals don't mix.'

He sat on his haunches, yawned, and gazed at her solemnly, as if he was willing to hear her out because he could tell this was very important.

She flung her arm to the right, pointing back towards the river. 'Go on, go.' His eyes were making her feel guilty.

He obediently glanced in the direction she pointed and then looked back at her, yawning again, as if to say, *Can I go back to sleeping on your feet now?*

All of a sudden, she felt hugely annoyed. 'Okay, that's it,' she hissed, in the shadows. 'I've tried to be polite, but it hasn't worked. So – *get lost*.' And she turned from him and hurried away.

He followed her, hobbling on his wounded leg, and for another unnerving second she felt how similar they were. She stopped and so did he.

'*No*,' she shouted. This time, the jackal did not wag his tail when she spoke; yet he stayed close. 'If there are two of us, it will be so much easier for me to be detected,' she explained. She glanced at his wounded leg and forced the tenderness out of her heart. 'You might slow me down. I don't want you.'

He whimpered, then licked her hand.

She hardened her voice with a huge effort. '*Leave me alone.*'

He stayed, gave one uncertain wag of his tail. Then he took one tiny step towards her.

Hating herself slightly, she raised her hand as if to strike him. He'd have learned to fear humans, she knew, at the factory.

It had the desired effect. He cowered at her gesture, and then got down on all fours, cringing very low on the ground, his stomach on the path. And there he stayed.

'Get lost,' she said gruffly.

She turned on her heel and walked quickly away, her jaw tense. When she had gone a few steps, she turned back. He remained in his prone position, resting his face on his front legs, watching her walk away. But he didn't follow her; he knew better than that now. She swallowed hard, and found herself walking on blindly in the darkness, unconcerned even about the No-Go giants.

'Only a stupid jackal,' she muttered to herself, hobbling towards the lagoon. 'I couldn't have looked after him. I couldn't have done.'

As she approached the lagoon, the darkness around

her grew thick. Her torchlight seemed to have no more power than a flickering flame from a candle. Coldness rose up from the earth and settled around her legs.

With a guilty look at the sign that shouted

'NO TRESPASSiNG!',

Minnie crawled under the turnstile.

- 24 -
THE LAIR

MINNIE FORCED HERSELF to take deep, calming breaths, then flicked her torch beam around, looking for any debris that might be dangerous, might trip her up. Luckily, the quake's greedy fingers had not reached as far as the lagoon. That was strange . . . She thought Mrs Primrose had said the quake had damaged *everywhere*.

It was a still night, and the screechers were quiet, and for that Minnie was thankful. Her body was as drained as if she'd travelled much, much further than the mile or two between the city walls and the lagoon. At least the air here was fresh and cool. She filled herself up with the smell of the lagoon water, and her racing thoughts calmed a little.

What had Speck told her? *Take the track to the right of the lagoon and carry on walking down it. It will skirt the back of the lagoon, into what looks like a solid wall of bramble, where no one ever goes.*

Minnie swept her torch to the right and stared into the darkness, past the waterslide, past the old sunloungers . . .

Finally she spotted it; a tiny telltale scattering of pebbles that wound their way into a dark thicket of spiky, thorny undergrowth. No wonder no one knew about it.

Minnie shook her torch a little to make its feeble light stronger. Thus armed, she took the dirt track. She was immediately assaulted by the strange clammy scent of sap and a million tiny thorns tearing at her skin and clothes. After struggling through it for what felt like an hour, the path widened beneath her feet, and she felt, rather than saw, something cold and huge ahead. Her torch revealed the opening of a cave, a gaping, sinister hole. Now she understood why they called it a cave mouth. And Speck wanted her to go in *there*? She peered at the darkness warily.

Suddenly, all her strength left her. She stared at the cave mouth and felt her entire body slump, too tired and too scared to continue.

Nasty voices inside her brain began to speak. She was an embarrassment to the island – how dare she try to defy tradition! Just who did she think she was, anyway, to delay a ceremony, to try to hold on to her giant for a little longer?

'I'm a bad person,' she moaned into her hands.

The nasty voices agreed. She was *selfish*. All the other

children, all the *better* children, had willingly agreed with the fast-track idea, and she – she alone – was too much of a coward. Why, here she was *crying* about losing her giant, like a baby . . . She curled up on her side on the dirt floor and became a scrunched-up ball of self-hate.

She was so still, and so quiet, for so long, that she attracted the attention of one of the lagoon's residents: one that didn't think she looked useless at all, not when she was so temptingly arranged like that on the ground. He could *entirely* see the point of her. She was there for meat. And she'd just ended up in his lair! How incredibly convenient.

When she looked up, she was only a bit surprised to see a screecher bird on the ground, cocking its black head at her. It was huge – its body as tall and as wide as a carriage wheel, and its head one huge, ruthless killing machine.

It opened its beak.

Sickly terror flared within Minnie. The screecher kept its mouth open like a taunt. Minnie braced herself. The moment the screecher bird called its signature cry, she would be covered by others within seconds. Screechers liked to share their treasure, and she was, she remembered (all too late), slap bang in the middle of one of their biggest nests.

Move, Minnie! She scrambled to her feet, thinking she would make a run for the cave mouth, but, to her dismay, the screecher bird flew towards it at the same time, determined to block her escape. It unfurled its wide wings, fixing her with a mocking glare, until its wingspan covered the cave mouth completely. She had nowhere to flee. Both she and the bird knew it. In vain, she gave it one last beseeching look. The bird threw back his head and sounded the hunting bugle to activate the kill.

It hadn't even finished its second screech when it was joined by a companion. Then another. The three screechers now squatted within the cave mouth. Minnie whirled round, planning to run down the path back to the lagoon. Too late! From the stench of old meat and the flapping wings in front of her, she knew there were now birds blocking that path too, although it was too dark for her to see how many exactly.

For a terrible moment, they merely stared at her, sizing her up. The air grew swollen with menace. The attack, when it came, was thick and fast. Talons outstretched, wings at full span, the screechers dived at her again and again, aiming to blind her with feathers and claws, to force her into an easier position to dine from.

It didn't take many repeated assaults to push Minnie back to the ground. She put up a fight as best she could, but the climb up the rubble had drained her of most of her strength, and fear took the rest. Once she was down, the pecks began in earnest: all over her back, her legs, her arms. The screechers took great beakfuls of her, and shook their heads from side to side, attempting to flay her. Screaming with pain, and with a final burst of adrenaline, she rolled from her back on to her front and then back again, trying to shake them off. This made something crack and break inside her backpack. The sound was loud enough to scare the birds off her for at least a second, before they attacked her again. Then she spied something, she spied something else flying through the air with killer determination. She shuddered at the prospect of one more predator, one more beak.

But this flying creature was not a screecher.

It was snarling, not screaming, and had two large pointed ears flattened against its skull. It did not have wings either, just an astonishingly fast leap.

The screechers were astonished, and not a little taken aback.

They had never seen a jackal roaming free on the island before. Locked up in metal cages, down by the factory, yes. But unshackled . . . and able to run? Able to attack? *Outrageous!* An insult to the ways of the island! They were going to complain. Unless . . . The screecher birds shot clever gimlet eyes at each other. Unless they just *ate him too?*

A fierce battle of fur and talons and beaks followed. Fortified by the presence of the jackal, Minnie stumbled to her feet and joined the fray. A beak punctured the skin just above her right eyebrow, and in a fever of fury she lashed out with her fists, thumping wherever she could, trying to aim her punches into the black whirlpool of feathers rather than fur. Through bright fireworks of pain she beat and kicked blindly, trying to get closer to the cave mouth all the while, struggling to see properly as blood streamed into her right eye and the shadows tricked and wrong-footed her.

But the one who fought the longest was the jackal. He leaped and pounced on the birds again and again, snarling and baring his teeth, ignoring the wound in his back leg and the hunger in his belly. Even as Minnie's punches grew weaker, the young jackal pounced and bit and tore when he could, always going for whichever screecher was threatening Minnie most.

When four of the screechers had given up and flown back to the safety of their own nests above the cave mouth, and the jackal had both paws on the neck of the remaining one, pinning it to the ground and baring its white teeth in a terrible warning, Minnie knew that she and the jackal had won.

'Let it go,' she said, gently. And, to her surprise, he did exactly that, and lifted his feet off the screecher's scrawny neck. The bird stumbled, staggered and gave them both a look of total disgust, before flapping away in a dishevelled state, shedding several feathers as it did so.

In answer, the jackal bared its bloody teeth at the bird.

For a moment, Minnie and the jackal looked at each other, united by what they'd done. 'You – you saved my life,' she stammered.

He dipped his head briefly in acknowledgement.

On trembling legs, she walked over and, without thinking, lifted her hand into the air. He flinched and she dropped her hand immediately, remembering with a guilty pang how she'd treated him before. Yet he stayed, standing still, as if he remained on guard, and up close she could smell his sweat and the aftermath of the battle. He was shuddering, clearly exhausted by his efforts.

Then she gently, so gently, put her hand on to the top of his head. It was the first time she had ever touched a jackal. She let her hand stay there, and he allowed it. She took in the solidity of his skull, the warmth of his flesh, and the softness of his fur, all at once – all this strength and fragility under her fingers, and she was humbled by what he had done for her, after she had rejected him.

For a moment both panted heavily, exhausted by the fight neither had prepared for, shocked by this unfamiliar tenderness between them. She had never patted a jackal before, and he had only ever experienced pain at the hand of a human. But he knew that Minnie was different, and so he forgave her; he felt the apology in her hand, and that was enough. He turned his head and peered into the depths of her eyes, unafraid of her.

It wasn't quite so simple for Minnie. Not only had she spent her entire childhood being told that jackals were food and nothing else, but she'd also been taught to fear them. She'd spent the last eleven years of her life looking at their snarling faces on food labels. Having just seen him fight off several huge vultures, snarling and ripping at them ferociously, she understood he was not an animal to be trifled with, even when young, injured and hungry. So what should she do? Trust him, or reject him?

He cocked his head and glanced towards the cave

mouth. In his clever face she saw a question that was also a plea.

She made up her mind. 'Yes.' She gave a small smile. 'That way.'

Then they walked into the cave, together.

- 25 -
THE CAVE

ITS DARKNESS AND shadows seemed to rush at them both, eager to wrap them in its forever embrace. There was a soft, spongy wet smell of minerals and secrets. A dripping sound.

The torchlight sputtered within the entrance. Minnie and the jackal's shivers grew more pronounced in the damp. Despite the comforting presence of the small creature beside her, she still hesitated when she peered ahead. Did Speck really want her to walk in there? But she had gone too far to turn back now. She needed a space to hide, and somewhere to sleep, very soon.

The jackal made a soft whine.

'You're tired too,' murmured Minnie. 'I know.' With one last glance back out of the cave towards the night sky, they limped on.

Before long, they came to the start of three tunnels; the two on either side were slightly narrower than the largest one in the middle. Minnie tried to remember what Speck had told her to do. Her head swam with exhaustion. Was it through the middle tunnel? She peered into it, heart thudding. Or the one on the right? She took a step to the left, then retraced her steps. A dismayed whine came from the jackal.

'Hold on,' Minnie murmured. 'Let me concentrate.'

Speck had said, *Walk through the—*

Ice-cold fear flooded her.

'I've forgotten!' she muttered, lips trembling. The jackal sniffed, deeply, as if he could detect something she couldn't. Then he walked into the middle tunnel, and panted eagerly.

'That way?' she said. 'Straight ahead?'

He gave a small whimper, which she hoped was of confirmation.

'Okay,' she whispered through dry, cracked lips. 'Why not?' As exhausted as she was, everything seemed slightly unreal to Minnie. Why not follow a jackal's directions? It made as much sense as everything else.

Crossing her fingers, stumbling and limping, Minnie followed her companion down the middle tunnel. Her breath, ragged and quick, repeated itself, which combined with the sound of his exhausted panting, made the tunnel feel full of voices. *It's just us here, no one else.* But having already been followed by a jackal and set upon by screechers, Minnie could easily imagine that, for a hat-trick, she was now being stalked by cave creatures, or even a bloodthirsty giant from No-Go. The island, it seemed, was always on the prowl.

The tunnel grew darker, seemed to wind in circles. *Had they taken the wrong turning after all?* Speck hadn't said anything about how long she'd have to walk. Had they accidentally gone through a smaller tunnel in the dark, without realising it? Were they stuck in an airless chamber, deep within a cave?

And yet the jackal staggered on. He'd pause, occasionally, to sniff the air, then glance at her over his shoulder, then take another step forward. He seemed to know something.

A minute later, she heard the sweet sound of trickling water, and, looking up, saw the blinking lights of a thousand stars ahead. Here was the clearing Speck had told her about – right in the middle of the tunnel. The floor was coated in a soft green moss that the jackal had already curled up on. She could have cried with relief at the sight of it. She crawled on to the moss next to him, expecting it to be cold, but it gave up its own warmth, as if it had been storing it for her.

Without another word, she curled on to her side,

put her rucksack under her head for a pillow, and comforted by the warmth of the jackal next to her, fell into an exhausted sleep under the stars.

- 26 -
SMASHED GLASS

WHEN MINNIE NEXT opened her eyes, it was to beauty. Through the hole in the cave's ceiling, Minnie found herself looking up at the most colourful sky she had ever seen, with streaks of vivid reds, oranges and pinks. She had never in her entire life back home seen the sky like that; normally, by the time she struggled awake in her shuttered bedroom and left for school, it was either just blue or grey. Did the sky do that trick *every* morning?

She was just about to call Speck to see if she knew about this, before she remembered where she was, and why. Her limbs grew heavy with sorrow as the events of the last few days came flooding back. Today was the day of her assigned ceremony. She had to stay hidden for at least the day. Even if it only bought her and Speck a couple more days together, or a week at most, it would be better than nothing. 'No matter what,' she promised out loud. At her words, the jackal opened one eye, and then wearily closed it again.

But Minnie could not go back to sleep. And not just

because of the beauty of the astonishing colours curling across a background of the softest blue. The agony in her body was unimaginable. She'd been too tired to remember to inject herself the night before, and now her body was beginning to protest, desperate for the numbing relief of Mr Straw's medicine.

She winced and doubled over, dawn forgotten, and reached into her rucksack for her supply, while the jackal slept on beside her. Gritting her teeth against the onslaught of pain, she pulled out the folded-up T-shirt in which she'd wrapped the bottles. But on unwrapping the material she blinked several times, willing the broken glass and soaked fabric in her hands to be just an illusion.

Every single bottle of medicine had been smashed into pieces.

How? They hadn't been broken when she'd packed them, and she'd been so careful . . .

Then she remembered, moaning with fear.

The screechers. She recalled how she'd rolled on the ground, trying to get away from them; she remembered that deadly *crack* she'd heard.

It had been then. She'd broken them then. And, without her medicine, she could black out from the pain. It had happened once before, when she was five, when Mr Straw had left the island for the weekend. (After that, they always kept supplies in the house.) And if that happened, would she ever wake up? Or would she lie there, getting weaker and weaker?

She lay on the moss, crying feebly. *Terrible, terrible trouble*, she thought, desperately. Animal moans, noises like something caught in a trap, came out of her mouth. She began to shiver all over. Without any medicine, she could barely walk.

She was dimly aware of a triangular black nose pushing its way towards her face, a pair of piercing golden eyes ringed with black looking at her in a puzzled, concerned way.

'Hurts,' she moaned, grinding her teeth slightly against the agony that bloomed, unchecked, within her. The jackal whimpered a little and licked her cheek. She closed her eyes and tried to think her way through the pain. What should she do next—?

Her thoughts were interrupted by the faint but definite sound of dogs barking. The effect of this sound on the jackal was immediate. The fur on his back stood up, and he began to growl and shake.

Dogs? thought Minnie, terrified. Why? Speck had said no one ever came . . .

BARK BARK BARK. Definitely dogs.

She stayed as still as she could, with an arm over the

jackal to keep him quiet. Ears straining, she lay on the moss, trying to work out where the sound was coming from.

The dogs barked again, and this time, Minnie realised, the sound was coming from the cave mouth, and it was accompanied by the unmistakable sound of her own name being shouted.

'Minnie Wadlow? Minnie?'

The voices belonged to adults, none she recognised immediately. They were faint – perhaps they had yet to enter the tunnel – but they – *whoever they were* – had definitely got as far as the cave mouth. If not past it already.

I can't be found. I mustn't be found. I have to hide.

The voice that said this came from both versions of herself: the one that felt as familiar as her skin, and the other, newer version growing just beneath it. And they were both right. She didn't want those people to find her at all. *Because if they find me, I'll have to turn my giant to stone.*

But inside her was another reason for hiding that had nothing to do with Speck. It was terror of something that she couldn't understand. They must have fought off the screecher birds. Speck had been wrong about that – the safe space wasn't safe after all. The only thing that lay between her and those hounds was the possibility that they might first go into one of the two other tunnels and not the one she was hiding in. But if they picked up her scent, then the game would be up.

For a moment she lay cowering on the moss, overwhelmed by fear and pain. And then that other Minnie inside her rose up and began to shout at her.

If you stay here and they find you, you know what they'll do to you, don't you?

Minnie whimpered. *They'll make me do the ceremony, as soon as they take me back. And then they'll punish me. And my parents.*

So move. Run!

I can't. It hurts too much.

Move as much as you can then. Better than just lying there and giving up.

So that's what she did. Slowly, Minnie forced herself to her feet and stumbled down the tunnel, holding on to the walls with one hand, dragging her feet behind her.

She turned, half-expecting the jackal to be beside her, but to her consternation he had turned in the opposite direction. Back towards the sound of the snarling dogs.

'No,' she hissed, in the half-light. 'Not that way. They'll rip you to pieces.'

He gave her one final look of adoration from his black-rimmed eyes, and padded slowly away from her. Shaking her head, Minnie had no option but to carry on down the tunnel, stumbling and moaning with exertion. After some time had passed, she heard the terrible sound of a dog fight, and snarling and ripping. The tunnels filled with the whines of a creature in pain, and the shouts of men, urging the hounds to go in for the kill.

He doesn't have a hope, thought Minnie, stifling a sob. The jackal had fought one more fight for her, but this one he had obviously lost. She hesitated, blinded by her tears, and then carried on her desperate way, staggering.

- 27 -
THE RIPPLE

SHE HAD NO idea when she emerged from the tunnel; all she knew was that the sun was beating down on her, and she was barely conscious because of the pain inside her bones. She could hear the men and the dogs behind her, gaining on her with every second, but they hadn't found her yet. Ahead was a path that led she knew not where; to her right was more bramble. *There'd be more cover there*, she thought, and, biting her lip to stop herself from screaming, she plunged into the thicket.

She found herself lurching into the shallow waters of the lagoon, fully clothed, Papa's rucksack still on her back. For a brief, melancholy moment, she remembered the last time she'd been in the water and who she'd been with.

Do you miss me, like I miss you? Are you cross with me, or have I done the right thing? Oh and by the way, if I ever see you again we are going to have words about what you define as 'safe'.

The voices and the barking behind her got louder and louder. They were just a few feet away. Seconds.

There was only one thing for it.

She took a deep breath and paddled, as noiselessly and slowly as she could, to the furthest edge of the lagoon, as far away from the path as possible. From the bank grew a large tangle of huge tree roots. With her breath coming by now in quick, terrified gasps, she squeezed behind the roots. They pressed against her face and her chest, and made it even harder for her to breathe.

But that was a small price to pay if they kept her unseen.

Her eyes darted round frantically. For a second, her vision grew dark and ragged around the edges. *Don't faint, don't faint, don't faint in the water, Minnie,* she told herself fiercely, blinking fiercely to stay awake. The pain by now was raging all through her body as if a million tiny needles were stabbing her skin repeatedly while unseen assailants pulled hard on her limbs from all directions.

She took a deep breath, forced herself to count to three, and breathed out again. If she'd judged it right, even if her pursuers peered into the water, the combination of the dappled shadows overhead and the roots in front of her would conceal her from their sight.

If she hadn't – well . . . The hunters would bear her

back to Quake Quarter and everyone she loved most would suffer.

A moment later, three sets of legs and two large dogs came crashing on to the path where she'd been standing moments before. She could just spot their dark uniforms through the brambles.

The legs stopped. So did the dogs, who whined and snapped at the air. There was no sound of the jackal, and she thought with a wrench of grief of his beautiful face, and what he'd done to buy her these few more seconds of precious time.

Another spasm of agony began to twist its way through her body, and she had to use every ounce of willpower not to gasp. Any sound she made now would give away her location.

'Well, she made it out here, but we've lost the scent,' said a man, sounding fed up.

'Shame,' said a second, idly stamping his boot on the path. 'I thought we'd found her.'

'She can't be far away,' said the third. 'She's very small. And usually she limps. I'm surprised she's got as far as she has.'

'Well, wherever she's got to, whoever finds her will give her up, eventually. There's a thousand island pounds being offered as a reward if any member of the public finds her.'

'They want to make an example of her. Stop the other children doing the same thing.'

'As if any other child would try to delay their ceremony! It's an honour to serve the island. Funny sort of thing she's doing. I mean, who wants to save their giant?'

'I blame the parents,' the first one said, spitting on to the path. 'Funny couple.' For a minute, the officials went quiet, thinking this over. One of their dogs lifted its nose in the air, sniffed, and began to whine.

It's smelled me, thought Minnie, desperately, shrinking back in the water.

'Crying about its injuries,' said the second official, with a laugh. 'But he won that dog-fight. Strange to see a jackal in a cave.'

'Let's see if they pick up her scent further down the path,' said the third.

Yes, go, she urged the men. *Move on. Please*. The combined sound of her breathing and her heartbeat sounded, to her, about as quiet as a seven-piece musical band with trombones and drums. There was something about her fear that was just as terrifying as the fear itself. It had depths and a quality she couldn't understand. She tried to reassure herself. The hunters were, underneath it all, her fellow islanders. Good people. Part of her knew this, but somewhere beyond that, in a place she could not explain, was a fiercer instinct to hide, something that felt huge and frightened and desperate, and her heart beat in a way that scared her too.

To her dismay, she saw one of the men pull out a flask of tea from his bag. 'Just for a minute,' he protested. 'It's been a long morning.'

The water was cold. Minnie had been still for a long time, and now she began to tremble. With a flicker of horror Minnie saw a tiny ripple move out from her body and lap across the water. The men didn't seem to see it, but then one of the dogs bent down and began to sniff the path, fervently.

'Hold up,' said a voice. 'Looks like there's a scent nearby.'

The dog's pacing was wild; it was pawing the bank of the lagoon. Minnie tried to make herself as small as possible behind her shield of roots. With a pang of dread, she saw another ripple move slowly across the surface – the clearest sign that there was someone in the water. The ripple got closer and closer to the men and the dogs.

The chief dog began to whine desperately and sniff near the water in the direction of the water. Minnie saw one of the men get down on his haunches and peer into the lagoon, blinking at the shadows. She held her breath and willed herself not to move another muscle. His eyes roamed the darkness, and she nearly cried out when he looked straight at the tangle of roots covering her.

'He's seen me,' she thought in despair. 'I'm done for.'

'Oh, shut up,' shouted one of the men, kicking the hound. 'I know you got bitten, but stop complaining.'

The dog whimpered, cowered and stopped barking. Minnie held her breath.

After a pause, the same guard said, 'Perhaps she's aiming for Black Sand Beach: her parents said they sometimes went there.'

'She can't be far away.'

And finally they left. Minnie watched through the undergrowth as the men walked away, and then, moaning from the torment, pulled herself out of the water.

- 28 -
BLACK BOOTS

ONCE THE HUNTERS and their dogs had gone, and Minnie had got out of the water as fast as she could, gasping, sobbing and shivering all over from cold and pain, she stood hunched, trying to warm herself. The jackal had given up his life for her, she thought, hanging her head with remorse. He'd bought her enough time to hide. She'd never forget him.

Blearily, she peered down the path – if it skirted all the way round the back of the lagoon, it would probably end up just outside Red Bridge. She gave a despairing look up at the sky, now thick with cloud. How could she stay hidden without her medicine?

I've failed. She couldn't save her giant; she felt as if she would die without Mr Straw's pain-numbing medication. The agony was getting worse by the second, as if her insides were twisting around each other.

What should she do? *If I stay here*, she thought suddenly, *I will die.* She would lose consciousness and be eaten by screechers.

Or get discovered by bad giants on one of their sinister nocturnal expeditions – then they'd bundle her up and smuggle her to No-Go to meet a grisly end.

I should have let myself get caught by the hunters, she thought bitterly. At least they could have taken her back to Mr Straw, who'd be able to fix her. She had to move, she knew that at least. If she sank on to the floor, she'd be finished.

Grinding her teeth, she forced herself to walk.

I have to get home. Maybe I can find some medicine in Old Town. Or I might see Hester, and persuade her to—

But it seemed so far away. It might as well be another island, across an ocean made of a million agonised footsteps.

What a useless runaway she'd turned out to be. A jackal had died because of her. With every step, Minnie grew weaker, and eventually she stumbled and fell to the ground. As the convulsions tore through her body, she writhed on the track, crying softly to herself.

She saw a pair of black boots stop next to her face. Through teary eyelashes, drifting in and out of consciousness, she thought she saw a face she knew.

His eyes widened with recognition too.

'Stone's breath, it's you!' he said, astonished. 'The girl from Quake Quarter. Noble giant defender. Friend of monsters. Minnie, isn't it?' His scathing voice flickered in and out of concern. She saw him take in her sickness and her dirt, and felt ashamed.

Now she could place him. Robin Scragg – the ungrateful rubbler; the boy who hated everything apart from his chickens. Her heart sank. The last person she needed.

He squatted on his haunches, wincing, and bent lower. 'I heard you were a runaway,' he said, thoughtfully. 'They were talking about it outside the pub. Someone said there was a cash reward on your head. Strange: would never have thought it of you. What have *you* got to run away from?' She was faintly aware through the fog in her head that he was looking at her scratched face and torn clothes. His eyes widened with concern. 'You're injured . . .' he said. 'Were you kidnapped by a No-Go giant? Did – did a *monster* hurt you?' he whispered in shock, staring at her wounds. 'Were you attacked?'

'No! I *am* running away,' she gasped. 'Listen – Robin – have you got any medicine?' And then she finally fainted, overcome by her pain.

*

Sometime later, she came to. Everything ached, but the spasms and cramp had, for the time being, ended. She opened her eyes hesitantly, felt the dirt caked on her face crack a little, and looked up into the green-grey eyes of the rubbler boy, who was sitting a little distance away from her.

'Well, that answers that question, at least,' he said.

'What question?' mumbled Minnie thickly.

'Whether you're dead or alive. You're not dead. I didn't fancy carrying a corpse. My back hurts enough already.' A coughing fit made him bend over double, then he stopped.

'Can you sit?' he said gruffly.

She pushed herself up to an awkward sitting position and drooped like a broken doll, damp unwashed hair falling over her face.

'So, if you weren't kidnapped, and you weren't attacked by a monster – *fine*, giant – why did I find you you rolling about on the floor?' said Robin. 'Seems a funny way to go on the run.'

Gritting her teeth, she said: 'I broke my medicine bottles.'

'Oh,' said Robin, matter-of-factly. 'What do you take it for?'

'Pain,' she said, curtly. 'And it helps me grow as best I can.'

He looked doubtfully at her.

'If it wasn't for my medicine, I wouldn't even be this

height. I've got defective muscles. Born with them.' Minnie stared at him, woozy from the pain's aftermath, suddenly suspicious. 'What were you doing just now, while I was out cold? You could have told an official you'd found me. Did you?'

'I didn't.'

'There's a cash bounty on my head, isn't there?'

Robin nodded.

'So?' Minnie was mystified. 'Why haven't you told anyone you found me? When I first met you, you were stuffing bread rolls into your pocket. Couldn't you do with the money?'

He stared at her, then said bluntly: 'I'm not a sneak.'

'But – money is money.'

'And what would I do with it?' he said, flatly. 'Buy my way into polite Quake society? As if they'd ever let me through the gates. Spend it on a fancy dinner in the Old Town? Do you think anyone would serve me?' He glared at her. 'Their money won't bring my family back. I won't tell them I found you.' This boy seemed to hate money as much as he hated giants, and the island and the Giant Management Company itself.

'Thank you,' she said.

He took a deep breath, then seemed to come back to himself. 'Can you tell me one thing, though?'

She owed him that, at least. 'What?'

'Why *are* you on the run? I thought you *loved* living in Quake Quarter, *loved* the ceremonies, the traditions . . .'

He was mocking her. She'd had enough. Every time she talked to this difficult boy who loathed everything around him, she regretted it. Awkwardly, she got to her feet. A look of shame flickered across the boy's face.

'I'm sorry,' he said, and he took a deep breath. 'I haven't chatted to people much since my family died. I get conversations wrong.' Underneath his abrasive manner, Minnie realised, Robin Scragg was the saddest person she had ever met, with no one to love and no one to love him.

'It's okay,' she said, more softly. 'But I do need to get home now. I've got to get my medicine.' She hesitated, as she glanced down the path.

His clever face filled with understanding. 'You don't *want* to go home.'

'No,' she admitted. 'I don't want to go through with my ceremony.'

Robin stared at her, wide-eyed. 'Rubble dust! *That's* why you're on the run. You're – you're actually bunking off from your own ceremony?'

She gave a tiny nod, ashamed.

Robin's eyes flickered with questions, and he glanced

up at the darkening skies then back at her.

'That's a new one,' he said, finally. 'I've *never* heard of a child who didn't want to have their ceremony – who wasn't excited about the festivities, and the dancing and the welcoming into society. You might as well admit to treason.'

'I am excited about all that stuff,' she protested, trying to sound like she believed it. 'I do want to do it, but *not just yet.*' Minnie gasped the last sentence as the cramps began again.

Robin's eyes narrowed. 'Did you say you needed medicine?'

Minnie nodded, unable to speak.

'I have some at my house,' he said, blushing.

Minnie peered at him, hardly daring to hope. 'Really?'

Robin rubbed his nose with a grimy finger. 'Yeah. My parents had lots of painkillers, to help with their twisted muscles. Decades of rubbling does that to you. Would they help?'

Relief flooded Minnie. 'So much! If they help these – argh! – cramps go, I can stay hidden a while longer. Until all the fast-tracking is done and dusted, hopefully.'

'All right,' he said. 'But – but you can't stay. If I get caught harbouring a rich girl run-away . . .' He let the sentence die. Minnie thought of the whips and the dogs and understood. 'But you can come and get what you need.'

How well did she know this strange boy, though? What if he really did want the reward money?

'This definitely isn't a trap?' she asked.

His face blazed with emotion. 'Look, I hate the people in charge,' he said. There was no doubting the truth that rang like a bell in his voice. 'So them not always getting their way will be a triumph to me. And – well, ever since my family . . . ' he swallowed. 'My cottage has been really quiet. This isn't a trap. Come and get what you want. But don't outstay your welcome.'

Despite the ferociousness in his glare, Minnie could also see the plea. She gave a tiny nod. 'All right. Thank you.' She weakly got to her feet.

Then Robin said something strange.

He said: '*Run.*'

Minnie frowned. 'Are you mocking me *again?*'

'*Just do it,*' he said, face white with fear, staring at a point just behind her.

She twisted her head to see what was so terrifying, and was astonished to find the jackal behind them. He hadn't died! Relief and affection were quickly replaced by surprise. Because he was no longer the cute, big-eared pup who had saved her life. In his place was a snarling, wild-eyed demon. His ears and fur were freshly ripped, and for the first time since she'd met him, he looked a bit like the vicious predator from the label on the cans of jackal meat. His teeth were bared at Robin, as if he wanted to sink them into his throat.

- 29 -
ROBIN AND THE JACKAL

THE CLOUDS RUMBLED with distant thunder. It was as if time had stopped. For a while, the two children and the jackal merely held their places, wondering who would make the first move. Minnie shot confused looks between the blood-soaked jackal and the shaking boy. 'But – but I . . . I know this jackal,' she said, softly. *What had got into him?*

Even though Robin was rigid with fear, he managed to give her a quick, terrified glance. '*You know* it? How?'

'He saved my life, last night! We, er . . . we even shared the same moss, to sleep on. He was really harmless, apart from with the screechers.'

'Well, it's not harmless now,' hissed Robin. 'It's looking at me like I'm dinner.'

The jackal took a deliberate step closer to them, his eyes fixed on Robin the entire time. He stank of fresh blood and fear and fight. There was a nasty bite mark on his cheek. His hackles were up and his front legs were bent. Minnie recognised these signs. He was seconds away from attacking.

'What's wrong?' she murmured to the young pup.

The animal's eyes flickered for a moment towards Minnie, and she caught a flash of recognition in them. Then they resumed their laser-like intensity on Robin. Minnie took a step towards the jackal, as if to soothe him.

Robin flinched. 'Careful,' he urged. 'Don't get too close. It might kill you first.'

'He,' she muttered. 'He's a boy.'

'I don't *care* what it is: it's got murder on its mind,' whispered Robin.

Robin had a point. The jackal's entire body bristled. A terrifying growl grew in the back of his throat. He treated Robin to a front-row view of his teeth, still flecked with blood from when he'd sunk them into the dogs.

Robin turned deathly white. 'He . . . wants . . . to . . . kill . . . me,' he moaned. The thunder cracked again, closer this time.

An angry sort of exhaustion swept through Minnie. She just wanted to go to Robin's and stay hidden. Every second out here made them more vulnerable. Frustration made her brave. She bent down on her haunches, reached a hand out and placed it on the jackal's neck. He flinched a little, but stayed where he was.

'What are you doing?' hissed Robin.

'It's all right, he trusts me,' she murmured. 'Now, Robin. Walk over to us.'

'Are you *insane?*'

'I think he needs to sniff your hand.'

A scornful silence greeted this.

'It was the only thing that calmed him down last night,' went on Minnie. 'He was exactly the same with me when we met. Then he sniffed my hand, and he changed. I think he just has a thing about scent. And – oh, can you just get on with it, please?' She glanced nervously around the lagoon. 'We're really exposed here. Anyone can see us.'

'If it bites my hand off, you're going to do all my rubbling work *for ever* while I sit around and eat grapes.'

'*Fine*,' said Minnie. 'Just hurry.'

As Robin approached, the jackal shook all over. 'Easy,' she soothed. A low, continuous warning rumble began in his throat, as if he was trying to out-thunder the thunder coming their way.

'Are you sure about this?' said Robin. Minnie nodded, trying to look confident.

Showing admirable bravery, the boy got down on his knees and offered his hand. Likewise, the jackal was bold enough to inch forward and take a tentative sniff of the boy's scent. This was the moment when they would become firm chums, thought Minnie.

A second later, the jackal seemed to twist rapidly in the air, there was a strong snapping sound and blood was running down Robin's wrist. The jackal growled triumphantly, and then twisted slightly towards Minnie, cocking his head as if looking for a pat on the head. Minnie's cheeks burned with embarrassment.

'I'm sorry,' she stammered.

Robin rolled his eyes wearily, as if nothing could surprise him any more. 'Never mind. That's the island through and through, isn't it? If it doesn't hurt you one way, it'll hurt you another.' He glanced at the torn skin on his hand. Minnie remembered her first impression of the boy who hated everything, and suddenly felt a pang of sympathy for him.

As if aware he sounded too miserable, and not wanting to lose her company, he gave a rueful grin. It was as if a cloudy day had suddenly brightened. 'Don't worry, Minnie,' he said. 'I can't actually feel much pain in my hands. They've been bashed by so many bricks over the years most of the nerve endings have gone. Still –' he shot a warning sign at the jackal – 'if your friend tries that again, I'll stick him in a can with the rest of his pals.' In answer, the jackal bared his teeth at Robin. As the beginning of a beautiful friendship, it wasn't promising.

Minnie got to her feet wearily, glancing up at the slate sky, darkening by the second. 'Let's keep going,' she urged.

The jackal began to walk alongside her, drawing a disgusted look from Robin.

'You're not serious?' he spluttered.

'*He's* coming with me,' said Minnie, firmly. 'He saved me last night. He helped me when I was lost. He bought me time today. I owe him. I need him.' *And I might need him to do those things again, once Robin and I have parted ways.*

Robin broke eye contact first. 'Have it your way,' he said, shoving his hands in his pockets and turning abruptly on his heel.

The jackal continued to pad softly alongside Minnie, snarling occasionally at the boy in front, but mostly turning his head to look at Minnie with adoration in his eyes. Minnie wondered what the jackal had smelt on Robin that had made him so agitated, and why he'd not reacted that way to her. She shook her head at him, with affection.

'I just can't work you out,' she murmured. 'You're loyal to me, but not to him. You're small, but you win every fight. You were caged, but now you're free.' He wagged his tail. She smiled a little. 'You're full of defiance,' she added. 'Always moving in and out of trouble. And just when I think I know who you are, you twist and change again.'

He twisted his head towards her and gave her a sly grin. And even though she hadn't been looking for one, his name presented itself to her right then.

'Twist,' she said. 'That's you.'

He stopped in his tracks and cocked his triangular head at her, as if trying the name on for size. Despite the blood in his fur and the bite mark on his face, she thought she had never seen anything quite so ferociously beautiful in her life.

Moments later, a thick rain began to fall.

'Brilliant timing,' Robin said, and it appeared he meant it. 'It will make it harder for you to be spotted.' He looked appraisingly at Minnie's hair, now plastered to her skull and cheekbones. 'That's good cover, for starters. But give me your rucksack.'

Then he glanced at her shoes. 'Take those off,' he said.

Minnie hesitated. The path they were on was horribly stony. 'Why?' she asked.

'Because whoever is looking for you – and it could be lots of people by now – will be looking for a nice presentable Quake Quarter girl, wearing good shoes, carrying a bag. Not a barefoot girl, with no bag, walking next to a rubbler. If you want to stay hidden in plain sight, you're going to have to confuse them.'

She did as he asked and stuffed the shoes in her rucksack, which Robin then shouldered. Another wave of fire ripped through her body. 'It's coming back,' she slurred, her eyelids flickering as her eyes rolled in agony. 'I'm . . . sorry. I can't . . .'

Robin turned and walked towards her. Twist growled. Robin ignored him. 'Put your arm around my neck,' he said to Minnie.

Minnie did as she was asked, swaying slightly.

'Well done. Now listen to me,' said Robin, and his voice was gentler than she expected. 'That's all you have to do, all right? Just listen, and try to do what I say.'

She gave a small whimper of assent.

'Left foot,' he said. Minnie moved it, wincing.

'Right foot.'

Her right foot dragged a tiny bit in the dirt, then fell back again. Twist nudged at her foot with his nose, as if to guide her. Her thoughts were fading, swallowed up by pain. She had forgotten what she was doing, where she was going . . .

'Right foot,' repeated a voice in her ear, as soft as the rain. 'You can do it.'

She moved it.

'Left foot . . . Right foot . . . Can you manage another

one? . . . Well done. Go on.'

This went on for some time. As the rain hid them and kept them safe, Twist and the children made their way slowly, so slowly, down the path.

- 30 -
MINNIE'S MYSTERIOUS ILLNESS

THE GROUND BENEATH Minnie's feet changed from a dirt track to a sodden river path. The two children made their way down this until it rose into a high arch that she faintly recognised, even through her haze of agony. 'Red Bridge,' she muttered.

'Not long now,' said Robin.

When her arm slipped off his shoulder, he reached for her hand and placed her arm back. 'Nearly there,' he said. 'Hold on.'

They crossed the bridge. The rain had stopped. Would anyone see them? She hoped not. They reached a path made of broken rubble. Her skin was so tender, felt so inflamed, she felt as if she was walking across broken glass.

Minnie saw, as if they belonged to someone else, her bare muddy feet drag their way down the path, then over a rough mat, and then finally shuffle across a tidily swept dirt floor. She was dimly aware that there was one wooden chair and an old sofa.

'Take the couch,' said Robin, and Minnie sank

gratefully into it. Robin disappeared. Twist's wet fur filled the small room with a pungent musky smell. She nearly swooned, felt blackness nibble at the edges of her vision. A few minutes later, two small white tablets were put into her hands, as well as a glass of water.

Minnie was about to take the tablets when a wave of ferocious pain, like something she'd never felt before, erupted out of her. The pills fell tumbling to the ground and, a second later, so did she.

The next few hours slipped by in fever. Sometimes she knew she was lying on a makeshift bed of towels and blankets, but a lot of the time she was not even aware of that. Occasionally a bucket was held to her mouth. Sometimes something cool was pressed against her forehead. Robin said things softly, things that sounded like 'temperature' and 'poisoning' but she couldn't find language anywhere inside her to reply.

Odd visions ran through her mind – Mr Straw's face bending over her while she cried and resisted; Mama and Papa whispering in corners while they looked at her; huge bottles of sunblock dancing across lagoons, out of which stretched stone arms, as if begging for help . . .

Eventually, her fever broke, and she opened her eyes.

'Speck?' she said.

She cried weakly when she realised her giant wasn't

there. But Robin was. He was crouched on the floor at her feet. The room was dark apart from the light thrown by candles, barely more than stubs. The pain had been everywhere, like a thief that had crept over her bones all night, stealing whatever it wanted. Now it had gone, and her muscles were aching but blessedly empty. She could have cried from the sweet relief.

'Better?' said Robin.

'A bit.' She sat up, feeling thirsty, and squinted into the candlelight.

He stared at her, frowned, blinked and rubbed his eyes. 'You look more like yourself, at least. You were really sick there, Minnie. It was like when one of our chickens ate some poison and fell into the same kind of convulsions. Has that ever happened before?'

'Never like that. What happened?'

He launched into a long, passionate anecdote about the bravery of the chicken, but she was distracted. 'What's happened to my clothes?' she demanded.

Robin, a little crossly, said: 'Nothing's happened to them. Anyway, on the fifth day, Feathers laid an egg, but—'

Minnie shook her head. 'No. These don't feel right.'

'You're still feverish. They *are* your clothes. Perhaps they've shrunk in the rain.' He yawned. 'What a night.

You were talking all night long. Saying strange things. Begging someone not to take you away. Sounded like a nightmare.' He leaned his head against the wall and closed his eyes.

'I must have been dreaming about a No-Go giant stealing me.'

They were quiet for a while. Blue light inched its way under the rough curtains at the simple window, and Minnie saw the dark circles under Robin's eyes. Twist paced around them, whining softly.

'He's been doing that for hours,' said Robin, flatly. 'Growling at me whenever I dabbed at your face with a flannel. Nipping my legs whenever I got close to you.'

'Sorry,' said Minnie. When she looked at him, the jackal heaved a huge sigh, as if with relief, and grinned. With the dirt and old blood washed off his coat by the rain, he gleamed quite golden in the room, like a small ferocious sun. Minnie realised suddenly that this humble room held two of the most unlikely friends she was ever likely to make, and both of them hated each other. She would miss them when she went back home. *Whenever that would be.*

'How are you feeling?' Robin said.

Minnie knew that behind this question was a bigger question. *Are you well enough to leave my house?* He had nursed her through a fever; she didn't want to outstay her welcome, or get him into any trouble.

'Much better,' she said, realising as she said it that she really did feel stronger; and less jumbled up and squished down inside than she had in a while, too. She glanced at the jackal. 'Can I have a quick wash – and give Twist a drink of water – and then we'll both go?'

Wearily, Robin got to his feet. 'There's a water pump in the yard.' He picked up a discarded rag from the floor. 'But tie that round his neck first.'

'Why?'

'My chickens,' he said, simply, with devotion.

Minnie did as he asked. The jackal strained and snapped at the makeshift leash, but thus restrained, he was led towards the back of the cottage into a simple dirt yard, where four scrawny hens pointedly ignored them.

Robin bent down over them, tenderly stroked their heads. He scattered them some food from a bucket, and then, after a moment's hesitation, threw some chicken feed in the direction of Twist, who fell on it ravenously. 'I don't like to see a starving animal,' he explained, bluntly, noting Minnie's raised eyebrows, 'even if it's a total pain in the neck. Now for water. Can you see the water pump by the door? Push it down.'

Minnie saw a small water pump next to the cottage.

She reached for it and it broke in her hand. Robin looked at her, then down at his broken water pump, now leaking into the yard.

'I'm sorry,' said Minnie.

Together they stared down at the broken-off handle.

'Right,' said Robin, carefully. 'I'm going to make some tea, and in return for you breaking my water pump, and your friend biting my hand, and me not getting much sleep last night, you're going to tell me *exactly* why you're on the run. And you're not to touch anything else.' One of the chickens, who Minnie presumed was Feathers, gave her a look of warning and clucked.

'Deal,' said Minnie.

'And then you'll go?'

'Then I'll go,' promised Minnie, to Feathers and to Robin.

- 31 -
THE CONFESSION

ONCE SHE'D FINISHED explaining about the fast-tracking, and how giants could get trapped between stone and flesh if the ceremony went badly, and all about Papa's futile attempts to get more investment, and how she couldn't risk bringing any more disgrace to her family or they'd be fined, thrown in the dungeon and suffer social rejection for ever – Robin was rolling his eyes.

'Talking to you is always so rewarding,' she snapped. 'You've such got a gift for sympathy.'

He took a gulp of his tea, stared at the chickens, then said, 'Sorry. But. You're not running away for your *family*.' He reached into his pocket and threw more chicken feed on the ground for Twist, who gave him an elegant look of astonishment, before devouring it.

'Yes I am,' said Minnie.

'No. You're running away because you love . . . *her*. You're not "saving your family from disgrace". You just don't want to lose your *monster*.'

Minnie stood up quickly, flushed. '*Stop* calling her

that. Anyway, you're wrong.' She held her hands up to her cheeks to cool them. 'I don't – um – love her. I'm not *allowed* to. It's against the rules in the manual. Any child can tell you that.'

'You're not allowed to run away either, but I don't see that stopping you,' Robin said. 'Look, I understand. I've always thought it horrible – how people make giants look after children and then tell them both they can't have any feelings for each other. It's just one of the ways this island is such a mess.'

Minnie bit her lip.

'You're wrong. It's not . . . not like that.' She wished her cheeks would stop burning. 'I'm just buying myself some time so I can do my ceremony properly. That's all.'

Robin took a deliberate sip of his tea. 'Sure. Time. Properly. Whatever you say.'

'It's true. I . . . I . . . *will* be able to turn her to stone, one day,' said Minnie.

There was a long silence. Twist looked at them both and cocked his head. Truth crackled between them.

'You just don't want that day to come,' said Robin.

Their eyes met. He was too sharp for her.

'No. I don't. Not ever,' whispered Minnie. 'Don't tell anyone.'

His eyes widened, but his gaze was steady. She stared

at the ground. 'Me and my parents – we'd be in so much trouble if anyone found out,' she whispered.

'I don't think anyone would believe it, anyway,' he whispered back. 'You must be the only islander in our history who cares so much about their giant they'll run away to keep them safe.' He wrinkled his nose. 'Makes no sense to me, of course.'

'It's hard to explain,' said Minnie, stammering and feeling terrified. 'She's just – ' she struggled to find the right word. 'She's . . .'

Like my family.

Like a part of me.

She looked at him, wary of his scorn if she put any of that into words, knowing she was breaking an ancient island code, but, to her surprise, he gave a weary nod, as if he understood. Then he rubbed his eyes. 'I've got no one to tell, anyway, Minnie,' he said. 'Your secret's safe with me.'

He yawned so widely his face nearly split open. Minnie remembered her promise not to stay too long.

'I'm going to go now,' she said abruptly. 'Thank you for the tea, and . . . and everything. Thanks for looking after me. I really do feel better. I'm so grateful.

Twist, who'd finished his food and had been lying in the sunshine, licking his wounds and generally looking happier for being fed, suddenly got to his feet, growling. Robin observed him, and Minnie thought she saw a tiny flash of affection on the boy's tired face

'Do you think that's his way of asking for more food?' he said, grinning wearily at the pup. 'We need to work on your manners.'

But a second later, the cottage behind them was shaking in its foundations as a loud, forceful knocking on his front door began. They both got to their feet, startled. Twist bared his teeth.

Then a stern, angry voice reached them from the other side of the door. 'Open up, Scragg. We've heard reports you're hiding Minnie Wadlow. If it's true, we urge you to give yourself up now, before we throw you in the dungeon—'

Minnie and Robin shared a terrified glance. 'The hunters,' she whispered. 'How are they here? Who told them?'

Robin was deathly pale. 'Any of my neighbours might have done it,' he whispered back. 'The one on the right has five mouths to feed. A thousand island pounds is a lot of—' The knocking had turned to kicks and blows.

'Minnie Wadlow's ceremony is a day late, thanks to her little escapade,' came the angry voice again. 'We need her giant to repair the city walls.'

Bang, bang, kick, kick.

'Bring her out immediately!'

Guilt for what she'd brought to his home flooded Minnie. Instinctively, she knew that neither she nor Robin could be there when the men came in. They wouldn't harm *her*, she was sure of it – she was protected, because of where she came from – but Robin was in a huge amount of danger. They'd threatened him with the *dungeon*. Were they really just going to chuck him down on the floor with all the bones of old bad giants and leave him there? For a moment, she wondered what sort of island she was really living on.

Robin was shivering like a frightened mouse, unable to move.

'Robin,' she whispered. 'Come on. We've got to *go*.'

Her words roused the boy. 'Not out the front,' he muttered.

'Then where?'

She followed his glance towards the scrubland at the back of the tiny yard, beyond which could be seen the saw-toothed peaks of No-Go.

'Please, not there,' she pleaded. 'Anywhere but there. That's where the bad giants, who hunt children, live.'

'We have to,' urged Robin. 'They'll throw me in the forgetter if they catch you here – and they'll force you to do your ceremony this afternoon.'

It was clear there was no other option. They were penned in on both sides by rubbler cottages, where betrayal lurked behind every tiny window. The only way out was through the scrub.

The battering resumed on the front door, followed by the sound of splintering wood. Minnie suddenly saw Speck, as if right in front of her, trapped in the city wall, all stone apart from her eyes, moving left and right as if to say: *Why couldn't you do this properly?*

She ran to Twist, who had been writhing and snapping at the air, and untied him. Then all three of them scrambled into the scrub. Seconds later, there was a cracking, snapping sound, followed by squawking.

- 32 -
THE PATH TO EVIL

WITH THE SILENT stealth that comes from true fear, they raced barefoot through the scrub, thorns catching at their faces and clothes. Eventually they broke through to a narrow alley, bordered on one side by scrub and on the other by old wooden fences. They skirted the backs of these, stooping as low as they could to avoid being seen. Breathing raggedly, they looked over their shoulders repeatedly to see if the dogs and the men were on their tail.

Minnie couldn't help thinking of the snarl in the men's voices as they taunted Robin. Did everyone on the island speak to the rubblers that way, when there was no one to overhear them?

'I need to stop,' Robin said, wheezing. He looked dreadful.

'I have some water,' Minnie offered, reaching for her rucksack, before realising with a pang of dismay that she'd left it at Robin's. 'Oh no,' she said. 'My food – water – torch – I've left *everything* behind. Even the medicine!'

They looked at each other, now totally aware of how ill-prepared they were for their flight. Twist threw his tiny head back and gave a soft howl.

Robin flinched as sounds reached them of furniture being thrown around and glass breaking. 'Come on,' he urged. But Minnie was terrified – both of what was in front *and* behind them. If they were caught by the hunters, her giant would be stone and Robin would be dead. Yet if they ran on into the mountains, something even worse might happen to both of them. For a second, she understood why Robin seemed to hate the island so much. Outside Quake Quarter, life seemed to be made up of only bleak options, and men who spoke with hate in their voice.

On their left, the earth rose sharply, and all of a sudden the mountains were right there. The air around them was cold and forbidding.

They reached a series of large, flat, granite stones, the undeniable beginning of a mountain path. Minnie eyed it, nervously. Everything she had ever been told about the horrors that lay within the mountains started at that path. An entire lifetime of fear had suddenly taken shape in front of her. *And she was meant to walk up it?*

'I'm frightened,' she said quietly.

'Me too.' Robin rubbed his head. 'But, listen: when I

was an apprentice, just starting out, Dad said the most important thing for me to learn was this. If you hear a building complaining, groaning and stuff, you have to *get out*. You can't sit around, waiting to see what happens next.' He glanced up at the mountains. 'Get it?'

'Not really.'

A coughing fit overtook the boy. When it was over, he said, 'I *know* what they'll do to me back there. It's dungeon time, no questions asked. But up ahead – I don't know what might happen, and I'll take my chances.' He sniffed. 'There's a possibility of survival if you keep going. If you stay, you're going to get crushed. Dad always said, once things start falling, don't wait around hoping things will get better. They won't. Get out when you can.' Shadows of grief fell across his face, and Minnie saw he was half with her, half with his lost family. Then he lifted his chin. 'So I have to keep going.'

As for her? She wanted to stay very far away from that stone path. And yet her feet were inching forward all the same. She had a dreadful longing to scramble up the mountain and plunge head first into the place that frightened her the most.

As if he could sense her hesitation, Robin said, thoughtfully: 'Have you actually ever *seen* a giant from No-Go? In real life?'

'I've heard their screams once they're thrown into the dungeon. But I've never actually seen one.' Minnie gulped. 'You?'

'I hear their footsteps,' he admitted. 'Late at night, as they walk over the bridge, and back again. But all the rumours about them snatching children – I know they get repeated a lot, Minnie, but it's never happened where we live. We might be able to outsmart them. Maybe they can't catch children very well. Maybe they're stupid.' He looked up at the dark peaks and set his jaw. 'That's my only option, anyway. You can go back, if you want.'

The injustice of life on her island finally dawned on her. Robin was right. She *could* always go back, and she'd be protected by the fact that she'd been born in Quake Quarter. But all Robin had done was look after her, and he was a fugitive for ever – no adult would fight for him.

Robin and Twist waited.

She glanced behind her. She thought about Speck. Then she looked at the boy and the jackal, both panting from their exertions, both grubby, loyal and utterly brave.

'We'll go up,' she said.

Robin gave her a weak grin.

'After you,' said Minnie.

'No, I insist,' said Robin.

In the end it was Twist who first took the plunge,

leaping up on to the first stone. When he'd gone a little way, he circled round to stare right into Minnie's eyes, and dipped his head slightly, in a question.

'Coming,' she muttered. Minnie scrambled up the first large boulder, and then the next, pulling herself up as she went. It wasn't as hard as it looked.

PUBLIC SERVICE ANNOUNCEMENT

CHILDREN: if you value your life, never go near the No-Go Mountains. The giants who live within these peaks are bloodthirsty animals, and will chew you up and spit you out for breakfast.

- 33 -
CLOSER AND CLOSER

THE MOUNTAIN TRAIL was relatively smooth at first. But it wasn't a pretty path. The land was barren – no plants, flowers or grasses grew on it. Instead, there were scorch marks, burned-out scrub and blackened tree stumps. These offered no shelter and worse, no cover from prying eyes. Yet the path was dry and easy, and within an hour they were roughly a thousand feet above ground, with still no sign of the hunters below them.

'Perhaps they've given up,' suggested Minnie.

'Or gone to get backup,' muttered Robin. 'Why have you stopped?'

'The path –' stammered Minnie. 'It's vanished.'

Twist whined and paced in distress. He did seem *extremely keen* to go up the mountain, thought Minnie, momentarily distracted by his behaviour. For a moment, the three of them simply stood and stared in dismay. The route had . . . disappeared. All they were faced with was a sheer, vertical slab of smooth black rock, shiny and ruthless and as impossible to climb as ice.

'As if the mountain is making itself as difficult to enter as possible,' muttered Robin. They examined the slab, looking for any crevices to help them climb, but all they saw was flat and merciless rock.

'Like it's been carved,' said Minnie.

'Must have been done by the monsters to keep us away.' Robin rubbed his eyes. 'Perhaps they're not stupid at all.'

Minnie still wished he'd stop saying that word. For here it seemed to carry a grain of truth. She craned her neck backwards. The sheer, shiny expanse of unpassable rock, as high as the city walls, looked down at them triumphantly, as if to say: *Ha! Try finding a foothold on this!* Minnie and Robin exchanged an uneasy glance.

'We could start from the bottom again – see if there's another route up?' said Minnie.

A terrible coughing fit racked Robin. *He looks dreadful,* she thought, not for the first time. The climb had been long and his face was pale and clammy. Minnie knew how much the vigil he'd kept over her the night before must have cost him. 'I'll keep watch,' she said, firmly. 'You have a nap. Then we'll decide.'

They sat, side by side, with the stone behind them. After a moment, Robin curled on to his side. Twist lay on the other side of her and, within minutes, both were asleep.

The sun beat down on them all, and, exposed by her shrunken clothes, Minnie's wrists and ankles began to burn. *I forgot to pack my sun cream*, she thought, turning her wrists this way and that, watching as they went pink in the sun. She tugged at her top, trying to make it stretch back over her skin as it used to, and her fingers brushed against the darn Speck had sewn in the left sleeve, only a week ago.

At the thought of her, Minnie scanned over the landscape beneath her, hoping she might catch sight of Speck somewhere below. What would be happening to her? And what would Mama and Papa be doing? Were they looking for her, too? She gulped.

To distract herself from her ever-spiralling thoughts, she stared at the island stretched out beneath them, swathed in an early-morning light that made it look beautiful. How small everything looked! Beneath the mist she glimpsed the small cottage they'd run from and, beyond that, just visible, lay the broken remains of the jackal-meat factory. Past that stretched the edge of the island, ending in black sand that tumbled into the ocean.

Sunlight glinted off the Five Bridges river as it slowly bubbled its dirty way down the landscape below, cutting it neatly in half. Minnie wondered for the first time why the earthquake hadn't pulled down the Red Bridge. She squinted through the morning haze and realised she was quite right. Even though the bridge was old and dilapidated, as crumbling and unsafe as it ever was, it remained arched over the river, clinging on as before.

But Mrs Primrose had said that the earthquake had happened *all over the island*. So surely the bridge should be smashed to pieces by now? How could it have endured something so strong?

Minnie squinted against the sunshine. It wasn't just the bridge that had survived. Nothing had been broken at the lagoon, now she came to think of it – the sunloungers and the old water slide had been in their usual places yesterday. Robin's cottage had been intact. Even the cave she'd escaped into hadn't been shattered. From where she sat, she could see that the only damage had been to Quake Quarter and the meat factory.

Minnie rubbed her gritty eyes, then concentrated on the path below her, keeping on the lookout for the hunters.

- 34 -
THE VOICE OF THE MOUNTAINS

ROBIN WOKE WHEN the sun was high in the sky and they were all thirsty.

'Are we safe?' he said, quickly, struggling into a sitting position and wincing a little.

'We're safe.' She tried to sound reassuring. *For now.* 'No sign of the hunters.'

Robin wrapped his arms around his knees and gave her a curious look. 'You mean the search party.'

'Yes.'

'I've just realised – you've been calling them hunters for a while. Did you know that?' *That's because they're hunting us*, thought Minnie, with a pang of that deep, instinctive fear again. *I feel hunted. I feel like prey.*

But she didn't want to add any more to Robin's plate, so to him she said, as casually as she could: 'Look, it doesn't matter what I call them, does it?'

Robin cocked his head to the side and looked at her. 'It's a weird thing to say for a girl who loves *her island* so much. Would you call them hunters if you felt safe around them? Or liked them?' He nibbled at a bit of skin near his thumb.

'Look, are you just going to sit about overthinking everything, or are we going to climb this mountain?' Minnie tried to sound as commanding as possible.

'*Fine*,' he said, pulling himself up to standing position. He stood stiffly and rubbed the small of his back, in a gesture that was now familiar to Minnie.

Robin's unsettling questions echoed in her mind. *Do you feel safe, Minnie? Do you love where you come from?* She tugged at her sleeves nervously.

Another coughing fit made him shake and contort. He thumped at his chest. 'Rubble dust,' he said curtly. 'Gets in my lungs.'

'Right.' Minnie glanced up at the sheer face of rock and began to pace along the ledge, Twist loyally sticking to her heels. Robin went up to the sheer stone face, and, unnoticed by Minnie, began to press it, expertly, with his hands.

'There's got to be a way up,' she muttered, pacing nervously. 'Perhaps there's another trail, that circles the mountain—'

'I've found a way,' came Robin's voice, from deep within the smooth slab. 'It's right inside.'

'Inside . . . the *rock*?'

'Yes,' came the voice again. 'It looks solid, but there's one place it isn't. Like an illusion. Walk up to the rock and you'll see.'

Minnie did as he said, and found herself staring at the slab in frustration. 'I can't see anything,' she said.

'There's a vertical slit in the rock. You just can't see it because the rock behind it is exactly the same colour, so it takes a while to spot. Press your hands on it and you'll find it.'

Minnie pressed her fingers on the rock, and, after a few false attempts, was astonished when her hands went through it.

'I've found it!' she gasped. *Now* she could see it – an opening in the rock, almost impossible to spot unless you knew where it was.

'It's too narrow,' she said.

'You have to walk in sideways, like a crab. Then it opens out,' came the instruction.

Once she had walked sideways for a few moments, with Twist right behind her, the opening widened, and Minnie found herself in a dark but relatively roomy chamber. It was a relief to be out of the sun, where her skin had been turning progressively pinker and more freckled.

Robin stood in front of her, looking proud.

'Well done,' said Minnie. 'How on earth did you work that out?'

He gave a tiny shrug. 'Rock is what I know. We've always got to test walls for weakness,' he said. A note of reluctant admiration crept into his voice, as he pointed to a series of vertical granite grooves carved into the mountain itself. 'Found their hidden ladder. I reckon that will take us right over.' He looked at her. 'If we want to go.'

The two children stared, and hesitated.

'What choice do we have?' muttered Minnie, glancing down at Twist for luck. He was pawing the ground restlessly, as if impatient to get going. 'What if he can't manage?' The steps cut into the stone looked challenging enough for a human, let alone a young injured jackal. 'He's come this far – I can't bear to leave him behind.'

To her astonishment, Robin addressed Twist directly. 'Go on,' he said, in that rare tender voice he'd last used when helping Minnie back to his cottage. 'Give it a go.'

To her even greater surprise, Twist didn't bare his teeth at Robin's voice, but, after staring up the ladder for a bit, put one paw on, and then another, and then scrabbled up.

Robin and Minnie's eyes met.

He blushed. 'Must have been the chicken feed,' he said quickly, before following the jackal without saying another word.

Smiling faintly, Minnie went last.

After a long, dizzying climb, Minnie felt a breeze ruffle the hair on top of her head. She pulled herself out of a hole in the stone and, panting, joined Twist and Robin as they squeezed on to a tiny, ribbon-thin ledge right on top of the mountain. They were standing between two worlds, and buffeted on each side by strong winds. One particularly strong gust nearly blew Robin over, and he grabbed hold of Minnie for balance. After a second, she held on to him too, and turned her head, heart racing, to face the nightmare within.

'Doesn't look that . . . scary, does it?' said Robin, after a while.

'No,' agreed Minnie, looking down into a natural basin inside the ring of peaks.

The floor of the mountain bowl was dusty brown and black, as if scorched. Here and there, plumes of smoke lifted up. They caught the odd sound of habitation; a jeering laugh, the sound of calling, the sound of glass breaking. But they weren't sounds full of gore and bloodlust, or battling giants and simmering cauldrons. They were full of something else, that they couldn't quite understand.

Yet the effect on Twist was electric. The young jackal paced up and down along the ledge, wagging his tail, looking up at Minnie and then glancing back into the basin. From his mouth, a howling started, and he pawed at the ledge, not caring that by doing so he was making it crumble beneath them.

'Maybe he can smell food,' Robin said, mystified. 'Stop that, will you?'

The jackal's behaviour grew increasingly strange. He'd paw at the ledge, then lift one paw slightly, body as straight as an arrow, staring down into the mountain basin with a look of intense concentration. After a few minutes of this, he lifted his triangular head far back and emitted a howl – a sound of such melancholic beauty that it seemed to hover in the air even after he had finished, lingering like a question.

Minnie couldn't work out if the howls she heard afterwards were merely the echoes of the jackal's howl, bouncing around the mountain and coming back to them, or the replies of other jackals on the loose around the island. Either way, her temper frayed.

'*Stop* drawing attention to us,' she hissed at him. 'And get back. You're going to make us fall down if you keep pawing at this ledge.'

Robin snorted. 'He's not going to do what you say. He's not *tamed*, he's a wild—'

Minnie felt a wild rush of love and pride as the jackal took one last lingering look at the inside of the mountain and then padded reluctantly towards her. Just as Minnie gave Robin a smug smile, the narrow path of earth gave way beneath them and they were plunged into icy-cold darkness.

*

After rolling and falling for several minutes, during which time all three added more bruises and cuts to their collection, they landed with a bang on a damp dirt floor.

'What was *that*?' gasped Minnie.

'We fell down a hole, I think.'

'It didn't look like a hole,' said Minnie. 'It was a ridge.'

'Until it wasn't,' said Robin.

They were quiet as this sunk in.

'We were meant to fall in,' whispered Minnie, ice-cold with fright. 'It was a *trap*.'

'A concealed trap!' gulped Robin. 'A concealed ladder . . . Maybe the mountain giants aren't so stupid after all . . .'

'Have you broken anything?' said Minnie, gingerly moving.

'I – I don't think so. Something broke my fall. Something quite hard and painful, though.' He gulped. 'Almost . . . bony.'

Minnie spoke very loudly and very quickly to drown him out. 'Where's Twist? Is he here?' She heard him give a soft whine nearby, and scrabble over to her. A rough tongue licked her hand and then her face. Twist sniffed her all over, as if checking for any cuts and bruises, and then settled down next to her, his warmth a huge source of comfort. Minnie stroked his fur and tried to comprehend their new reality.

It was so dark they could barely see each one another. It appeared they had fallen right into a lair. They were helpless. Things did not seem good. Minnie noticed a tiny pinprick of light, coming from a distance. The opening of the chamber they were in, perhaps.

'Can you see that?' muttered Robin.

'Yeah,' said Minnie.

'Is it me, or is it moving towards us?'

*

She was just squinting into the distance, trying to work it out, when a new wave of cramps ripped through her body – a fresh torment, one that felt like her muscles were tearing. Her hand tightened on the fur on Twist's back, and he gave a tiny yelp. 'If . . . the . . . No-Go giants do eat us,' Minnie gasped, 'can you ask them to start with me?' At least it would put an end to her pain. How much longer would she have to bear it?

By now the pinprick of light had grown to a swinging orb and was getting nearer.

Twist's fur began to rise, but then, mystifyingly, she heard the tell-tale thump of his tail wagging.

'What *is* that?' murmured Robin.

'A lamp,' whispered Minnie through chattering teeth. Twist growled and thumped. The floor shook as footsteps got closer. The orb swung nearer.

The loudest voice that Minnie had ever heard in her entire life said: 'Oh, we have fresh droppings. I wonder who it is today. More officials?'

Suddenly, the light was shining directly on them and they were exposed under it unable to see who held it, blinking like moles as it picked its way across their faces.

And then there was a huge gasp, so large that Minnie felt the skin on her face sucked into it for a moment.

'But you are *children*,' boomed a huge, surprised voice. 'Actual human children.' And the lamp fell to the floor, as suddenly as if whoever was holding it had dropped it in surprise, and the echo of the metal clanging against the bony ground seemed to go on for ever and ever.

Minnie's heart boomed as loudly as the voice, as if it

wanted to burst out of her chest and run for cover. All her life she'd been told that pure evil lurked within the mountains, and now she was hearing its voice.

- 35 -
BLADE

MINNIE REACHED OUT for the comforting warmth of the
jackal, but her hand met cold air. Where had Twist gone?
She reached out for Robin instead, only to find his hand
was already reaching for hers. She held it gently, mindful
of his rubbling injuries. He squeezed her hand in return,
and then they waited.

To Minnie's surprise, the giant in front of them gave
a delighted, low chuckle, and as the lamp was picked up
again it revealed Twist's black nose nuzzling a giant hand,
larger than even Sandborn's had been, dotted with red
hair and puckered all over with scars.

It was the most terrifying hand Minnie had ever seen.

And Twist seemed to love it, licking it with total
abandon. She could practically hear him purring as he
nudged the big hand again, butting it gently for attention.

I should have called you Traitor, not Twist, thought
Minnie.

'I've never seen one of you out of a cage before,'
boomed the voice, as the hand gently patted the jackal's

head. 'You're a beauty, aren't you, boy?'

Twist's yellow eyes closed in bliss. Then the giant swung the lantern back in the children's faces.

'You really are children, aren't you?'

'Y– yes?' said Minnie, croakily.

'Look at the size of you,' said the voice in reply. 'Fascinating. How do you not just break?'

'Um—' said Robin.

'Did you say something?' said the voice.

'N– not really,' confessed Robin.

'It's like listening to mosquitos,' muttered the giant, as if to himself. 'Very tricky.' There was a massive shift of air and light as the giant crouched down on his haunches. When he next spoke, Minnie was blasted in the face by warm air.

'Do you have . . . names?'

'Minnie and Robin,' said Minnie, as loudly as she could.

'And where are you from?'

'I'm . . . I'm from the rubbler district,' said Robin.

'I live on Quake Avenue,' said Minnie.

The light stayed fixed on their faces.

'Where d'you get the jackal?' said the voice.

'He found me. On the river path. I think his cage at the factory was broken in the quake.'

'And he hasn't attacked either of you?' said the voice, sounding sharp and surprised. Minnie's ears had begun to ring.

'Me,' said Robin. 'Once. But – then we got used to each other. And I fed him.'

There was a lengthy pause.

'You are very odd,' boomed the voice. 'And very young. What are you doing in these dangerous mountains?'

'We – we – I mean – I—'

The children were nearly swept to the back of the cave on the strength of the giant's sigh. 'Come on, I haven't got all day. Are you here on purpose?'

'Yes,' admitted Minnie.

'Why on earth would human children come to our mountains?'

'It was our only choice,' whimpered Robin. 'We were being chased.'

'We wouldn't have come here voluntarily,' added Minnie.

'Few do,' said the giant agreeably. Minnie shivered; they still hadn't seen their inquisitor's face.

'We were trying to stay on the ridge—' said Robin.

'But our trap got you.' The giant bent down to stroke the jackal again, and Minnie caught a glimpse of a wily, smoke-smeared face, and of a huge red beard, threaded with gold strands. 'What do you mean, this was your only choice?'

Minnie and Robin went very quiet. The giant harumphed. 'You'd better tell me quick. You're in enemy territory, and the only thing you have to trade is the truth. Vastly underrated as a thing to barter with, in my experience.'

Beside her, Robin held his breath, as if waiting for Minnie to speak.

'Well, if you won't tell me in the dark, maybe you'll talk more in the light. Come on. Up you get.'

The orb swung, as the giant turned and began to walk away, followed by the jackal. Minnie stumbled to her feet, trying to work out what hurt more, her body from falling fifty feet, her newly painful muscles or how quickly Twist seemed to have switched his allegiance.

Robin was overcome by a bout of coughing. Minnie was racked by another agonising cramp that ripped through her muscles. As they both coughed and moaned, stumbling after the giant in front of them, he laughed mercilessly.

'I hope you look better than you sound,' said the giant, turning and walking away without bothering to look back. 'Follow me. And watch out for all the bones. They can be a real trip hazard.'

The mountain giant led them out of the tunnel, over a carpet of things which crunched and cracked. Eventually, all four of them emerged into a clearing, furnished with a home-made stove, a battered copper kettle the size of a small tree and a rough blanket on the floor. It looked for all the world like a sentry post. He put down his lamp, and then he turned round, and Minnie and Robin got to see who they were speaking to.

He was quite a sight.

Up till then, both of them had only *ever* seen giants in the black-and-white uniform handed out to servants by the Giant Management Company: neat, tidy, with not a hair out of place or a wrinkle in a sock. But the towering giant in front of them looked as if he'd eat a uniform for breakfast and then belch it out in the next breath. Brightly coloured scraps of material were swathed around him in haphazard knots; he was caked all over in grime; his red beard was matted and filthy; but he had one thing neither of them had ever seen before in a giant, *ever*. Swagger. It was a tired, faded swagger. It had a shaky quality that suggested it might not last much longer. But it was there.

He put his hands on his waist and looked down at them with a roguish glint. 'Every time I see representatives of

the human race,' he pronounced (in a voice that would have got him into trouble back in the Quake Quarter for being louder than the regulation volume servants could speak at), 'I thank the earth, sky and everything in between that I dodged that particular bullet.'

There was an awkward pause while the children absorbed this insult.

'You know our names. Now, please, can you tell us yours?' Minnie asked.

'Eh? Speak up, child.'

She repeated herself, shouting.

The giant peered down and looked at Minnie properly for the first time. 'I am Blade,' he announced.

'They call you that on account – of your knives?' stuttered Robin, looking warily around the giant's massive frame.

'On account of my wit,' said Blade. 'Although – funny you should mention it – I also love a good dagger.' And he lifted up a flap of material which might have once been a waistcoat, and treated them to a glimpse of shining knife-edges nestling in a leather pouch.

Robin made a tiny moan which he covered up with a cough.

Blade's face twitched. 'Very good for opening tricky nuts. Don't suppose you have any, do you?'

'Sorry,' said Robin, relief flooding his voice. 'Not today.'

Blade looked visibly disappointed. 'Shame,' he sighed, nearly blowing them all over again. 'I love nuts. Such a great snack and source of energy.' Then he seemed to remember why he'd brought the children out. 'You are trespassing here,' he said, reasonably. 'Why?' A huge finger the length of a desk was pointed at Minnie. 'Speak.'

Somewhat reassured that they weren't going to die, at least not immediately, Minnie swallowed. 'I'm on the run,' she shouted. 'And he's with me because . . . well, because he helped me, and now he's in trouble.'

Blade frowned. 'You? On the run? A nice girl from a respectable part of the island? With everything to live for?' It was almost skilful how he made that sound like an insult. 'Why?'

Maybe it was the heat, or maybe it was Blade's actually quite kindly eyes, but Minnie decided to just be honest. 'I have a giant. I was meant to turn her to stone today.' To her horror, tears began to spring from her eyes. She put both hands to her face and went quiet, struggling not to sob.

'She didn't want to go through with the ceremony,' whispered Robin.

'You didn't want to? Well, well, well,' said Blade again, and this time his voice was soft and wondering. He looked into Minnie's eyes. 'I've never heard of that before. Perhaps there are some hearts behind those city walls.'

Minnie blinked back her tears. She tilted her head back and stared up into Blade's face, even though it hurt her neck to do it, and she saw only wonder and sadness there.

'Did you say you were being followed?' said Blade, suddenly, his yellow eyes narrowed.

The children hesitated. 'The Giant Management Company are looking for me,' admitted Minnie.

'Do they know you're here?' said Blade, his voice taut.

'I don't know,' she admitted. 'There was no sign of them behind us, though, once we got to the mountain.'

Blade seemed to weigh up what to do. 'Well, this is a tough one,' he admitted. He pointed up to the ledge. 'Usually, if anyone falls into my trap and survives, I pick them up and fling them back over the ridge as best I can. And if the GMC know you're here, then you'll have brought us trouble, and we can do without that. But –' he eyed the children, and the jackal – 'if an animal of the island has stayed with you this long, you can't be all bad. And I have to admit, you intrigue me. Especially *you*.' His yellow eyes blinked at Minnie. 'Very much you. Fancy you running away from your own ceremony! This is . . . new. And you live right inside Quake Quarter, as well, which could be very useful for our search—' Abruptly, he bit off the rest of his sentence, as if he thought he had said too much. 'Never mind.'

'Your search?' Minnie gulped. Had Blade just *admitted* they were looking for children to steal? 'Searching for what?'

But the red-haired, nut-loving, knife-carrying giant turned away, surprisingly nimble for one so vast, his many ribbons and strips of fabric whirling with the movement, and he took huge strides down a wide scorched path. 'Follow me,' he said, curtly. 'Please.' He looked at Twist, and grinned, and Minnie gasped at the sight of all those giant teeth. 'You too, boy.'

The jackal wagged his tail and plunged after him.

'He wants us to follow him even deeper into No-Go?' Minnie said.

'Seems like it,' said Robin, slowly.

'He didn't even try to persuade us.'

'He doesn't have to,' said Robin. 'Or are you forgetting the knives?'

Blade turned around and smiled graciously. 'I'm not sure if I mentioned this amid all the excitement, but you have no choice here. I just added the "please" next to "follow me" to be polite. Can't *believe* I had to spell that out,' he grumbled to himself, turning down the path again.

So they followed the giant into the heart of the lawless mountains; the place which had haunted Minnie's nightmares since she was tiny. And with every step she took on the black earth, that feeling of destiny grew stronger.

- 36 -
A SURPRISINGLY LARGE CAKE

MINNIE HAD ALWAYS assumed the inside of No-Go would be overgrown and scary with wildness. But the track Blade led them down was just as scorched as the mountain path they'd taken earlier. With every step they took into the belly of the place, Minnie felt increasingly helpless, at the mercy of the strange giant thundering away in front of them. How on earth would they escape? Perhaps if she'd paid more attention during geography, she'd have an idea of how to flee this bleak place. But they'd never really learned that much about No-Go, apart from how terrible its inhabitants were.

Blade's gold-flecked beard swung as he marched on. Why had he decided to move them on? And, more importantly, *what would happen once they got there?* While she fretted, the sun beat down on them. *I'm going to burn*, thought Minnie, glancing at her ankles and wrists.

They reached a vast square, at least three times the size of the Old Town. Around the perimeter were burned-out, hollow tree stumps, on which rough planks of wood had been nailed. On these were goods, the size and type of which made both children gasp. Medicine bottles the height of a pony, mammoth bouquets of dried herbs that would have made a bed collapse, shrivelled slices of fruit the length of her arm, dusty barrels of various liquids, huge tankards . . .

A few giants were desultorily browsing these stalls, talking in low voices with the traders behind them.

They had reached the giants' market.

Around a makeshift bar, in various stages of wakefulness, were giants of all ages. Some were hunched over half-empty tankards; some were beginning to drain full ones. As they watched, one woman gulped down the contents of a glass before throwing it to the floor, making it smash. As her companions clapped, Minnie remembered the sound of breaking glass she'd heard from the mountain ridge. This, it appeared, was as good a game as it got within No-Go. She eyed the group fearfully. They were the *fugitives*. The lawless ones. The rebel ones. Right up close. She held her breath a little and shuffled a bit closer to Robin.

In between the few transactions, the stall owners spent their time glancing at the mountain peaks above them, fearfully. Minnie remembered, with a pang of surprise, that she'd been doing exactly the same thing at Florin's ceremony. She'd never thought the giants on the inside would *ever* do the same thing.

What could they possibly be frightened of? Her thoughts tumbled through her. She'd always thought No-Go was a place of pure evil, but all she saw was fear and sadness. The only thing that seemed to cheer any of them up was the sight of Twist. All the giants in the market noticed him, and tried to tempt him over, holding out titbits and whistling. Twist gave them all a sweet gaze from his almond-shaped eyes, held his head proudly and trotted on, as if to say he was flattered by the adoration and not at all surprised by it, but he was quite busy, unfortunately, and couldn't stop.

The four crossed the market and followed another charred track, Blade barely bothering to check that the children were behind him. On either side of this path grew a few short golden grasses, which eased the landscape's misery a bit, yet the air still smelled of smoke.

'Do you – have a lot of barbecues?' asked Minnie.

Blade snorted, but said nothing.

Finally they reached a clearing, an area of grass stubble which had been flattened. And within this space were two giants.

The older one, a woman, was sitting on a wooden

stool. She had elegant hands which were resting calmly in her lap, although Minnie noticed the backs of them were puckered and twisted with scars, like Blade's.

The other giant, a younger woman, was sitting on the ground next to a mound of old rags. She was ripping these into long thin strips. Both had the same clothing as Blade – that is, garments made entirely of strips of fabric knotted to each other, then fashioned into loose tunics. They looked, Minnie thought, oddly comfortable. She found herself comparing the clothes to the tight, ill-fitting dress she'd had to wear to Florin's ceremony, and knew which she preferred.

At the children's approach, the two giants regarded them calmly. It was only when they got a bit closer that Minnie saw how still the women held themselves; their yellow eyes seemed to flicker with a million thoughts, one after the other.

'Blade,' said the older female giant, bringing her scarred hands together in gratitude, 'you brought them speedily. Thank you.'

'You heard the news then, Issa?'

'We did. Something this rare travels fast.' She looked at Minnie and Robin, as if sizing them up, and then said, to Blade: 'Have you got a sharp knife?'

Blade beamed with delight. 'I do! Let's see now . . .'

Minnie and Robin shared a terrified glance. They'd been tricked! All their wildest fears had been right. While Blade reached into his peculiar multi-coloured waistcoat and pulled out the longest, shiniest knife he had, Minnie's blood turned to ice. *We should never have come*, she thought, furious and scared at the same time. *I was right all along.*

- 37 -
REFRESHMENTS

BLADE HELD UP a knife that was as long as a carriage, and sliced it slowly through the air, grinning with menace.

'Something like this?' he said, turning the knife edge this way and that. Robin made a tiny whimpering noise. Minnie grabbed his hand and tugged it, but her legs were too wobbly to run.

The older giant looked at Blade's offering and smiled gently. 'Yes, that will be perfect. Chesca, please bring out the cake.'

Minnie and Robin glanced at each other. *Cake?*

'You must be hungry and thirsty, children. We took the liberty of preparing you food and drink.' Issa smiled ruefully. 'It's simple fare, as we can't grow much, but it should fill you up.' Behind them, the younger giant was carrying a large tray. On this was heaped a huge circular object, the size of which made Minnie and Robin gasp, for the sponge underneath was at least the width of a carriage wheel.

'That's a cake?' said Robin.

Issa beamed proudly. 'It is indeed. An old recipe, going back hundreds of years.'

'I – I've never seen giant food before,' murmured Robin.

'Me neither,' said Minnie, realising it for the first time. Back at home, Speck ate what they ate – except more of it, if it was available. Minnie used to think there was something undignified about the way Speck had to gobble several portions of food to feel full. Now she wondered if there was something wrong instead with the way humans fed giants such tiny portions. Wasn't there something cruel about it? *Was Speck permanently hungry?*

'Bark cake,' said the older giant, breaking into these thoughts. 'We grind the bark of trees for flour. Then we soften it with any seaweed we can salvage from the beaches. Those trips aren't made many times a year, as, if we are caught, we get thrown into the dungeon. Please, I'd like you to have some.'

Minnie grimaced at the mention of seaweed.

'Giants have *died* for that cake to be made,' Blade growled. 'Eat some.'

'Sounds delicious,' said Minnie, hastily.

'Wait,' said Blade, agreeably. 'Let me cut you a slice each.'

Blade sliced down into the sponge with obvious

enjoyment at the excuse to use one of his knives. Once he'd finished, he placed a slice each into Minnie and Robin's outstretched hands. Each piece was as big as a pillow, and required both hands to hold it, so Minnie found herself staring, for the first time in her life, at a literal armful of cake. It smelled a little of seaweed and salt, and it was extremely heavy.

The children shot surprised looks at each other. It didn't take long for their arms to begin to shake. Robin raised an eyebrow, said, 'Here goes nothing,' opened his mouth and plunged straight in. Within seconds, his face had disappeared into the slice. He made a tiny surprised noise, hesitated and then continued eating. Without any cutlery or plate, Minnie realised she had no option but to do exactly the same . . .

It wasn't a sweet cake. It was barely, really, a cake. It tasted exactly of what it was made of, and she couldn't say she hadn't been warned – and it dried her mouth out, but it was food, at least, and she didn't want to appear rude by spitting it out. When Twist nudged her leg pointedly, Minnie was happy to accidentally on purpose drop most of her piece for him. She thought longingly of the pastries in Quake Quarter, and glanced over at Robin, but the boy was licking his lips.

'Reminds me of the mud cookies Mum used to make,' he said, 'when times were really hard.' He blushed a little. Minnie looked down at the ground, embarrassed for a moment.

While he ate and the jackal snuffled on the ground for more of the bark cake, Blade and the two other giants muttered to one another. Fragments of their conversation came to Minnie.

'In the trap,' Blade was saying. '. . . Quake Quarter . . . wants to prevent . . . ceremony, she said.'

There was a loaded pause.

'Interesting. Thank you, Blade,' said the older female giant, who wore a faded collection of light turquoise fabrics, gathered and tied round her in a series of tight knots. She plucked at one of the strips and Minnie noticed, again, that scar on the back of her hand.

Blade reached for a slice of cake, finished it in two bites, wiped his knife on his sleeve, and put it away carefully. 'I won't stay. There are only two other lookouts patrolling the entire barrier. Goodbye, children. Don't forget to speak up.'

He saved his warmest smile, however, for the jackal, who gave a whine as Blade walked out of the clearing, but stayed where he was, much to Minnie's relief.

'I am Issa,' said the older giant pleasantly, reassembling herself on her stool. 'I suppose I am the elder of No-Go. And this –' she indicated the young giant who had brought over the cake, but who had now gone back to ripping fabric – 'is Chesca. She reached us last year from the GMC, and has stayed with us ever since.'

'She ran away from the compound?' gasped Minnie.

Chesca gave her a loaded look, and nodded, while a dark thrill ran through Minnie. Chesca was a *criminal*. Minnie felt guilty just looking at her. Once Robin had finished his cake, there was a pause.

'And so,' said Issa, matter-of-factly, 'what can we do for you?'

'P– pardon?'

'You must be here for a reason. No one ever just strolls through. So what is it? If you tell us, maybe we can be of some assistance.' Issa smiled. 'And in return – perhaps you can help us.'

Robin swallowed. 'How would we do that?'

'Oh, there's always something. Knowledge, usually.'

Minnie took a deep, shuddering breath. 'Can I just check one thing?' she said, nervously.

'Yes,' said Issa.

'Are you going to harm us?'

'Or eat us?' said Robin.

Chesca snorted, but said nothing.

'Harm you? Eat you?' said Issa mildly. 'No. Whatever gave you that idea?'

Were they teasing?

'Well, we know that you try to steal human children on a regular basis,' Minnie said, tentatively. Issa didn't deny it. 'Why would you be doing that, if it wasn't to do something – nasty?'

A flicker of pain raced across Issa's features. She took a deep breath. 'You're partly right,' she admitted. 'But we don't want to harm a child. We're not trying to steal anyone. We're searching for one.'

'Isn't that the same thing?' said Robin, going a bit pink at his own daring.

'Not really,' said Issa. 'But enough of that, for the time being. Why are you here?'

Minnie remembered what Blade had told them: how the truth was their most valuable currency in No-Go. She puffed her cheeks out, and decided she had nothing to lose. 'Well, I have a . . . giant. A servant. Like a lot of people have, where I live.'

Chesca ripped a piece of fabric extra loudly. Twist's ears swivelled in alarm, but he settled on the ground, watching them all.

Issa nodded. 'Yes. We know of your customs. What is

the name of the giant who cares for you?'

Minnie's lips trembled. 'Speck. Well, that's her nickname. I don't know her real name.'

Issa and Chesca looked at each other.

'My ceremony was meant to happen yesterday.' Minnie paused. 'Do you know what a ceremony is?'

'Yes,' said Issa. 'We know. We see the statues that preserve your bridges and mansions. We see them every time we venture down on to the plain. The giants who gave their lives.'

'Y– yes. For the good of the . . . well, anyway, I – I decided that I wasn't ready for my ceremony. It was sprung on me, last minute, because of the quake. Did you feel it?'

The two giants shook their golden heads, slowly. 'It didn't quite reach us,' said Issa after a while. 'They generally don't.'

'Oh.' There it was again; that earthquake glitch that Minnie was only just beginning to realise existed. Why did the quakes only target bits of the island, and leave the others alone? And why would Mrs Primrose lie about it? 'Most of Quake Quarter was destroyed,' Minnie continued. 'They needed an urgent supply of statues. They wanted me to do my ceremony earlier than planned. I didn't think I could. So I ran away.'

'Why?' said Issa, and she and Chesca seemed to go very quiet.

'Because if I stayed away, then – then my giant wouldn't—'

'Be murdered by your barbaric tradition?' suggested Chesca, quietly.

No one here likes islanders very much, thought Minnie. 'Well, um, they don't like the word "murder" – it's not true and it's not nice; and it's an old, much-honoured tradition, and ceremonies are for the, um, the good of . . .' Her voice trailed off. She couldn't bring herself to say it any more. Minnie thought of the giant who had raised her, and her heart pounded with love and grief.

'I don't want to turn her to stone, ever,' said Minnie quietly. 'Because I love her.'

There was a tiny gasp from Chesca. Issa blinked, rapidly, as if trying to hold back tears. 'We've never heard of such a thing,' she said quietly.

'Love is a punishable offence,' agreed Chesca, staring down at her lap for a moment. 'You might be the only child in the history of the island who loves her giant.'

Minnie's lip wobbled. 'Well, I do. A lot. As much as I love my parents. Perhaps a tiny bit more, sometimes. She taught me to read, and tucked me in almost every night, and took me to school, and swam with me, and . . . lots of things. So many things. I can't be without her. That's why I ran away.'

She hung her head. It was the first time she'd ever admitted it out loud. Here, in the burned-out basin of the No-Go Mountains, admitting she loved the giant who'd brought her up somehow didn't sound so bad. When she lifted her head, Issa and Chesca and Robin were all staring at her. Twitch bared his teeth a little, ready to defend her.

'P– please don't tell anyone I said any of that,' stammered Minnie. 'I'd be in so much trouble.' She winced. That horrible stretching feeling was back in her muscles.

The pain moved up into her arms. Minnie had a flashback to the feverish night she'd spent at Robin's cottage, vomiting and shivering. She couldn't bear for that to happen again. She steeled herself against the oncoming cramps and was relieved when they softened.

Issa glanced towards the mountain peaks and then looked back down at Robin and Minnie. Then, hurriedly, she said, 'Thank you for being honest with us, Minnie. Now – perhaps you can help me with something. You're from Quake Quarter, aren't you? Would you be able to look at this map and let us know if any houses are missing?'

The elderly giant produced a large, faded scroll from the bag beside her, which she unfolded carefully and laid out on the ground with her scarred hands. Minnie peered at it, and caught her breath with amazement. On it were all the houses in Quake Quarter, drawn with great care in many different types of ink, as if added to bit by bit over many years. Next to each house were written, in painstakingly tidy writing, the names and ages of the children inside the house. Some of the names had been struck through. A few of the houses were missing, including her own, but it was an almost complete record of all the children on the island, and where they lived.

Minnie bent down and gasped in amazement. 'This is – incredible!' she said. 'How have you done all this?'

'It's not been easy,' said Issa, looking solemnly at the faded, soft paper. 'We have lost many along the way. But we think it will be worth it, if we're to ever find who we're looking for.'

Now that Minnie had told them all her deepest, darkest secret, she felt the least they could do was share one in return. *Finally*, she thought, with an uneasy thrill, *I can find out why the No-Go giants keep looking into children's bedrooms.*

'Who are you looking for?' said Minnie.

'A child.'

'What could you possibly do with a child, though?' stammered Robin.

Minnie nodded in agreement. She now knew that no one in No-Go wanted to harm her or Robin; the giants were sad, but not murderous. So why were they so keen on finding one human child? Her heart began to thud. She felt as if she was on the brink of a huge discovery. Her skin broke out in goosebumps.

'Why are you doing this?' she asked. 'Why do you creep over the bridge and look into children's windows, and get thrown in the dungeon for doing so? Why do you want a human child so badly?'

Issa looked into Minnie's face, and hesitated.

'We're not looking for a human child,' she said, tentatively. Minnie frowned. 'But we *are* looking for a child. An infant from *our* race. A giantling. Who was stolen from her mother.' Real, almost unimaginable pain flickered across Issa's features. 'My granddaughter. That's who we're trying to find.'

- 38 -
THE CHANGE

MINNIE AND ROBIN exchanged puzzled looks. There was something about Robin's face that made Minnie nervous.

'Someone stole your granddaughter?' she stammered, looking around the clearing. 'But who? And why?' Despite the heat she began to shiver. And then those awful cramps resumed in her limbs with a terrible vengeance. 'Issa,' she said, softly, her eyes fluttering. 'Have you got anything to numb my pain? I broke all the bottles that my healer made . . .'

At the mention of the healer, Issa's manner changed. She bristled all over with fear, as if Minnie had just summoned a ring of demons to surround the clearing.

'Your healer?' said Issa. 'What does he look like?'

'Quite short. Rubbery lips. He normally has – egg on his tie,' Minnie stammered. 'Do you know Mr Straw?'

'You stay away from him,' said Issa, urgently. 'He's a bad, bad man.'

'He's – but he – he gives me medicine,' gasped Minnie, through her pain. 'Ever since I was little. It . . . helps.'

'She was born with defective muscles,' added Robin.

'The medicine helps her grow, but she's been without it for a while now, and she keeps doing this.'

In a daze, Minnie noticed the way her wrists had begun to shimmer in the sunshine, through the sunburn, as if she was coated in lots of golden freckles.

Issa seemed to notice it too, and her eyes blazed suddenly with emotion as she looked at Minnie full in the face.

'It was *you*,' she whispered. 'You're the one we've been looking for, all this time. We found a lot of other children, but they were always the wrong ones.'

Wrong un, remembered Minnie, dizzily. That was what she'd read in the paper that the giant had said, when he'd seen Milton Yellowtongue. He was the 'wrong one.' They'd been looking for … *her*?

'We wanted to find *you*, Minnie. You were the stolen child. We'd just about given up hope of ever finding you. And then –' Issa clapped her hands together – 'and then you walked right here. The island brought you here.' Issa looked fondly at Robin and Twist. 'Everything that happened, and the friends you made, played their part in bringing you home.'

'H– *home*?' gasped Minnie. And then she could no longer speak, for her arms and legs felt as if someone invisible had put her on a rack and was stretching them all. She finally began to change into the shape her body had been reaching for, and denied, her entire life.

Her eyes closed as the sensations overwhelmed her.

'You're so nearly there, Minnie,' she heard Issa say, softly. 'Your body is doing what it needs to do. Don't be frightened.'

'Wait – is that your response? Let's all just sit around and do *nothing*? Why aren't you helping her?' That was Robin, she could tell, who sounded like the boy she'd first met – tired and sad and angered by everything around him. 'You're *monsters*—'

Twist began to bark, and then there was the sound of ripping clothes, and then the final stage of her pain blotted out the rest.

Some time later, it was over. She blinked her eyes open, groggily. Someone had thrown a large blanket over her. She felt entirely strange. But that dreadful pain was completely over. There was an ecstatic snuffling on her face and a wet nose was pushed into her eye sockets and then all over her face.

'Mmmff,' she said. 'Hello, Twist.'

She craned her neck back, and saw that Robin had scuttled as far back as he could to the edge of the clearing. His hands were over his mouth. His eyes were wide.

'What's wrong?' she said. *I sound different. Why do I sound different?* To Robin, she said: 'Why are you looking at me like that?'

'You –' he raised a trembling finger in her direction, and dropped it. 'You.'

Minnie peered down at herself. Shaking all over, hardly daring to do it, she brought out one arm from underneath the blanket. The minute she saw it for the first time, she understood.

She was a giant. Her skin was covered with golden freckles. Everything about her was bigger.

Nausea rose in the back of her throat. The world spun. She closed her eyes again, hoping it was just a bad dream.

'Has she gone to sleep?' said Chesca, sounding surprised.

'Shock,' murmured Issa. To Minnie, she said: 'Why don't you try standing up? See how it feels?'

'I don't want to,' Minnie moaned. Of all the nightmares she'd ever had about the No-Go Mountains, and there had been some dreadful ones, *this* particular version had never come up, and it was truly the worst of all. She'd been turned into a *giant*.

'Just try,' said Issa gently. 'Go on. You can't lie under that blanket for ever.'

Minnie hated everything, but she knew Issa was right. With her new giant hands, she pushed down the blanket, then, blushing – for her old clothes had ripped right off her and were lying around her in rags – she pulled it right back up again. Awkwardly, holding on to the blanket as best she could, she got to her knees, clutching it round her like a towel.

And then, hardly believing what she was doing, she staggered to her feet and unfurled her full length, wobbling a little as she adjusted to the feel of her new body. She felt like she was on stilts, and grew a little dizzy.

She looked down at Issa and Chesca, and gulped when she realised that she was even taller than them. Robin, who had stumbled to a standing position with a wide-eyed look of trauma, wasn't even the height of her knees.

Chesca nodded approvingly. 'Over nineteen feet,' she said quietly, looking up into her face.

'I'm – I'm taller than Sandborn?' stammered Minnie.

'Just like your mother,' said Issa, eyes sparkling with pride. Minnie wished she'd stop talking like that. Twist cocked his head and blinked at her, as if trying to get used to her new height.

For a few seconds, no one said anything. Minnie looked at Robin again. *Does he think I'm a monster now, too?* She felt an unspeakable sadness. He'd always said how much he hated giants – did that mean he hated her now?

Glancing away from him for a moment, she was astonished to see how much her horizon had changed. From her new, unfamiliar height, the market stalls and its customers were clearly visible in the distance.

I feel, she thought wildly, *like a screecher*.

She forced her attention back to the clearing. Robin was still wide-eyed and disturbed. It flipped a switch in her. 'What have you *done?*' she demanded, hating the sound of her new giant voice. She felt loud and ugly.

'Done?' said Issa, mildly. 'You are our beloved stolen child. We haven't done—'

Making sure her right hand was still clutching her blanket, Minnie used her left one to point, furiously, at Issa. 'Stop. That's gibberish. I don't believe you. *You've* done this to me. I don't know how – maybe you put something in the cake – but you've put a spell on me! You've *poisoned me!* And I – I demand that you change me back! Now!'

She whirled on Chesca. 'Stop fiddling with your strips and look at me! Look at me! Why am I like this?' She looked at her left hand and wanted to be sick.

'I've even got the same sparkling freckles as you! This isn't fair! Make me a girl again!'

'I can't do that,' Issa said. 'Because you've always been a giant.'

'I'm not a giant. I'm an islander.'

'You are both,' said Issa. 'It isn't just humans who are islanders, despite what they would like us to believe. And a giant is who you are, Minnie,' said Issa. 'You've *always* been a giant. You just weren't allowed to be one.'

'Tell me,' she shouted. 'Tell me why you've done this.'

'We haven't done anything, Minerva,' said Issa, sounding sad. 'The only thing that's been done to you has been done by . . . others.' She glanced at Chesca, who nodded, and then seemed to make up her mind about something. 'I've got somewhere to show you. Follow me.'

'Nice try,' said Minnie, with a scornful laugh she hoped Robin would be proud of. 'I'm not falling for that trick again. Last time I followed a giant, he led me to *you*, and that turned out pretty badly. I'm not going *anywhere* with a giant from this awful place.'

She took a step away from the clearing, barefoot,

with only her blanket round her. Twist dipped his head sorrowfully, unsure what was happening. 'Come on Robin,' she said, begging. 'Let's leave this place. Maybe I can go back to Mr Straw, and he can give me something to turn me back . . .'

But Robin lowered his eyes and shook his head. She wanted to cry.

Issa took a step closer to her. Her eyes were soft and full of love. Minnie glared at her. 'You have to trust me,' said Issa. 'Please. Come with me. It will be the final bit of the puzzle. Everything will make sense.'

'You'll understand your past,' said Chesca, nodding solemnly.

Minnie hesitated. She looked once more at Robin.

'Will you come with me?' she asked him.

He bit his lip. Then he got to his feet, not quite looking her in the eye. Minnie thought she'd be comforted, but she wasn't. She wasn't sure if he was coming because they were still friends, despite her turning into a monster, or just because he didn't want to be left in the clearing with Chesca. Perhaps, she thought sadly, she was the least worst option of all the monsters around him.

'Show me, then,' said Minnie, heavily. Then she

glanced down at her blanket, wincing a little. 'But first – can you lend me something to wear?' She blushed. 'Nothing fits me now.'

- 39 -
MINNIE'S BEGINNING

Chesca deftly swooped in to dress Minnie.

'All our clothes are hand-me-downs,' explained Chesca, hands swiftly moving around her, binding the strips into knots until Minnie was clad in a dress. 'We have no clothes shops here. Our clothes are worn and handed down from giant to giant, and then we rip them up and use them again. Every bit of fabric on you has been worn by at least thirty giants before you.'

Chesca stood back and looked at her, smiling a little at her handiwork. Now she was dressed, Minnie allowed the blanket to drop to the floor. 'What do you think?'

Minnie nervously regarded her new body, clad in a multi-coloured arrangement of shades and materials, knotted together repeatedly. 'Well, it fits,' she said, reluctantly. The dress was actually surprisingly comfortable, and the fabrics, although threadbare, were soft and kind against her skin. She saw patches of different clothes and different lives everywhere she looked – here the scraps of a dark blue jacket, there a pink braid which must have edged a skirt once – and she thought, for a moment, of all the giants who had come before her. For a second, a small bond began to form, a feeling of connection to those long-gone giants whose clothes she now wore. *But I'm not like them*, she corrected herself. *This is a mistake. They'll turn me back in a second.*

'Let's go, if you're ready,' said Issa. 'Chesca, stay here and watch the peaks.'

Chesca nodded, and raised a hand in farewell.

Minnie followed Issa past the shelter, followed by a silent Robin and Twist. They went down trails that wound and curled like ribbon ends, far away from the market square, towards the opposite side of the range from where they'd climbed up.

Minnie was horribly captivated by the sensation of walking at her new height. Once, she had been so small she had looked up into everyone's face, apart from Robin's. Now, she was taller than her house. She had to concentrate hard on not wobbling. Her muscles felt brand new and vulnerable, as if someone had peeled a shell off her. And her skin! She kept catching glimpses of golden freckles peeping out from her extraordinary new clothes.

Now she was walking behind her, Minnie saw that Issa's hands weren't the only things that were scarred. The back of her neck and legs were shiny and puckered, the skin riven with scar tissue. She couldn't stop looking at them, or comparing them to the scars she'd seen on Speck's back. Those had been thinner, longer, more deliberate-looking, while Issa's scars were wider and more haphazard.

After walking a mile or so, Issa began to slow down. The air had grown much colder, and all at once Minnie began to tremble. A sense of dread crept into her. 'I can't go on,' she said, suddenly. 'Don't make me. I'm frightened.'

Issa turned, her eyes kind, but firm. 'If you want to know the final truth about yourself, granddaughter, we must go on.'

Minnie exhaled. This stranger really did believe they were related. Perhaps, if she did go on, she could prove that was a mistake. She took a deep breath and nodded. They continued.

The air around them grew heavy and stifling, thick with secrets. The ground they walked on was so brittle it seemed to snap and crack under their feet, as if they were walking on broken glass. Not even a screecher bird broke the oppressive silence around them. They were walking towards death, Minnie was sure of it.

They came to a small clearing, shrouded in shadows cast by the mountain peaks. It felt like a place someone had hidden in; someone who didn't want to be found.

There was one dwelling; a simple grass shelter, made of long, brown, dead grasses tied together in an arc. Minnie found herself walking towards it, as if she was tied to it by an invisible string and it was pulling her in. She stood in the open entrance of the shelter and peered in. Within it was a crumbling mound of straw in a large rectangular shape, like a mattress. On top of this was a doll; a doll with yellow eyes and golden hair, in a faded dress.

Just in front of the shelter were some clumps of grass and long finger marks, as if someone had been scrabbling at the earth. Issa, Minnie noticed, was careful not to walk there; she walked around the grass and the finger marks, as if it was sacred ground and should not be disturbed.

The air was very quiet, and thick with menace.

Twist padded over to her, and whimpered.

'Where am I?' said Minnie. In the strange place, her words sounded like rocks falling on to ice.

Issa's pale yellow eyes shone. She pointed inside the shelter, towards the bed and the doll. 'This is where you were born.'

Then she pointed at the flattened grass. 'And that is where you lay with your mother, as she suffered with a fever.'

Minnie shook her head, roughly. 'I have a mother. Back in Quake Quarter. She has never been here and neither have I. You're – you're lying,' she said, desperately.

Issa held herself very still, and her mouth trembled as she said: 'The woman in Quake Quarter is not your mother. Your mother was a giant. And she was my daughter.'

Minnie looked at the torn-out clumps of grass, at the gouge marks in the earth and her heart began to pound. *Mama is not my mama?* It sounded nonsensical, and yet, deep down inside her, she knew it was true.

She regarded again the patch of earth outside the grass shelter, large enough for a giant to curl up on and writhe in pain. *I had another mama.* She thought, with a terrible pang, of how often she had longed for Mama to kiss her, to hug her, and how rarely she had got her wish. Would her real mother have hugged her? And kissed her every day?

'My mother – had a fever?' she whispered.

Issa said softly, 'She did. And, as your mother lay there sick and in need of help, a medicine man came walking through the grass. I was there. I was with her.'

'Mr Straw,' said Minnie, in a voice that was hollow with truth. She shuddered a little, thinking of his greedy eyes, and the next thing she said seemed to come from a very deep, buried memory. 'Bending over me. Face right up close to me. Big and . . . scary. Reaching out for me.'

Issa nodded, and then glanced up the path, trembling, almost as if he was coming again.

'This medicine man would come to our market a lot. He would buy herbs and our potions. Sometimes he would buy up all our stocks and medicines, then it would be months before we could heal ourselves.'

'Why did he buy so many herbs and potions?' said Robin, quietly.

Issa looked at him. 'Because he wanted to experiment,' she said simply.

'With what?' said Robin.

'With giants.' Issa swallowed, then went on. 'He was interested in whether he could create medicine to make us weaker, or stronger, or shorter, or taller, depending on the need.'

Minnie had a bad feeling about whatever was coming her way. Issa gave her a gentle smile, as if she could feel her terror.

'During one of these periods, when we had no medicine in stock, Mr Straw came back. He overheard talk about the giant who'd fallen ill during childbirth, and had no medicine to cure her fever. He stood in the market square, and he heard.'

Minnie looked at the doll again, and felt tears begin to fall down her face.

'He came to see us,' said Issa. 'I begged him to help her. And he knew her. He knew who she was. She was a runaway giant.'

'She'd run away from the Giant Management Company?' whispered Minnie.

'Yes. The minute she found out she was expecting you. She knew that if she stayed, she would not be able to keep you. The GMC always separate mothers from their children, so they can pair adult giants with human children instead. She risked life and limb to come back here, Minnie, and she hid out here for months. When you were born, it was the happiest day of her life. But then she fell ill. And Mr Straw came.'

Minnie glanced at the shelter, her heart thudding. Her mother had run away. She had been a servant. She'd risked punishment, in order to stay with her.

'By the time he came your mama was so sick, Minnie, and no matter what we did, without medicine we couldn't help her.' Issa's voice was low and breaking. 'He bent down, and he tried to take her temperature, but she was terrified, and she pushed him away. I begged him for medicine. But when we tried to give it to her, she thought he was trying to poison her.' Issa blinked away some tears.

'After a while, he noticed you,' said Issa, bleakly. 'And

he bent down and he picked you up, right out of your mother's arms.'

'Why did he take me?' whispered Minnie, through trembling lips.

'He said that he knew of a couple recently arrived on the island, a couple who were childless, who longed for a baby, but could have none. He told me that he might be able to change you into a baby who could pass as human. He tried to persuade me that he was going to give you a better life.'

Minnie could almost hear her mother's frightened breathing, could almost feel her final embrace as she had reached for her baby daughter and cried, softly, into her skin. Minnie looked at those marks on the ground and shuddered and wept. Those marks told her that her mother had tried to lift herself up and pick up her baby. But she hadn't been able to.

Robin took a step back and looked up, his tear-streaked face full of sadness. 'Mr Straw stole Minnie away from her mother,' he whispered, as if to himself.

Issa nodded, wearily, and said: 'He bundled you up, and he walked back down that path as boldly as if he owned the place. You were crying so hard. He walked right through the market square, as brazen as anything.'

'Why didn't you try to stop him?' Robin gave Issa

a look of fury. 'You were right there. She was your granddaughter.'

'I did. We all did,' said Issa. 'Many of us.'

Robin gave one of his scornful laughs. 'A group of giants couldn't overcome *one* man? On their own turf? You didn't try hard enough.'

'Oh, we did,' said Issa, and she held out her arms and legs wearily, displaying the scars that ran up and down her skin. 'But he had fire, Robin. And we couldn't fight that.'

Minnie remembered the burned-out tree stumps in the market square, and then, with a pang of dismay, the lit torches that accompanied every single Goodbye ceremony. Suddenly she realised the dreadful truth.

Whenever the islanders lit torches, it wasn't to celebrate. The flames were to *intimidate*. The islanders used fire to scare and oppress the giants. 'Mr Straw set fire to everything as he walked,' she gasped, suddenly realising.

Issa nodded. 'We couldn't get through the flames and the smoke quickly enough. He stole you and he set fire to the market square as a warning. And he took you down the mountain and away for good. It was after that that we began to set traps, and carved the mountain's cliff-face, but . . . we'd lost you by then.'

Robin gave a low whistle. 'What a . . . monster.'

He glanced at Minnie, and gave a tiny nod.

Issa nodded too. 'We heard reports that the stolen child had been sold to a couple.'

Robin and Issa looked down at the ground, as the full force of Issa's words hit Minnie in the chest. She'd been *stolen and sold*. To make someone *money*.

'We heard what had happened to you over time. Some of the servants were brave enough to send messages to us. We knew you were being brought up as a human by a couple in Quake Quarter, but we just didn't know who they were. We would come and try to find you – we looked through so many windows, tried so hard to steal you back. But the guards are plentiful in Quake Quarter, and we were never successful in finding you.'

'You never stopped trying, though,' whispered Minnie, finally realising. The bad giants from No-Go, who looked through windows to find her and who had haunted her nightmares hadn't been bad at all. And she had dreamed about them all her life, because some part of her had always remembered. And her nightmares hadn't been, in fact, about the giants at all. They had always ended with being stolen away.

Issa nodded. 'We never stopped trying, no.'

Minnie hung her head, for the giants who had tried to find her and paid with their lives in the dungeon. Twist walked to her quietly and nudged her ankle with his nose.

'And then . . . you came to us.' Issa smiled, lovingly, and, despite everything, Minnie smiled back, and then she was struck by a thought.

'How did I stay so small?'

'He was always experimenting with potions, Minnie. He must have kept your growth suppressed somehow.'

Minnie and Robin exchanged a glance of pure horror.

'The medicine!' she said, wanting to throw up. Twice a day she'd had to inject herself, for as long as she could remember. All her life she'd been told her muscles were weak, that she shouldn't overdo things, and for eleven long years she had suffered, and limped and screamed from the pain. That pain had been her body trying desperately to grow but not being able to.

'His muscle-strengthening, pain-killing medication,' she said, again, wanting to hit something. 'It was a lie, wasn't it? It stopped me from growing. And when my body was in pain because of it, the medicine also numbed the pain. And – and they knew.'

An image of her parents floated into her mind, and it brought a pain as bad as anything she had ever felt in her bones.

Robin gulped, suddenly, his eyes full of understanding. 'I've just remembered that awful fever you had. I *thought* you'd been poisoned. And, it turns out, you had.'

Issa, glancing between the two, said: 'Did Minnie have a terrible reaction recently?'

'You could say that,' muttered Robin. He told her about the evening Minnie had spent in the cottage, shivering and hallucinating.

Issa said, 'It sounds like your body was in shock. If you were shivering and sweating, that was all the medication concocted by Mr Straw finally leaving your bloodstream. He was never making you better. He was experimenting on you.'

Finally it dawned on Minnie that she had never had a weak body. That her muscles had never been wasted. That it had all been a huge lie. She was overcome with grief, and tears ran down her face as she tried to make sense of what she had just learned. Robin and Issa let her cry, and said nothing at all, and for that she was grateful. Then she stood up and gently wiped at her face, her fingers exploring its new dimensions with wonder.

'Thank you,' she said. Then she reached out, and tenderly touched her grandmother's burned face, the puckered scar that ran up her neck. 'That's for trying to protect me.'

Issa grasped her hand, and squeezed it, and for a

moment her eyes burned golden in the light; and by the way she stared at Minnie, Minnie suspected hers were golden too. And she thought of all the times she'd caught people staring at her, back in Quake Quarter. That tiny fleck of gold deep within her pupils must have confused and worried the residents around her.

And, finally, she understood why her parents had never hugged her or kissed her. Why they had always been so terrified of a boy falling in love with Minnie, so terrified of it that they deliberately made sure she was always a bit grubby, dressed in ill-fitting clothes and with unbrushed hair.

'They didn't want *anyone* to kiss me,' she said aloud, 'in case I turned to stone, too. They tried to keep me as unappealing as possible.' She thought of all the times she had felt plain, remembered how teased she had been, and felt a fury within her.

'You must have been lonely,' said Issa, softly.

'Not all the time. I had my . . .' Her sentence tailed off. She felt odd, claiming ownership of Speck. 'I had Speck,' she said, and she closed her eyes.

She felt a small hand pat her on her leg, opened her eyes, and saw Robin standing by her. He only came up to her knee. He looked up at her, and in his face was an understanding, and a plea.

'Minnie,' he said gently, 'I'm really sorry all this was done to you.'

'Do you think I'm a monster, Robin?' she whispered.

And he shook his head and pulled back. 'No,' he whispered. 'I don't.'

She saw in his eyes that he meant it, and that was enough.

- 40 -
A WARNING

THEY WERE QUIET for a moment, in the remnants of her mother's last hiding place. It was still a sad place, but now that the truth had been told, and Minnie understood so much more, it felt less oppressive. In fact, the air seemed to be waiting for her to do something. And what she wanted to do, more than anything, was to see Speck. She alone would know what to say, and what to do and how to comfort her.

She had a sudden flashback to that puzzling morning in the garden, when Speck had been so adamant that Minnie needed to know about a safe place. Had she known who Minnie was? Had she guessed somehow?

She turned, blindly, consumed by her need. 'Which way . . .'

Robin cleared his throat. 'But – Minnie, wait.'

She whirled on him, impatient to get going. 'What?' she snapped.

He winced at her louder voice, then went on: 'Will it be safe for you to go back?'

'Safe?'

'Minnie,' said Robin gently, 'you're a giant now. Going back to a place where giants are turned into servants, and servants are turned to . . .'

'Oh!' She slumped; suddenly, all the fight left her. In the heat of her fury, she'd completely forgotten what she'd become.

'Bu– but I'm still Minnie,' she said. 'I'm still – technically – their daughter. A girl from Quake Quarter. Surely I'll be all right?'

'I'd like to think so,' whispered Robin. 'But . . . who knows?'

Twist gave a soft howl, as if to remind her of the islanders' barbarity.

'I don't know what to do next,' she admitted, hanging her head.

'You are welcome here,' said Issa, instantly. 'But I have to tell you something, Minnie, so you know everything. You've been lied to a lot in your life, and I'm not going to lie to you too.'

Minnie felt her stomach plummet. 'What?'

Issa glanced around the clearing, grief etched into every wrinkle on her face. 'No-Go will always be your home, but it's not safe.' She gestured at the burned-out land with her scarred hands.

'But . . .' Robin frowned. 'You've got the traps, and Blade.'

'They keep a lot of would-be intruders away, this is true,' said Issa. 'But not always. When the Giant Management Company wants to frighten us, they find a way. They like to let us know who's in charge.'

'Why were you so desperate to steal me back here, if you couldn't guarantee my safety?' hissed Minnie.

'Because we didn't know how long you'd be safe over there either,' admitted Issa. 'If the only thing keeping you small was Mr Straw's medicine, there was always a risk that, one day, that might stop working,' she said.

'Or I might run out of supplies,' added Minnie, understanding.

'Exactly.'

And Minnie thought about the urgency in Speck's eyes all those days ago. 'When . . . when Speck told me about a safe place to run to –' her thoughts snowballed, faster and faster – 'she was also afraid for me. She wanted me to find somewhere to hide, in case I changed in the middle of Quake Quarter.'

'Speck *knew?*' gasped Robin. 'Knew what you were, all along?'

'She might not have known,' said Issa, quietly, 'but she would have heard the rumours about a giant child in the community. All the giants would have known. Perhaps she had her suspicions it was you, and wanted to keep you safe in case it was.'

She looked at Minnie, and smiled gently. 'Because she loves you, too.'

And Minnie was about to reply, when there was the sound of dogs barking from the mountain ridge.

- 41 -
ON THE RUN AGAIN

THEY LOOKED UP.

Encircling the entire mountain bowl was an army of Giant Management Company officials. They were too far away for anyone to see their individual faces, but the flaming jackal-skin torches in each hand were plain enough. Issa looked exhausted, but not surprised that they were there at all.

'They always find a way, sooner or later,' she said, with an air of bleak resignation. 'They might have found the hidden entrance, or speared the rock with pickaxes, or forced servants to throw them up to the ridge – all of which they have done before. They always scale the mountain when they want to.' She shot a look at the two children. 'Quick, get in the shelter,' she said. 'You don't want them to recognise either of you.' Robin and Minnie scrambled inside, followed by the jackal.

'We believe you might be harbouring a Quake Quarter girl,' shouted a voice, down into the mountain bowl. 'We last saw her coming up here early this morning.'

The entirety of No-Go went deathly quiet. Finally, a voice that Minnie recognised as Blade's was heard, shouting from about a mile away. 'We've seen no one of that description,' he said.

'We don't believe you,' said the official. 'We are also looking for a rubbler boy, who goes by the name Robin Scragg. He has been assisting Minnie, and for that he must be punished. If you give them both up, we'll throw down some food and some of those nice caskets of wine that you like.'

Not one word was said in reply. Minnie thought of the giants in the market square, and Chesca and Blade, all of whom had seen them both, and realised that none of them were going to reveal her.

'Well, we tried to be nice,' came a shout. 'Now we'll be nasty. If you don't give up the boy, and the girl that you are keeping, no doubt against her will, then we will smoke them out. You know how we'll do that, don't you? But if you tell us where she is now, then we won't. Perhaps you might even be able to grow some vegetables this month. Cultivate your fruit—' There was the sound of jeering laughter, high up on the ridge.

They're enjoying this, thought Minnie, and suddenly she realised that everything to do with giant management was an absolute *game* to the people that ran the island.

They loved it. They loved keeping the giants trapped in the mountains, and throwing them in the dungeons once in a while. They loved the ceremonies. They loved frightening and ruling and scaring them.

'Come on,' came another shout. 'Give up the girl and the boy who has aided her, and we won't throw the flames down.'

For an agonising pause, the entire mountain bowl lay quiet, the silence of giants refusing to speak.

'Okay, last chance. We're going to speak to Minnie directly,' shouted a voice, and Minnie felt her heart beat violently in her chest, and sweat instantly pour out of her. 'Minnie,' cried the official, 'until you come back to us, we've got your giant held in a rather . . . uncomfortable place.'

Minnie started, and gulped. What did *that* mean?

'She's fixed into the city walls, Minnie. Tied in there with chains, and dogs are circling her. She doesn't look very happy. She keeps saying you've abandoned her. Why don't you come and put her out of her misery, Minnie? Turn her to stone with one little kiss, and do your duty to the island. This little escapade has gone on long enough, don't you think? And now you're making your giant suffer.'

Minnie gave Robin a look of sheer terror. 'I have to

go,' she said, starting for the exit of the shelter. 'I have to rescue her.'

Robin put a hand on her. 'But what if they're lying? What if they're just saying that to get you out of here?'

Minnie hesitated. 'You might be right,' she admitted. Minnie felt a pang of grief for her old life, where she'd known nothing that could hurt her, had thought everyone was kind and everyone was happy. And while she faltered, unsure about the best thing to do, the officials cresting the rim of the mountain basin made up their own minds.

'Very well,' shouted one of them. 'The usual then.'

And the first flame was thrown. A few seconds later, the earth began to shake with the thud of the giants inside, running from the fires.

Issa hurried to the shelter and looked inside. Her eyes were wide with love and sadness, but her voice was firm. 'You must run. It's too dangerous for you to stay now. I know a way out of here.' The giant elder pointed, trembling, past the grass shelter. 'Go that way, until you get to the remains of the sacred bough—'

'Sacred *what*?' said Minnie.

'Where will it take us?' said Robin.

'Away from here,' said Issa quickly, as if she didn't

have time for details. 'And once you get there, go *down*. And hurry.'

'Come with us,' said Minnie. She gulped. 'Please, grand– grandmother.' *I've only just found you*, she thought. *I can't lose you too.*

'I can't, my love,' said Issa. 'I have to stay.'

'Why won't you come?' Minnie was sobbing.

'If we leave, we'll have *nowhere* to live, Minnie. This is the only place that we can stay. If we run, we'll be servants, and then there will be nowhere for those who try to fight.'

'F– fight?' stammered Minnie. 'What fight?'

Despite the flames racing up the path, Issa grabbed Minnie's hands with her own. 'Some of us believe we have one more fight left, Minnie. A rebellion. And staying here lets us believe that one day we might be able to stop all of this. That we'll change things for good.' Her yellow eyes bored into Minnie's. 'Maybe, one day, you'll help us.'

Then Issa reached out and tenderly picked up Robin's hand in her own. Robin's eyes widened at being touched by a giant, but he held on. 'Robin, I cannot thank you enough for looking after my granddaughter. You are a very special islander. I'll never forget what you've done.'

Robin blushed. Behind Issa, there was the dreadful

thudding sound of more flaming torches landing on the ground. Smoke was beginning to thicken in the air. Issa coughed. 'Now go,' she said, with difficulty.

She gave one final loving look at Minnie. And then Issa was gone.

Minnie blinked away her tears and glanced at Robin. Breathing was beginning to get harder as the smoke and stench of burned land grew thicker around them. 'Robin – if you come with me – I don't know what might happen or where we'll end up. I can't guarantee you'll be safe.'

He nodded hastily, and Minnie suddenly saw a gleam in his eyes. 'Maybe,' he whispered. 'But –' he indicated the smoke around them – 'I'm not safe here, either. Besides, I have a feeling about you, Minnie.' His eyes were streaming from the smoke swirling close to their shelter. Twist snapped and snarled at it, full of distress and fight. 'I've spent my life watching things fall down,' said Robin. 'All I deal with is broken things. But I have a different feeling about you. So I'll come with you. For as long as I can.'

'Despite the dungeon?' said Minnie, shakily.

'Despite the dungeon,' said Robin.

They grinned at each other, and for a moment their fear lifted, despite the torches thudding to the ground around them. It took a burning wad of lit jackal fat landing at their feet to galvanise them into action, and the giant, the boy and the jackal ran out of the shelter, through the black smoke, and in the direction that Issa had pointed them.

- 42 -
UP IN SMOKE

WITH FIRE AT their heels, surrounded by smoke so thick it was like fog, eyes streaming, they ran blindly. And so the mammoth tree trunk seemed to come out of nowhere, more an apparition than a reality. One minute it wasn't there, and then it was; distorted and ancient, as wide as Minnie's classroom. Its dimensions were hard to understand; it was the biggest tree they had ever seen in their entire lives, and even the smoke that had followed them reared back a little, as if in fright, giving them valuable space in which to catch their breath.

Within their souls, where instinct reigned, they somehow understood that this place was holy. As they gazed at the grey tree, the men and the flames and the fear all suddenly seemed a little bit further away than before.

The tree was as tall as it was wide, at least six feet taller than Minnie. The canopy offered by its huge branches was the size of Florin's lawn, at least. It had no leaves – it was wood, and wood alone – but knotted to its twisting branches were tiny scraps of parchment, charred at the ends and tied on with remnants of old fabric. Standing on her tiptoes, Minnie reached for one. Handwritten messages were written all over the material in what looked like an ancient language, impossible to decode. This was where giants had written their secrets and wishes and hopes and dreams for many years and tied them to the tree.

Panting, thumping his chest, Robin wheezed out his next sentence. 'Issa said we needed to look out for a sacred bough.' He pointed at the strips of fabric tied on to the branches. 'Look at these! Maybe she meant sacred bows?'

The sound of men shouting from the mountain ridge reached them. Minnie glanced up through the branches full of parchment scraps, beyond the top of the tree, where the smoke hadn't reached yet, and saw with horror that the Giant Management Company officials had reached this part of the mountains, too. They were high up on the ridge, and their band had grown in numbers.

'They're *above*,' she whispered, putting her hands up to her face.

'We see a *giant* down there,' shouted one of the men. 'Why are you hiding, little giant? Come out from under that tree and introduce yourself.'

Minnie began to quake. She shot a terrified glance at Robin.

'Well, if you don't want to be polite,' shouted one of the men, 'maybe you need to be taught some manners.'

There was the sound of jeering laughter, and then the whistling sound of a flaming torch being thrown. Moments later, the branches of the tree began to sing and pop as they burned, and then the little pieces of parchment and knots of fabric were ablaze.

'Can't hide under that tree for ever,' shouted an official.

Minnie and Robin gave each other terrified looks – how long before the flames reached the trunk and blew their cover?

Twist began to tug at Minnie's clothing with his teeth, and pulled her round the tree trunk. Baffled, exhausted, she allowed him to manoeuvre her.

All of a sudden Twist stopped and pawed at the tree, and looked at Minnie.

They had missed it – but here, on this side of the vast trunk, the tree was hollow. It nursed a large oval opening: a doorway! An escape route.

Minnie peered down inside the trunk. The hollow went on, down into the earth. She glanced at Twist, and loved him more ferociously than ever.

'Get in,' Robin hissed, hopping about anxiously. 'And hurry. I think they're getting ready to throw another one.'

Minnie climbed into the vast hollow. Seconds later,

so did Robin and the jackal. It was dark and cold, and smelled of damp and soil. The hollow led to a wide, dark tunnel that twisted downwards in a spiral, as if into the earth.

Above them, the sacred bough of No-Go began to blister and pop. The ancient tree, which must have stood in the same spot since time began, took a long time to burn completely, for its wood was strong and its will was even stronger. By the time it began to totter, the island's officials had long gone, bored by the display and tired of waiting for it to explode, so that when finally it tumbled to the earth, groaning, there was no one there to witness its fall.

And there it lay blazing for several hours. All the secret wishes and prayers that had been tied to its branches over time also went up in smoke, and flew up into the air, and that was how the island heard them and grew thoughtful.

- 43 -
A NEW LAND

THE TUNNEL WAS dark and quiet. Unlike the caves at the lagoon, which had been cool and damp, this passageway grew hotter and more airless with every step. It was like walking deeper and deeper into an oven. The roof was rough earth, and soil kept falling into their eyes and mouths at regular intervals. Barely able to see or talk, by silent agreement they decided to just grit their teeth and plough on, unsure of what lay ahead, their heads still full of the men and the flames, and of what had happened to Minnie, and the story of her mother.

Every now and again, Robin would bend over double with a gut-wrenching cough, but, despite that, he led the way, for he was the only one who found this way of walking familiar. Moving through the earth's darkness was, to him, like finding his way into a collapsed building. So he walked quite naturally any fear of the dark and the danger having been worn away a long time ago.

An hour passed, maybe more. There was no light; they moved in darkness, guided only by the sound of each other. They grew tired, coated in sweat and grit. Even Twist's seemingly endless energy began to leave him, and the padding of his feet grew slow. Minnie stopped, waiting for him to join her, but in return she heard only a tiny whimper.

She turned and walked back. Then she crouched and held out her hands in the darkness. A few moments later, a small, dry, leathery paw pressed tentatively on her hand, followed by a second. 'That's it,' she urged, softly. 'Go on.'

The loyal jackal climbed into her cupped hands, circled a few times, which tickled very much, and a few moments later lay down on her palms – a handful of such softness that she held her breath for a moment. Ever so slowly, Minnie straightened her legs and walked on, with the jackal curled up in her hands. She was still smiling tenderly when she finally glimpsed the end of the tunnel.

But neither she nor Robin ran towards it with relief. For the world outside didn't look very welcoming: they glimpsed a chain-link fence topped with shards of jagged glass, and three wild dogs shackled to a post. The earth was swollen with water and boggy. And, in the distance, where the land met the sea, Minnie saw from her new height the rigging of an old ship sticking up from the ocean, a rag of a sail on its mast like a vast rotting spiderweb: all that remained of the giant invasion several centuries ago. She contemplated that ship with new eyes. Once, she'd seen it as the ship of an attacking enemy. Now, she saw it differently. People – *giants* – like her had crossed the sea on it. Her ancestors.

In fact, she'd been so intently looking at the ship that she'd leaned her whole face out of the tunnel. At the sight of her, the dogs began to bark and throw themselves around the post, snapping their jaws. The sound roused Twist, who growled in reply. Minnie put a hand over him, to stop him from trying to wriggle out of her hand towards the dogs.

'You've fought enough,' she murmured. 'Where are we?' she added, making sure her head was back in the safety of the tunnel behind her.

'I don't know,' said Robin. 'Never seen this place in my life.' They glanced back out at the wetlands beyond the tunnel, thick with sludge and slick with a mustard-yellow oil. 'Not very pretty, is it?'

A memory blazed in her thoughts: that puzzling conversation she'd overheard, the first night she'd run away, when she'd hid from the townsfolk in the Old Town. They'd been talking about security after the quake and how strange it was that, instead of increasing security on the streets, people were being sent to work somewhere that no one went to. What had they said? Something about sending them to *a toxic old swamp no one passes through?* And: *What they got in there that's so valuable, anyway?*

She glanced at Robin. 'We've reached a bog – I mean, a swamp,' she said.

He frowned. 'A swamp? I didn't know we had one.'

'Neither did I,' she admitted, 'but I heard some people talking about it.'

She told Robin about the hour she'd spent hiding on the hill of rubble, while the islanders beneath her talked about a mysterious swamp and the guards sent to protect it. A swamp, she realised suddenly, that wasn't even painted on her Get-to-the-Castle board. Why would it have been left off? Everything else was there.

'So, after the quake, the Giant Management Company sent loads of security *here?*' Robin glanced outside. 'To guard . . . what, exactly?'

Minnie shrugged. 'I'm not sure. They said something about paperwork?'

Robin was peering out towards the bubbling swamp, curiosity in his face. 'Look,' he whispered, staring in the direction of the chain-link fence.

She followed his glance. Beyond the dogs, the fence and a battered black carriage, she saw a concrete one-storey building, in the shape of a perfect square.

'What *is* that place?' Robin said. 'What's that building?'

Minnie racked her brain. 'It's – I think it's the . . .' She tried to remember what the islanders had called it. 'The archives and records centre!' she burst out, proud that she had remembered.

Robin frowned. 'What's that?'

She shrugged. 'All I know about it is that it's guarded.'

Robin couldn't take his eyes off the flat grey building in the distance. 'And why would they guard island records?'

There was a heavy silence, during which Minnie watched her friend, his eyes flickering with thoughts too quick for him to articulate. They were shining when he finally turned to face her again. 'If they're guarding something inside that building, Minnie, it's a secret. A secret *they're* keeping from *us*. And I want to find out what it is.'

'Why?' she said, and, to her ears, her voice sounded scared and small.

'I've spent my life picking up rubble and fixing rich people's cafés and houses. No one has ever once thanked me. All I've got in return is a rubbler's cough and a rubbler's back by the age of twelve, and no family to speak of. I hate the whole sorry lot of them, and what they do. Look at what they did to you, for starters! Never mind the other giants, and the rubblers. They're *rotten*. You know I hate them.' His face burned with urgency. 'And when you pull down a rotten building, you have to understand the whole structure.'

'What do you mean, pull down—'

'Where it's most fragile. What its secrets and its weaknesses are.'

'Robin,' stammered Minnie, '*what are you talking about?*'

He jerked his head in the direction of the swamp. 'We have to find out what they're guarding in there.'

She licked her lips. 'Robin. No. I don't want to.' There was something about that squat grey building that made her blood run cold.

He blinked. 'You must.'

'Why?'

'Minnie –' he rubbed his temple – 'what if another giant tries to protect her baby, and doesn't manage to? Do you want anyone else to go through an entire life taking medicine that hurts them every day? Why do you think no one's ever interested in your dad's designs to stop the earthquakes? This whole island is *foul*, Minnie. I can practically *smell it*. It's creaking at the joists – can't you hear it? Don't you think we should try to find out what's going on in that building? Don't you want to smash it all to bits?' His face blazed with that yearning again, a terrible wanting that made her scared.

The silence between them grew and grew.

'Sometimes I wish I'd never met you on that lagoon path, Robin Scragg,' she said, quietly. 'I wish I'd just stumbled home and taken my medicine. I'd still be a – a girl from Quake Quarter. The smallest in my class.'

'Yeah, well, the feeling's mutual. You've brought nothing but trouble ever since our paths crossed again.' To her surprise, Robin suddenly smiled.

'What's so funny?' snapped Minnie.

'I just realised that, for the last two days, I haven't done any rubbling.' Almost absent-mindedly, he stroked the shiny swollen skin on his hands. 'I've never had a two-day holiday before in my life, not even at Christmas.'

Minnie frowned at him. 'Being on the *run*, people kicking your door in, being frightened, sleeping on mountains and fire raining down around you feels like a *break?*'

'Yeah. At least it's different. When we rubble, we just rubble. Hour after hour. Day after day. Our whole life. Carrying bricks, digging out stones, till we can't any more.' He sighed, and gazed out of the tunnel, towards the mysterious building in the swamp.

She looked at his tired, weary face, older than his

years, and made a decision. Minnie got up suddenly, still unused to her new height.

'What are you doing?' said Robin, a tiny note of hope creeping into his voice.

'You're right,' she said, sharply. 'Let's find out what secret they're guarding.'

'Brilliant,' he gasped, scrabbling to his feet.

Minnie glanced at the dogs by the fence. 'Twist,' she begged, 'please stay here. There are three of them and you've fought enough.'

In reply, he gave her a disdainful look from his beautiful black-rimmed eyes.

'There's your answer,' grinned Robin. 'Stubborn, isn't he?' and, to her astonishment, he reached out and patted the jackal. To her even greater surprise, Twist closed his eyes lovingly while he did so.

And then they walked out into the fading afternoon light.

- 44 -
ISLAND RECORDS

AT THE SIGHT of Minnie and Robin emerging from the tunnel, blinking and trying to get their bearings, the wild dogs behind the chain-link fence suddenly went quiet.

They are used to seeing giants and children together, Minnie thought with a pang. *And now I am the giant.* Twist growled quietly, but stayed by their side, and after a few hostile glares, the dogs plainly decided that the newcomers posed no threat, and stayed quiet.

The ground beneath their bare feet grew wet and squelchy, and damp fronds tickled their ankles.

'I wonder what's contaminating the swamp,' murmured Minnie, lifting one foot and then the other. 'Do you think it's poison?'

'I hope not,' he whispered.

As they walked towards the grey building, past the chained up wild dogs, Minnie had, once more, a glimpse of the ship, in the distance, and something about it unsettled her. There was something not quite right about it . . . but dusk was falling. *It must be a trick of the light.*

The swamp grew wetter and the mist grew thicker. Twist's paws squelched in and out of the bog, and he seemed to catch a scent that unsettled him. Still they pressed on, squelching all the way, keeping an eye out for guards, trying to be as quiet as they could.

By the time they reached the flat, grey building in the middle of the swamp, night had truly fallen.

*

From the roof, a sweeping searchlight moved slowly, circling the perimeter of the building. The beam was inches from Minnie's toes. Robin nudged her, and put a finger to his lips. She glanced at the roof, saw three security guards gathered there, one moving the light, two sharing a flask of coffee between them.

What could be so important inside that it needs three guards?

Robin silently pointed to the back of the building, and when the beam of light was as far away as it could be, they hurried in that direction, hoping the sound of their feet squishing through the mud wouldn't carry to the roof, or to any other guards who might be around.

In the gloom, they saw two small steps leading out of the swamp. Minnie was hugely relieved to finally step out of the quagmire and on to concrete. Next to an open door was an empty chair and a mug on the floor.

There was the sound of footsteps nearby, and loud laughter. Whoever had been in the chair was coming back, after swapping a joke with the guards on the roof. Robin moved immediately. He slipped into the open doorway without even looking back. Minnie took a deep breath, hunched her shoulders and squeezed through after him as quickly as she could, Twist sticking to her like glue. Here, for the first time since she'd met him on the lagoon path, the jackal looked frightened.

Once inside, they turned to each other, their faces lit by the eerie green glow of the emergency light.

'Ready?' Robin said solemnly, staring up at Minnie's face.

She nodded. 'Ready.'

He eyed the ceiling, then regarded the way she was bent over. 'Are you comfortable?'

'Not one tiny bit. It's like being in a doll's house.'

They grinned tiredly at each other, and walked down a cold hallway, Minnie bent double all the way.

It was the first time Minnie had been inside a building since turning into a giant, and she felt large and loud and wrong in a way she hadn't at No-Go, stumbling behind her friend in the dark, leaving large, wet, swampy footprints on the concrete floor. Her ragged breathing sounded too loud; she was sure the guards on the roof would hear it. But Robin moved deftly, never looking back – and his urgency soothed her, in a strange sort of way.

At regular intervals along the dark corridor were large mahogany doors that had small brass plates on the outside to announce their purpose. There was very little light, and Robin was in a rush, but even so she read snatches here and there, the lettering glinting in the gloom – GIANT BIRTH RECORDS, DIRECTOR OF HALF-TRUTHS, PROPAGANDA AND MISINFORMATION UNIT, ROUSING SONGS FOR CHILDREN.

These words swirled around in her mind in a jumble, and, without meaning to, she walked right into Robin, knocking him to the floor.

'Why did you stop?' she whispered, holding out her hand to pull him up.

He gave her an agonised look, and pointed. Just a couple of feet away, standing so still that for a minute she couldn't see her, was a security guard, her back to them.

Minnie, Robin and Twist went completely still. The guard seemed to sense something, and was on the verge of turning round, when the sound of howling filled the air.

Minnie's heart leaped into her mouth. She looked down at Twist, whose eyes shone as his body twitched all over with longing.

Then the air filled with another howl, and then another. Minnie swallowed; she'd never considered it, but if their jackal had escaped from the ruins of the jackal-meat factory, there was every chance others had too. Were there hordes of wild jackals out there now, circling the swamp? In another moment, the guard dogs outside had joined in the din, barking at the jackals, and the jackals replied with more howls of their own. As the sound intensified, Robin quickly opened the first door he saw, grabbed Minnie, and pulled them both inside it. A second later, the guard ran down the corridor in the direction of the barking and the howling.

Twist could barely contain himself, making whining, yearning sounds as he heard his kind outside.

'He's going to give us away,' muttered Robin. '*Shhhhh,* Twist. Be quiet.' He scrabbled around in his pocket and brought out a tiny fragment of bark cake. 'Eat that. Good boy. Now be quiet.'

Minnie stared at Robin. 'You take food from everywhere you go, don't you?'

He shrugged. 'Those animals are a perfect distraction – let's not waste it.'

As if in a dream, Minnie allowed him to lead her out of the tiny office and back towards the corridor, Twist, quieter now, following but shaking. The secret hidden within the building seemed to be calling to them now, pulling them towards it. They walked down a flight of concrete steps, and the air that came out of their mouths was laced with little puffs of mist.

'That must be it – I can feel it,' said Robin, suddenly, through chattering teeth, pointing to a large steel door. Minnie was so cold she thought she might shake the bones right out of her skin.

Robin reached for the door handle, but at the last moment pulled his hand away, then stepped to the side.

'You should open this,' he murmured.

Minnie reached for the door handle and tried to turn it. 'I can't,' she said, her voice small.

'You *can*. You broke my water pump without even trying. You're a giant.'

She tried to turn the handle again. This time she broke it, but the door stayed shut. She wanted to weep. 'I can't,' she said.

'Minnie,' whispered Robin, 'imagine Speck is on the other side.'

Minnie stared at the door, and took a deep breath.

She stuck out a bare foot, and kicked as hard as she could. The door fell with a bang on to a concrete floor.

'Nice,' muttered Robin.

Then they walked into the vaults.

- 45 -
THE SECRET

THE ROOM WENT on for miles – for as far as the eye could see. Three flickering strip lights on the ceiling cast a gloomy light on metal shelves that leaned haphazardly, screwed to the walls and filled with old containers and plastic boxes of yellowing paperwork. With no apparent end in sight, Minnie felt like the secret – for there was a secret here, of that she had no doubt now – had no end, either. It went on for miles – might even go on for ever; might stretch into the ocean and still go on, ploughing over the ocean bed, disturbing shoals of fish as it torpedoed its way across the world. The secret here was big and had been allowed to grow, unchecked, for a long, long time. There was no knowing where it would end up. But it started *here*. Of that she was sure. Every single hair on her body was standing up.

It was damp and cold. She could almost feel the swamp wanting to push through the walls. Twist was crouching low to the ground, his tail tucked between his legs. Minnie wanted to soothe him and flee. But first they had a job to do.

The earthquake had done some of the work for them. Previously locked safes were lying wide open, spilling out their white paperwork guts for them to find.

'I don't know where to start,' Minnie whispered.

'I know what you mean,' said Robin. 'This room alone is the size of the whole rubbler district.' Then, with a sudden, frenzied movement, he bent down and reached for the first paper he saw. He read it, frowned and held it out to her.

It was just names and words, written in old-fashioned writing, under three columns, headed: SHIPS, CREW, WEAPONS.

'Doesn't mean much to me,' she said. They shrugged at each other.

'Your turn,' said Robin.

In a daze, she walked to a shelf, and, with some difficulty, pulled out an old notebook. She tried to turn the pages and accidentally ripped one. It felt like handling a book in a doll's house. Suddenly she had a flash of insight into how difficult Speck – how difficult all the giants in Quake Quarter – must find handling human-sized things. She felt a pang of remorse remembering all the times she'd giggled when Speck broke a plate.

She handed the book to Robin instead. He opened it

at an architectural plan of a house. They sat on the cold floor and stared at the pages as he leafed through them. More drawings. A fountain. A city hall. Strange phrases, like *blank canvas*, and *unlimited opportunities for designing model-perfect city*, and *dangerous native animals could be reused for cheap meat*.

Restless suddenly, she got up.

In a hidden corner of the vault, in the darkest, dampest corner, was a small metal cabinet. It was so small you would almost not know it was there. Almost. It had fallen to the ground, and mildewed books and papers spilled out of it on to the floor.

Above it, Minnie saw the words:

Chronicles
Records of First Explorations,
Recommendations for Settlement

And when Minnie read them they almost seemed to pulse in the dark, as if to say: finally.

'Robin,' she whispered. He ran down the length of the vaults and joined her. Together they regarded the cabinet. Then, wincing slightly, Robin got down on his knees and picked up a large, leather-bound book with the words SACRED ISLAND, 1802 on the spine.

They stared at that for a while.

'Sacred Island?' whispered Robin, glancing at her with confusion. 'Not Scarred? This island had another name, once?'

They looked at the spine again.

'1802 is the year before the giants invaded,' added Minnie, her mind racing. In silent agreement, they sat on the floor. The book fell open as if it could not wait a moment longer. They found themselves looking at a map of an island, the outlines of which were familiar, if not what was depicted inside them.

Minnie had seen the shape everywhere – at her school, in Papa's study, in books, in atlases. She had drawn this map in geography lessons. She had baked *cakes* in this shape on special days.

It was, undoubtedly, their island. They could even see the Five Bridges river, running from north to south, all the bridges still intact, drawn with painstaking detail. But the rest of the island looked completely different.

In the top left, where Quake Quarter should have been, was one label: *Orchard – Native Trees*. There was nothing else. No Old Town. No city walls. No Quake

Avenue. Nothing.

Just that word, *Orchard*, surrounded by pencil drawings of large trees.

Minnie thought of those mysterious wizened tree stumps that lined Quake Avenue.

Below the orchard, in a careful pen and ink drawing, was a large blue body of water. *Lagoon*, someone had written, carefully, next to the drawing. Then: *We should keep this, for recreational pursuits.*

In the far right corner of the map was a rough sketch of a temple, next to the text: *We believe this is a sacred space for the current inhabitants.*

Below the lagoon, there was a drawing of a green wood, next to the words: *Undeveloped Land.*

She frowned.

'That's where the meat factory is, isn't it?' muttered Robin, looking where her fingers were. But she could barely murmur, because her eyes had skipped ahead, to the bottom of the map, where someone had written:

Expect much resistance during invasion.
All ships must be used. Strongest men for crew.

Who had written these words? She thought of the messages in the Sacred Bough, written in a language she had never seen before. Surely if the giants had written of an invasion, they would have written their plans in Giant, and kept them in much larger books?

Which meant there was only one other answer.

And Minnie suddenly understood. Everything around her went very still and very quiet, apart from a roaring in her ears.

'*This* is the secret,' she whispered to Robin. 'This is what they've been guarding.' Her throat was suddenly dry. '*People* invaded the island. The giants were here first!' She looked at Twist, and her heart gave a thud. 'And so were the jackals. Once, it was just jackals and giants. That's why Twist didn't ever attack me; he must have smelled that I was a giant, in my skin somehow.'

Twist closed his eyes, and rested his head on his front paws.

'This is – this is bigger than I even thought,' said Robin, quietly. 'I knew something bad would be here. I just didn't realise how rotten.'

They looked at each other as the full force of their discovery hit them. The islanders had *lied*. They had pretended that it was the giants who arrived in ships.

The ships, she realised now, that had looked far too small to contain giants.

'Humans stole this island from the giants, not the other way around,' said Minnie. 'The humans invaded. They built the castle, they learned that giants were frightened of fire, and they used their dogs and their flames to make the giants give in.'

And then the invaders had turned the truth inside out.

Robin let the book fall to the floor, as if he couldn't bear to have it on his lap a moment longer.

They both felt the tremor at the same time. A small but distinctive one; the island shaking itself. Around them, the vaults and shelves shook and trembled slightly, rattling in the dark.

And Minnie finally put the last piece of the puzzle in place.

'The earthquakes didn't start because of the giants,' she gasped.

'What do you mean?' stammered Robin.

'They began when . . . when the people invaded.' She stared into space. 'I think that, all this time, the island has been trying to shake the *humans* off itself.'

The minute she said this, she heard a great sighing sound whip itself up around the building.

'The earthquakes will never stop,' said Minnie,

wonderingly – 'not until the humans leave.' She spoke as if she was dreaming, as if her mouth was full of treacle. The knowledge came from deep within her.

And then she began to cry. 'All the giants,' she said quietly, 'that were turned to stone! Because they were told they were *bad*. That they needed forgiveness.' She gulped. 'And they didn't. It was the other way round.'

Robin closed his eyes and laid his head back against a shelf. One tear squeezed out from beneath his eyelid and ran down his cheek. His swollen hand, broken from years of rubbling, lay limp in his lap. Minnie knew what he was thinking, and was quiet for a moment. Then he swallowed hard and opened his eyes.

'Do you think the giants know?' he said, softly. 'Do they know the truth?'

Minnie thought of Issa and Blade. 'Perhaps. They might hand it down, by word of mouth, like a secret. The ones in No-Go probably know; maybe that's why they live in hope of an uprising. But the giants in Quake Quarter –' she thought about Speck and Sandborn, about the way they walked, how they'd been bred in captivity, ruled over with an iron fist – 'no, I don't think they know.'

She got to her feet and looked down at her friend. From outside came the sound of howling again.

'At least, not yet,' she said, ripping the map out of

the book and handing it over to Robin. 'Put that in your pocket.'

He scrambled to his feet and looked across at her.

'That feeling I had about you,' he said, going a bit pink. 'It's getting stronger.'

- 46 -
'WHERE IS MINNIE?'

THEY FLED THE vaults and ran back up the stairs. Minnie's skin had begun to crawl – she couldn't wait to leave the whole building, the whole factory of lies. They found their way back to the door, and when they stood outside panting in the dark, Minnie had time, briefly, to realise this was her third night away from Quake Quarter.

On her left, Robin yawned and rubbed his eyes, He hadn't slept properly for nearly forty-eight hours, and she was exhausted herself.

Robin squinted into the night shadows, but there was no sign or sound of the guards. 'It's so quiet,' he whispered. 'Coast is clear. We should get away from here, find somewhere to sleep for a while—'

All of a sudden, a flashlight swept across his face, and then Minnie's.

'You want somewhere to sleep, Scragg?' drawled a laconic-sounding voice. 'I'm sure that can be arranged. There's a lovely spot in the middle of the castle that's just recently been vacated; there's not much of a bed, but plenty of fresh air and solitude. It's great for your health – all our guests lose weight.' And someone began to laugh.

Robin gulped. All the colour drained out of his face.

'And don't even think about making a run for it,' added the voice. 'You're surrounded by guards, and dogs. Now, who's your giant friend? Why are you trespassing on land that you've no right to access – and with a giant from No-Go? And – most importantly – what have you done with Minnie Wadlow?'

Robin gulped and swallowed a few times. Minnie could feel him trembling, even though they weren't touching. She couldn't bear the thought of him in so much fear, after everything he'd done for her – *after everything he'd done for the island* – and she grew angry. She coughed, deliberately.

The flashlight moved to Minnie's face. She held her breath. Surely they would soon realise who she was?

'Who are you?' said an official.

'I'm Minnie,' she said, blinking in the light. 'I'm the girl you're looking for.' She pointed at herself, giant and huge in the night air. 'I've changed. It's a long story. But I'm Minnie Wadlow. And Robin was only looking after me, so please don't punish him.'

Jeers filled the air. They went on for some time.

'That's brilliant,' said one.

'Priceless,' said another.

'She's a liar,' said a third.

'But very funny,' said one of the others. 'Maybe we should book her for our Christmas party.'

Minnie gulped. Her voice shook. 'It's very cowardly, you know, pointing that light at us when we can't even see your faces,' she said. 'Now, listen. I'm from Quake Quarter – I promise. And I need to go back there. I've got to see my parents, and my giant, and then I have to tell everyone about what we just discovered—'

The jeering and laughing intensified, and then suddenly stopped.

'Very good, but let's go back to our original question. Who are you? Where is Minnie? She's got a ceremony she needs to attend, and if she doesn't hurry up, her giant's going to die before she's able to turn her into stone, and then she'll be useless to us.'

Minnie's heart stopped. 'Going to die?' she said. 'Wh-what do you mean? Is she sick?'

'Sick and tired of being stuck in a city wall, waiting for a child to turn her to stone,' said another voice, mockingly. 'She's been there since Minnie did a runner.'

So they *hadn't* been making it up when they'd said they'd stuck her in a city wall. *Speck, I should have come home earlier*, thought Minnie, feeling her heart crack.

I ran away to save you, but I failed.

To her surprise, Robin spoke up. 'Well, that's cruel of you. Why have you done a thing like that, to a giant who has served your company her entire life?'

'We had to make an example of her. Otherwise all the other children might get silly ideas into their heads about preventing their ceremonies, too, and then where would we be?'

Minnie's eyes filled with tears. 'Can I see her?' she said.

'You can join her, for all we care,' said one of the officials.

'Look, I really am Minnie,' she tried again. 'Except I changed into a giant. Actually – I didn't change. I've always been one.'

'Your lies are wasting our time. We don't look kindly on fugitive giants at the best of times, and certainly not ones who spin ridiculous stories out of thin air,' drawled the man, his voice as coldly languid as the mist that curled around their feet. 'Take them to the dungeon.'

Five men in dark clothes rushed at them both and put handcuffs around their wrists. There was an awful whine and the sound of boot meeting ribcage, and she realised, too late, that Twist had tried to fight off the men, loyal as always. She saw them bend down towards him and try to get a leash on him, and she couldn't bear it any more.

'Leave him here!' she pleaded.

There was another dreadful sound of kicking, a final whine, and then silence.

'Happy to oblige,' said a guard. 'He's not going anywhere now.'

'Twist!' she cried, looking into the gloom, trying to find him, but they were marched away, leaving him behind. Tears streamed down her face at the way the guards had beaten the most loyal and beautiful creature she'd ever known. Everyone she had ever loved was lost to her now, in some way or another. Her parents, Speck, her grandmother, the mother she'd never known, Twist... Robin was right. The island *was* rotten.

- 47 -
THE REAL ISLAND

FOR AN HOUR, Minnie and Robin were pushed, prodded and marched through the swamp at the mercy of the guards from the Giant Management Company. Minnie, sickened at Twist's death, had no fight left inside her. When the guards shouted at her for being too slow, adding that she was just another wicked giant, she dipped her head, not bothering to disagree.

By the time they got to the river, she was walking like a servant. Head down, shoulders rounded, eyes on the floor – trying to make herself as unthreatening as possible. There was no bridge to cross the river (the only existing bridge was down in the south), but this didn't deter the guards working for the Giant Management Company. Down the river bank they went and into its disgusting waters. In a rare moment of unity, everyone held their breath as they splashed through it. The humans sank into its toxic waters right up to their necks, and Minnie was momentarily very glad of her size, for the water only came as far as her knees.

Out of the water, stinking and cold, they all proceeded along the river path. Minnie could barely keep her eyes open: they'd been walking for hours. As the sky lightened a little, she finally saw Robin again, stumbling and shuffling in front of her.

The city gates of Quake Quarter loomed ahead, rebuilt and restored in Minnie's absence. As they approached, the gates opened slowly to admit them all into the city, and Minnie saw how much rebuilding had happened; many cafés and shops were operating again, fixed with stone statues that she recognised with a pang.

As Minnie walked, she made everything shake: the broken buildings; the tables outside the cafés; the glass in the window panes; the cups of coffee balanced precariously on trays held aloft by waiters; even the people below her.

'You're walking too heavily,' said the guard on her right. 'Tread softly or you'll make something fall.'

Minnie tried. She shuffled along, tiptoeing on the pavements, struck all of a sudden by how hard it was to be a giant in a human settlement. She remembered Speck's closed-lip smile. *I'm going to have to learn to hold my smile back, too*, she thought, then realised she wouldn't have all that much to smile about anyway. She cried a little.

'Stop that now,' said a guard, although not unkindly.

Everywhere she looked she saw new statues that had been created to prop up the crumbling buildings and sagging walls – many of them giants she'd seen just a few days ago, alive, at Florin's ceremony. Her eyes went from one to the next, desperately.

'Speck!' she shouted as loudly as she could, startling the few shopkeepers opening the blinds on their newly rebuilt shops. A moment later, she was rewarded with the sting of a lash on her left shoulder.

'Try that again and we won't be so gentle,' said the nasty guard.

They were marched over the cobbles. The deeper they went into the Old Town, the more activity she saw; a few townsfolk, but mostly long lines of rubblers, bent and hunchbacked, snaking in and out of the destroyed buildings, carrying out broken bricks and smashed rubble. She saw how many of them were small children. 'They're starting early,' she whispered.

'They haven't finished,' muttered the guard on the right. 'They've been working through the night. Repairing the damage caused by the quake – caused by *your lot*.'

Some of the little ones looked and waved at Robin, but most of them were yawning with tiredness. Robin, unable to wave back in his handcuffs, shouted greetings to them, with a bright, artificial cheerfulness. 'Can you look after my chickens?' he called. 'Help yourself to the eggs—'

'How long for?' shouted a little girl.

'Oh,' Robin said, casually, 'maybe quite a long time.'

Everything looked tiny, Minnie thought, from her new height; the cafés and newsagent's and city hall that had once loomed over her, she now loomed over. As people began to stare at her, thinking they were watching a new criminal (one shopkeeper even shouted: 'Was there an attempt on a child last night, guards?'), Minnie felt an intense longing to shrink back to her usual height, and to walk the shiny cobbles as the human she'd once been. As the only giant in a crowd of people, she felt lonely and conspicuous as if she didn't belong. It must have been awful for the servants, she thought, suddenly. To walk around Quake Quarter for their entire life, knowing that none of it was theirs.

You do belong, said a cross voice inside her, that other Minnie. *You belong here more than any of these people. This island belongs to the giants.*

It belonged once, but that was a long time ago, she replied to herself, sadly. There was no denying – looking at the stone statues, listening to the march of the boots on the cobbles – who was in charge now.

She remembered what she'd been told about Speck's whereabouts, and the longing for her grew too great to be contained any more.

'Where is Speck?' she said, desperately, to the guards. 'I need to see her.'

'Fair enough,' said the man at the head of the line, in a mocking sort of way. 'Let's show you.'

And they were marched away from the picturesque inner circle of the Old Town and into darker, more cramped streets that Minnie didn't recognise. Here, houses and food stalls jostled side by side against each other, and the air smelled of stale cooking and broken pipes. There were no gardens or roses or hanging baskets here, but overflowing refuse containers and scuttling rats. These were the outer limits of the Old Town, where the less well-heeled islanders lived, and the broken city wall that encircled this quarter cast a dark gloom. *The island I thought I lived in never existed at all,* thought Minnie. *It was an illusion. This, that toxic swamp, and its secrets, are the real island.*

A sweet, cloying stench filled the air. Stringy, scraggly screecher birds, the ones who were too old or too lazy to try and hunt, kept swooping down to pick at the black refuse sacks, dragging them partway down the road, and flying off with whatever they found within the bags.

'Here we are,' the man said.

Ahead of them, Minnie saw a weary giant, raising her neck with difficulty, and peering at her blearily from a gap in the broken city wall. And that was when Minnie found herself looking at the face she loved more than any other in the world.

For a moment, time seemed to stop. Speck was wedged into the wall, further fixed in place by the thick chains around her ankles and wrists that were drilled into the stone. She was drooping on the spot rather than standing, utterly pale, bruised and weary. Minnie had never seen anyone look so weak and beaten.

At first, Speck gazed at Minnie with an air of puzzlement, as if she couldn't place her. Then her eyes widened, and she brought her neck up a bit sharper. 'Minnie? Is that really you?'

'Yes!' Minnie stammered.

'You're – you're a giant!' she said, thickly. 'It happened!'

'You thought I might be, didn't you?' Minnie said. 'What gave it away?'

'I first suspected it at Florin's ceremony,' Speck replied. 'You don't usually see Quake society people dance like that. And then I couldn't open the coffee can, but you could. And your eyes went yellow, in certain lights. Speck's voice was raspy, and she appeared to swallow with difficulty. 'I wanted to keep you safe, Minnie.' She peered fuzzily at the guards. 'Looks like I failed.'

'It's not your fault that I got caught,' said Minnie. 'But I should never have run away at all. I wouldn't have done if I'd known they'd do this to you.'

She may have been weak, half-starving and thirsty, but Speck had enough of her old fire within her to flash her eyes. 'I'm glad you did it,' she whispered. 'I'm proud you tried.' She looked as if she wanted to say something else, but her eyelids fluttered and her head dropped.

Minnie's vision blurred at the sight of her favourite person suffering so much, pinned into broken stone, waiting for her misery to end. A screecher bird, who had been slowly circling the area, flew down and settled on the wall next to Speck, as if it knew it might not have to wait too long before it could begin to feast.

'There you go,' said the man in charge. 'Now you've seen her, let's go.'

Minnie looked over her shoulder as she was marched away, but Speck's eyes were closed. The screecher bird, on the other hand, seemed wide awake.

Up the mound they went. They were led down a flight of huge stone steps set into the ruined wall of the castle. She knew what lay ahead of them.

- 48 -
THE FORGETTER

ONCE, WHEN MINNIE had been eight, she and her classmates from Quake School had been shown around the castle ruins on an educational school trip. They had peered down from the broken battlements into the dark dungeon below – a patch of wet earth with a huge metal grille placed over it. She had shuddered at the sight of the giant bones, watched the screecher birds swoop on and off the grille, waiting expectantly for their next meal.

And now she was being led below the battlements, not to the top. *Were the birds waiting for her?*

'I really am Minnie Wadlow, you know,' Minnie said again, not really expecting anyone to listen as they walked towards a dark cold tunnel. 'My mama and papa will be desperate to see me. Our guard is called Marcus. He likes to drink beer.' A look of shocked recognition crossed the man's face below her, which made her add, encouraged: 'You might even know him. Papa is an earthquake engineer. Mama is called Nanette, she does lots of charity work . . .' Her life rolled off her tongue, as she tried to convince someone, anyone, of her identity before it was too late, and she and Robin were abandoned completely to die.

The guard on her left, who was young and passionate about his work, said: 'You telling us that means nothing. You could have tortured that information out of Minnie.'

Minnie would have laughed if she hadn't been so scared. They were halfway down the torchlit tunnel, and ahead she could see large white bones strewn haphazardly over a dark dirt floor.

Then they were led through a large stone archway and into the dungeon itself.

'Any trouble?' barked a dungeon guard, a thin, wiry woman with extremely white teeth.

'A little,' said a guard, blandly, 'but not much. This giant keeps saying she's Minnie Wadlow, though. And although we suspect this boy has hidden away Minnie Wadlow, he's not telling us where, or why.'

'That's because I'm Minnie Wadlow,' said Minnie. 'Mr Straw did it,' she added, almost incoherently, struggling to speak through her shock and her exhaustion. 'With his medicines.'

The dungeon guard cocked her head and stared at Minnie. 'Is she feverish?'

'She's been saying this for hours,' came the reply.

'Well, she can carry on saying it,' said the dungeon guard, 'because no one will hear her.' She gave both Minnie and Robin a look that was almost laced with pity. 'Goodbye, you two. May your demise be swift.'

'Wait, that's it? You're just going to leave us to rot?' gasped Minnie.

'That's generally what we do with criminals who don't tell the truth, yes.' The guard turned on her heel and walked back out, and a heavy metal gate dropped down from the archway, its spikes grinding into the dirt floor with a sickening finality. If they walked away now, Minnie knew, she and Robin would starve to death, and Speck wouldn't be far behind them.

A sudden, desperate idea occurred to her. If she wanted the truth to come out, she'd have to lie first. It was crazy, but it might ensure one more meeting.

'Wait!' Minnie hurried to the bars and peered through. 'Wait! You're right. I'm *not* Minnie Wadlow. But . . . I know where she is. Me and Robin, both of us do.'

The footsteps stopped. The dungeon guard came back.

'Tell me what you've done with that poor little girl,' said the guard, 'and I'll reward you.'

'How will you do that?' murmured Robin, swaying on his feet from fatigue.

'A quick bullet in the heart, painless death. Much

better and more merciful than starving away, believe you me.'

'No, thank you. Listen,' said Minnie, urgently. 'I will reveal her whereabouts, but on one condition.'

The dungeon guard frowned and regarded her through the bars. 'What's that?'

'I get to choose who I tell.'

'And who might that be?'

And suddenly, something inside Minnie woke up. An idea began to develop in her mind.

'Everyone,' she said, and her voice shook, but held firm. 'I want to tell everyone. And . . .' she took a deep breath: 'I'm going to choose where.'

- 49 -
AN AUDIENCE

WITHIN A FEW hours, under guarded escort once more, Minnie and Robin were taken out of the dungeon and back to the grubby section of the Old Town, to the section of city wall where Speck had been pinned.

Gathered on the cobbles were all the people Minnie had invited to witness the truth: Mrs Primrose, looking frustrated; Mr Athelstan; Mr Straw; the Lloyd family, who owned the jackal-meat factory; Hester; Florin; and all her classmates. Also invited was every family on Quake Avenue; people who worked for the Giant Management Company; all the shopkeepers; and the entire rubbler district. (Not knowing how long she'd have the upper hand, Minnie had taken full advantage of it and asked for them all to be given the morning off.)

Although many of the servants had been turned to stone in Minnie's absence, a few remained, and they were also there. As well as these, there were the giants in training from the compound. These giants were young and in immaculate uniforms, and looked baffled and terrified to be out of the GMC compound for the first time in their lives.

And finally, her parents. They stood in the middle of the group looking absolutely dreadful: dishevelled, sleep-deprived, still wearing the clothes they'd worn when Minnie ran away, their faces full of love, shame and guilt as they took in her new appearance and realised what that meant for them. Minnie thought she'd be full of fury when she saw them, but instead she felt pity. She wanted to hug them and ignore them all at once.

There were also a few who had not been invited by Minnie, but were there regardless: twenty Giant Management Company officials. Each one stood by a flaming jackal-skin torch. Each one held a snarling dog on a leash. And there were the screecher birds too, who were bored and sensed trouble, and when there was trouble there was usually food.

It was quite the crowd, and they were getting restless, in the midday heat, with the flames snapping and roaring between them.

Minnie glanced at Speck, who looked even more exhausted than earlier, and seemed to be struggling to keep her eyes open. She glared at the GMC officials, and said, 'I'm not going to reveal one word about Minnie Wadlow's location until that giant gets given some food and water.'

Mrs Primrose bunched up her wrinkly little face, and Minnie realised that she didn't have a kindly face at all – it was nasty, and mean, and pinched. 'Giant 581 is our property, and her welfare is nothing to do with you,' said Mrs Primrose.

'If you say so,' said Minnie. 'But if you want to know where Minnie is, you need me to talk, and I'll only talk once that giant has had some water and food. And some for me and Robin too, in fact. And – and for the rubblers, while we're at it. They've been working all night, I've heard.' She paused. 'Um, please.'

There was a furious silence. People looked from Minnie to Mrs Primrose. The people in charge at the GMC looked at each other, nodding with disappointment. 'This is what happens when bad giants and good giants mix,' one of them muttered. 'Nothing but trouble.'

And then, suddenly, a shopkeeper shouted: 'Oh, just give them some water! It's really hot! Don't be so nasty!'

Florin Athelstan nodded. 'Come on, Papa,' he hissed. 'Speck has done nothing wrong.' And there were a few nods among the crowd.

So Mrs Primrose gave a furious sign to some of her employees. As they rushed around, fetching water and food for Speck and the rubblers, Minnie looked out, beyond the walls, over the river. As a giant, she couldn't just see more of the island, she also felt more connected to it. It was as if every part of it, in some strange way, was also part of her. The ferns on the lagoon path, the clouds in the sky, even the dark plumes of smoke still rising up between the mountain peaks of No-Go – all of it seemed, somehow, to speak to her.

There was another spark in the air, something else trying to reach her, she sensed, but it would have required all her concentration to understand what that was, and there was an awful lot going on right under her nose, and so she had to turn her attention away.

While the rubblers and Speck, and Minnie and Robin made their way through long, refreshing drinks of lemonade and some pastries – Minnie looked, gratefully, at the baker – the crowd talked among themselves about whether Minnie Wadlow, the little girl with the big nose, had been killed, or kidnapped, or both.

Finally, the refreshments were finished, and Mrs Primrose looked up at her with a chillingly cold smile. 'Let's get on with it, shall we? What have you done with the girl? Is she alive – or dead?'

Minnie took a shaky breath. 'Well, both. I am her, and therefore she is alive. But the short, limping, always-in-pain, lied-to, believed-everything-she-was-told girl she'd once been – well, she's . . . gone.' She looked at the people gathered below. *Now*, she thought. *Tell them the truth now.*

'I'm Minnie Wadlow,' she said, to an accompaniment of gasps and jeers. 'I was born a giant. But I was stolen, and experimented on—'

She was pleased to see Mr Straw blanch a little, at the mention of the word 'experiment'. He gulped nervously and pulled at his tie, but said nothing.

'Do you know,' bellowed Mrs Primrose, cutting into Minnie's explanation. 'I'm almost impressed by how much trouble you're causing us, giant.'

'Pardon?' said Minnie.

'Let's look at your list of offences, shall we? I'm going to tick them off with my fingers, just in case you can't count.'

'I *can* count,' said Minnie. 'I learned at school, same as Hester and Florin.'

'Don't you dare mention my son,' barked Mr Athelstan. Behind him, Florin flinched. 'As you were, Mrs Primrose,' said Mr Athelstan, with exquisite politeness.

'Thank you.' The tiny lady held up a delicate manicured hand – *hands*, Minnie thought bitterly, *that once passed me biscuits and stroked my hair*. 'As I was saying,' continued Mrs Primrose. 'One: you *look* like a giant from No-Go – a crime in itself. Two: you were found in the swamp – again, unforgivable; no one is allowed there apart from officials with permits from us. Three: you were clearly meddling in business you had no business meddling in. And four: as if all that wasn't enough, now we hear that you – *you*, a filthy, lawless giant! – keep claiming to be Minnie Wadlow.'

'I *am* Minnie Wadlow,' said Minnie Wadlow.

'You're at it again!' said Mrs Primrose. 'So let me get this right. You're saying that *you* – a dirty fugitive from No-Go – are a much-loved islander, a human child, belonging to a respectable family from Quake Quarter?'

Minnie felt her parents staring at her, as well as Mr Straw.

She took a deep breath. 'Can I just explain?'

And as she said those words, there was a small earthquake under their feet.

- 50 -
THE TRUTH

THE SMOKE WAS still rising from within No-Go. The fire started by the GMC must have been a particularly bad one, she thought. This thought led to fury, which gave her courage.

'It's true. I've been a giant all along,' she told the crowd. 'I was born in No-Go to a fugitive giant. Not long after I was born, I was stolen from my mother. Then my parents bought me from Mr Straw. Mr Straw made me medicine to stunt my growth. He charged my parents for it; in fact, I think he charged them almost everything they had. And for a long time, only the three of them knew – and the giants from No-Go. But then I ran away from home, to prevent my fast-track ceremony, and I ran out of medicine, and so my body finally grew. It was very painful. It's true.'

It was the longest speech she had ever made in public. She thought she'd risk a joke. 'This nose,' she said, pointing at it, 'should have given you a clue.'

There was an astonished silence. The crowd looked

at her nose. They looked at each other. They looked at Mr Straw. A few looked at Mr and Mrs Wadlow, shivering in the middle of the crowd.

Speck gazed at Minnie, and mouthed: '*Well done.*'

'Well?' spat Mrs Primrose, addressing Minnie's parents. 'Did you buy her from Mr Straw and pass her off as a human, all this time?'

Minnie's parents were quiet for a second, and then Papa gave a tiny nod. 'Yes.'

The crowd gasped. This was turning out to be quite the show.

Mrs Primrose said: 'You'd better explain yourselves.'

Papa looked at Mama, and then, unsteadily, said: 'We were desperate for a baby, and . . . we bought her from Mr Straw. When we met her for the first time, we knew that she was perfect.' He turned to his daughter.

'Hello, Minnie,' said Papa, his lips trembling. Mama just sobbed, trembling like a leaf. 'We're so glad you're alive, sweetheart. We had no idea what might have happened to you when you ran away—'

Minnie blinked back her tears. She held up her arms. 'Aren't you disappointed with me?' she said, bitterly. 'I turned into the very thing you tried to stop me from becoming all along.'

But as she asked the question, Minnie saw there

was nothing but love and pain on their faces, and her bitterness dissolved a little.

'Disappointed with you? Never,' said Mama.

'If anything, you should be disappointed with us,' said Papa, sadly.

Mama nodded. 'If you ever long to have a child one day and can't, then maybe you'll understand why we did it. You were our miracle.'

'You lied to me for years,' said Minnie. 'And even though you knew how much pain I was in, you kept giving me medicine to keep me stunted.'

'We were doing it for you,' wept Mama. 'We were trying to keep you safe. We just didn't want you to ever be at risk. We didn't want to lose you. We tried so hard to have you, and we knew that if you ever changed into a giant – well – that came with risks.'

'You took me. You *bought me*.'

'We did. I know it doesn't sound noble. But we were so desperate for a child to love,' said Papa, and his eyes were hollow with longing. 'And when you're desperate, you do desperate things. Besides, we thought it was such a good idea, at first.'

'You, a little orphan with no parents of her own—' said Mama. 'And us, with so much love to give, and no child to lavish it on.' She sniffed. 'We believed that by taking you from No-Go, we were giving a child the best possible chance of a happy life. With us, you got an education, security, love—'

Minnie found her voice. 'You didn't always act as if you loved me.'

Mama hung her head at that, and after a second, gave a tiny nod. 'I was too distracted keeping the charade going. I was terrified that our secret would be discovered. It ate me up inside.'

'You kept me in *pain*.'

'Nothing compared to the pain of being a fugitive giant, surely?' said Papa. 'Stuck in those mountains for your entire life, always scared of having your house burned down, never having enough food, no education—'

'It wasn't easy,' explained Mama. 'Mr Straw kept blackmailing us—' She shot him a look of pure loathing. 'He was always making the medicine more and more expensive, every time we saw him. And when we realised that we could never allow anyone to kiss you, in case you turned to stone, let alone kiss you ourselves . . .' Mama cried – 'we realised we'd made a mistake. We did – but by then all we could do was keep seeing it through, to protect you as best we could.'

Minnie suddenly thought of their home, the repairs

that couldn't be done, the lack of decent food, how hard Papa worked, the endless shortage of money, and all the late-night discussions about how they'd pay the latest bill . . .

Mama looked up at her, and her face shone with yearning. 'You've really grown into your face. You look –' and she smiled, shakily – 'well, you look beautiful.'

Papa nodded. Minnie gulped.

'ENOUGH!' roared Mrs Primrose, sending the screechers flapping into the air momentarily. 'Let's get to the bottom of this. Where is the healer? Show yourself, Mr Straw.' The bald little man stepped forward from the crowd. 'Is this true?' demanded Mrs Primrose. 'Did you experiment on a giantling and stunt her growth?'

Mr Straw hesitated. His glasses were so smeared with grease it was hard to read his eyes, but Minnie could sense, all the same, that his brain was running through various different calculations, as if he was weighing his words.

'Yes. And I believe she was one of my greatest experiments,' he replied.

There was a shocked hush. Mr Straw lifted his chin and, when he next spoke, his voice was proud. 'Besides,' said Mr Straw, clearly on a roll now, 'I did you a favour. I pulled a filthy little giantling – an orphan – out of the criminal underclass, and gave her the best possible opportunity on the island. And not only that, but I gave a childless couple – a *barren* couple – the chance to be parents. The mess they made of it is not my responsibility.' He looked modestly around the crowd and held out his hands. 'I have nothing to apologise for.'

'So it's true,' said Mrs Primrose, looking at Minnie. 'Fancy that.'

Instead of anger in her eyes, there was, Minnie saw, greed. 'You really did suppress her growth.' She stared up at Minnie. 'You changed her nature.' She was silent. 'Can you make giants bigger as well as smaller?'

'I think I can,' said Mr Straw. 'With more money. And a better laboratory. I can make genetically modified giants.'

'Just think of what we could do . . .' whispered Mrs Primrose, the lynchpin of the GMC.

'Exactly,' said Mr Straw. 'We can weed out the runts like Giant 581 and breed them to the perfect size and height. We can create giants according to our needs and our measurements. Imagine that! Endless servants, endless statues, endless stone, endless money.'

They smirked at each other, and Minnie's heart turned to ice. As she watched them concoct plans for the giants of the future, she thought she heard, faintly in the distance, the sound of howling. She took a deep breath. She thought about what Mr Straw, with the support of Mrs Primrose, would be capable of – keeping entire generations of giants, like her, in endless pain, forced to take medication to grow up or grow down, depending on the needs of the GMC.

They *had* to be prevented.

But what she could do, to stop them? She was handcuffed.

Out of the blue, she remembered what Blade had told her. *You're in enemy territory, and the only thing you have to trade is the truth. Vastly underrated as a thing to barter with, in my experience.*

Minnie looked at the crowd nervously. It was hard to tell where their sympathies lay, and they were clearly intimidated by Mrs Primrose. But, down there, someone had told Mrs Primrose to let the rubblers have water. Her favourite baker had donated pastries. Hester and Florin were looking at her gravely, giving her time to speak. Perhaps they would listen. And she had one more truth to tell. That was all she had. She might as well use it.

'There's something else you should know,' she said. 'The No-Go giants aren't evil at all.'

The crowd stirred, restlessly. The man who sold newspapers frowned at her. 'That's a lie,' he said, grumpily.

'Yes,' said Minnie. 'We've all been lied to. The Giant Management Company are very good at making up lies.' She stared in the direction of the mountain peaks. 'I've been there. I've met the mountain giants. They're nice. They've *never* tried to kidnap or harm any one of your children – they were only looking for me. My grandmother's there. The ones who aren't nice, actually, are the people who repeatedly set fire to their homes, and they are the ones who are standing right here—'

'That's enough!' said Mrs Primrose, hurriedly. 'Guards, stop her.'

The guards snapped into action, and began to pick up their torches.

Minnie flinched when she saw them coming closer. 'What are you going to do, brand me?' she stuttered.

'Leave her alone,' shouted Speck huskily.

'Don't you dare burn our child!' yelled Mr Wadlow.

'One more word from you, Keyton,' said Mrs Primrose with a sigh, 'and you'll be going in the dungeon. Don't imagine for one second that you're not going to pay for what you've done.'

'P-pay?' said Mrs Wadlow.

'You've been carrying on under false pretences for a decade,' Mrs Primrose remarked, mildly. 'Allowing a giantling into school. Letting her spend time with decent, respectable children from the island.'

'And not only that, but you have both committed theft,' added Mr Athelstan.

'Theft?' stammered Papa, finally tearing his eyes away from Minnie and looking at Mr Athelstan in confusion.

'*Theft.* The giantling should have been handed over to *us* the moment her mother died. She could have had five years' training by now, in readiness for when she too became a servant.' Mr Athelstan gave Mrs Primrose an apologetic look. 'I can't imagine how much training Minnie will need to catch up with her peers.'

'Yes, it has massively inconvenienced us,' said Mrs Primrose.

There was an awful, shocked pause as the Wadlows finally realised what was being said. Mrs Primrose heaved a deep, pained sigh. 'She'll have missed out on so much valuable schooling. I can't guarantee she'll ever be as good as some of the other servants, or as biddable. But stock, as they say, is stock, and she'll make a stand-in for a family that loses their giant prematurely, if nothing else.' She looked at the guards. 'Seize her.'

'You – you *can't*!' gasped Mama, her mouth wide with horror. 'You can't just take her from us and turn her into a s-ser-servant. Please, no! She's a Wadlow. We've brought her up.'

'We *can*. She belongs to *us*.'

'B-b-but she's our family. She's our daughter.'

'She was never your daughter,' said Mrs Primrose. 'She's not your family. She belongs to the Giant Management Company. From now on, you will accept that.'

Mama and Papa turned to each other, horror in their eyes.

'Just be thankful we're not putting you in the dungeon as punishment for the fraud you've committed against the island,' said Mrs Primrose. She glanced at Minnie. 'Your training will start tomorrow.'

There was another faint but distinct rumble under Minnie's feet. 'Is anyone else feeling that?' she said.

'Feeling what?' snapped Mrs Primrose.

'That earthquake?'

But the humans around her shook their heads. Only Speck said, 'Yes, I feel it too. The island is speaking to you, Minnie.'

And Minnie finally realised what it meant to be a giant. Because the island really did belong to them. That was why they heard the tremors before they came.

The GMC – with their boots, and flames and wild dogs – could pretend all they liked that they owned the island. But the island had always tried to fight them off.

And perhaps now was the time to help with that fight.

She looked over the walls, towards the mountains, and then she called for help.

- 51 -
THE BATTLE OF FIRE AND TEETH

FOR A MOMENT, there was nothing but a scandalised stillness down at Minnie's feet. And then, to her amazement, she heard the sound of howling, less faint this time. *The same howls we heard at the swamp* . . . Could there be other jackals on the loose?

'Listen!' Minnie said, desperately. 'Listen. You've got to know this. This island was never yours. I found out the truth in the swamp. It was the giants' first. They were invaded, not the other way round. Our history is a lie – told to justify turning giants to stone. Just to make some people rich and powerful.'

A clamour erupted round the crowd. A few adults shouted, 'Shame!' at Minnie. But one or two turned to each other and seemed to mutter agreement.

'All this time?' said Speck. Her voice was dull and flat. 'All those ceremonies? All those giants, turned to stone? All the punishments, because we were told we owed them that? And it was ours, all along, and we'd never done anything wrong?'

'All this time,' said Minnie. Speck's face changed completely. *Let the guards do their worst to me now*, she thought. *I've told the truth.*

'I've got proof,' shouted Robin, struggling in his handcuffs. 'I was there too. We found a map! Quick, Posy, pull it out of my pocket.'

The smallest rubbler child, a barefoot girl with a twisted back, hobbled to Robin and pulled out the original map of the island. She held it aloft. A woman took it from Posy's hand, and passed it along and every time someone in power tried to grab it, it evaded capture and was passed on and read again.

Eventually, it ended in the hands of Florin Athelstan.

He looked down at it, and then up into the eyes of his father.

'Dad?' he said. 'Is this true? Did . . . we steal the island from the giants? Were our ceremonies –' his jaw clenched – 'based on a lie?'

Mr Athelstan hesitated, and as he was about to speak, Minnie realised that there was a new type of shaking under her feet, and it wasn't an earthquake.

It was the sort of tremor you get when an entire group of giants are marching at the same time.

'Hello Minnie,' boomed Blade. 'Hello Robin.' The city walls were so high that only the faces of the No-Go giants

could be seen. But behind the broken part of the wall Minnie saw that they had come in their masses; dusty, smoke-streaked, grim-faced, but there.

'You heard me! You came!' she gasped. 'I wasn't sure—'

'Of course we did,' said Blade. 'When a giant shouts for us like that, how could we ignore it? It sounded like you were in terrible trouble.'

'We lost you once,' added Issa, quietly. 'Couldn't bear to lose you again.'

Minnie saw Mrs Primrose whisper something to one of the guards, and saw him slip away from the dirty street. *What are they up to now?* she thought, tiredly.

Blade was staring at her. 'You look so much like your mother. Wonderful woman.' He sniffed, loudly, then peered over at the shaking islanders below him.

'Hello,' he shouted. 'Listen, before anything starts, can I just check – does anyone have any nuts? No? Never mind.' He sighed. 'Worth a try. Anyway, here, Minnie, I've brought you someone.' And he picked up a golden creature from behind the wall, and put him carefully on the top. Twist looked at Minnie, and gave a ferocious wail of recognition.

'*Twist?*' gasped Minnie. 'He's alive?'

'He was badly injured,' said Blade, stroking his back with one finger, lovingly. 'But he limped all the way to the tunnel and came and found me. What's more –'

and here Blade beamed so widely that all his teeth were visible, and all the islanders gasped, even Speck, at the sight of a giant smiling properly – 'we met even more of his pals. Aren't they beautiful? They've been gathering all over the island, clever little things.'

And in the next moment, a swarm of golden jackals leaped up on to the wall, and stood on it in a line. The Lloyd family, who owned the jackal-meat factory, made faint noises of fear, for the jackals were staring at them with loathing, peeling their lips back to reveal their teeth.

For a moment, the No-Go giants and the jackals stared solemnly over the wall at the GMC guards and their dogs. There was a heavy silence as they all contemplated what lay ahead. There had been a long war before. Would there be another one now? The screecher birds held their breath hopefully. Could there be bloodshed?

'You know, we don't have to fight—' started Issa.

'Seize them!' said Mrs Primrose, cutting across her. 'Grab them and kill them all, before they kill us.' She smiled menacingly. 'Here come the provisions.'

And then there was a squeaky, rusty sound behind them, like the sound of a hundred wheels rotating together across cobbles. Minnie turned, and realised that the Giant Management Company must have been preparing for something like this for a long, long time.

- 52 -
WiLD AND SNARLiNG

THERE WERE TOO many wagons to count, and no doubt there were many more lying in wait somewhere. Each wagon was piled high with jackal-skin torches. Some of the torches were falling apart on their sticks, as if the skins were hundreds of years old, but some looked freshly scraped and tied, as if they'd been made in the last month. It would have taken the GMC several decades, if not a century, to stockpile so many missiles.

At the sight of the torches and as the stench of petrol filled the air, every single giant on the other side of the wall paled and went quiet. Minnie thought of their scars, and how long they had been terrorised by flames. Desperately she squirmed and tugged at her handcuffs, but they held firm. At the formidable sight of the weapons in front of her, she was suddenly filled with a terrible misgiving. Had she called the giants and the jackals to their deaths?

'Fire!' ordered Mrs Primrose.

For a moment, it seemed as if no one would obey her. The guards hesitated. The No-Go giants waited.

'I said, *fire*!' repeated Mrs Primrose. 'Or be fired at.' She looked imperiously around the entire crowd. She pointed at the smallest child. 'Come. Now. Pick up a torch, and throw it over the wall at the enemy.'

'I – I don't want to,' said the small rubbler child.

'Then I shall throw you in the dungeon, you troublemaker.'

The little girl walked, quivering, to the nearest wagon, and was handed a torch by Mrs Primrose.

'Now throw,' said Mrs Primrose. 'Go on!'

The torch barely flew a metre, but it seemed to set the battle in motion. One by one, the others slowly walked to the wagon and picked up their weapons, too.

While the humans armed themselves, the giants and the jackals began to climb over the city walls, their flecked skin and fur combining together to make them look like a river of gold, pouring over the walls and into the city.

'We don't want to hurt you,' said Blade, to the smallest children, who were sobbing.

Twist, still clearly injured from the kicking he'd received at the swamp, made his way through the crowds, heading straight for Minnie, but, as he limped towards her, a pack of dogs leaped on him. In his injured state, he was no match for them, and quickly disappeared under the assault, snarling and biting as best he could.

A second later, a flame had landed in Blade's red beard, and as his hands flew up, desperate to untangle the torch from his face, wincing, five guards ran to his legs and began to tie them together with rope, so that he was bound. When the jackals around Blade flew at the guards, the dogs attacked them, too, and a wild, snarling fight began.

Vainly, Minnie struggled to break open her handcuffs, pulling and pulling at her wrists to be free. *My hands may be cuffed, but I can still walk*, she thought suddenly. And so she strode into the fray, kicking the dogs away whenever she could, pushing the guards off the giants on the ground. A guard held a torch near her ankle, causing the worst pain imaginable, and she flinched, and had to retreat, but then she rallied and went in again, hoping not to fall.

More flames were thrown. Some giants, dodging these, managed to move through the crowd, but as none of them wanted to hurt or step on any of the children, the guards throwing the flames were able to aim with better precision, and kept pushing them back to the city walls.

Cruelly, the servants were tasked with firing flames at their own kind. The torches flew and sang past Speck, still pinned in place. Each time they struck a giant or a jackal someone would cheer.

But others did not.

The mountain giants tried valiantly to reach Minnie and Robin, but the flames flew thick and fast, and the dogs were wild, snapping and biting and leaping up their giant legs, trying to bring them down by any means possible. Chesca managed to fight off the two dogs that were clinging to her skirts, growling, and, with one arm bent across her face, she nearly reached Minnie, but at the last minute three torches fired in quick succession sent her sprawling to the ground. The guards cheered at the sight of a fallen giant, and the younger servants from the compound were told to bind her in chains and take her to the dungeon.

When Minnie looked up, she saw with dismay that many of the No-Go giants had been beaten back or were retreating, terrified of being thrown in the dungeon to die. As the tiny street filled with smoke and snarling dogs Minnie's heart began to sink. She couldn't see or hear Twist any more. Chesca had disappeared. She couldn't see Robin or Blade or Issa.

At first, when she saw Papa reaching through the smoke with a look of furious anger, and Mama not far behind him, slapping at a giant, Minnie thought they were fighting on the side of the townsfolk. But then, when she squinted harder through the smoke and limbs, she realised that Papa was actually pulling a dog off Issa, and Mama was trying to put out the flames leaping up a giant's dress, patting at them with her bare hands in an attempt to stop them consuming the entire garment.

Minnie's eyes widened in amazement. The dog was ripped off Issa, and landed on the floor with a whimper. As if he sensed Minnie watching him, Papa grinned, and raised his hand to his forehead in a salute, before immediately plunging into a fight with one of the guards. Minnie strode over and joined him. With a combination of punches and kicks, they were able to push him back from Papa and Mama, and sent him running away down a side street.

'He's probably gone to get more wagons,' shouted Papa, panting slightly from the fight, his white shirt ripped at the collar and arm. 'But I think we can say we won that fight, Min.' They shared a grin, and, in that moment, Minnie felt more like his daughter than she'd ever felt before.

'I've seen you, Keyton Wadlow,' came Mr Athelstan's voice. 'Don't think you won't be punished for your treason!'

'Oh, working for you is punishment enough,' shouted Papa. 'I know now that you never wanted me to stop the earthquakes. I was wasting my life away, working for you.'

To Minnie, he said: 'Minnie – go and get Speck. See if you can free her. I'll try and stop them from throwing the flames.' Then he gave Minnie one final look of love, and turned back into the smoke.

Despite the bravery of the giants and the jackals, their numbers were dwindling. And still the flames kept being thrown. The servants from the compound, though young and frightened, were healthier and stronger than the weakened, battle-scarred No-Go giants. What's more, they were terrified of the GMC, and so ultimately they proved the better fighters, spurred on by what might happen to them if they didn't win. Minnie couldn't see Speck any more, and the flames whizzing past her head were getting faster and closer. When she wasn't dodging those, she was ducking frantically left and right, trying to avoid the screecher birds, who had decided the time was right to start pecking at the weak.

Things were looking desperate. Giants were being felled like trees by the flames. Their side was losing.

Then she felt someone prodding at her ankle. She looked down into the eyes of Florin Athelstan.

'I've got an idea,' he said. 'Bend down.'

Minnie got to her knees, and the boy who had never stopped loving Sandborn told Minnie what he wanted to do.

- 53 -
REINFORCEMENTS

'Minnie,' he shouted, into her ears. 'Minnie, remember our history classes?'

She shot him a look of baffled frustration. 'Florin, we're in the middle of a battle!'

'Listen. We were always told how our kisses would turn giants into stone, right?'

'Y-yes . . .' she said, shaking off a wild dog that had just sunk its teeth into her ankle.

'And they always said that our belief in the process would make it work more thoroughly, didn't they?' His face was lit up with urgency. 'What if a kiss could turn our giants back? If we kissed them believing they should be alive again? No one ever talks about that. But I wonder—'

Everything about him burned with a desperate question. 'D-do you think Sandborn is still intact? Did he avoid getting smashed to pieces in the earthquake?'

Minnie thought for a moment. 'The last big quake hit here the hardest,' she told him. 'The rubbler district wasn't hit at all. Mrs Primrose lied about that.'

Their eyes met. Florin's eyes were full of tears, and not just from the smoke.

'I think it's worth a try,' said Minnie, smiling at him. He gave a big, juddering sigh. 'Do you?' He looked as if he wanted to cry. 'I need to go to him now, before we lose.'

Minnie surveyed the dwindling number of giants. 'Blade,' she shouted. 'Blade!'

To her relief, his head loomed out of the smoke. Parts of his beard, she noticed, had been cut away, perhaps because blazing missiles had landed there – and there was a screecher bird on his head, pecking furiously at his scalp, making blood pour down into one of his eyes. But he was alive, and, she was amazed to see, that tired swagger seemed to be burning just as before.

'Blade, can you carry Florin down to the rubbler district? And run!'

*

Still the fighting went on. Mrs Primrose was shouting instructions at all the children to go around and kiss any fallen giant on the lips, but she shouted in vain. All the children, sickened by the sight of humans burning giants, refused to do it.

A group of No-Go giants had surrounded Speck and were pulling and pushing at the wall around her to bring it down, valiantly persisting despite the many burns now blossoming on their backs, but Speck had been wedged in so deep, and the giants were by now so weak, that theirs was a losing battle.

Robin was surrounded by snarling dogs, pinning him in place. Minnie could hear, somewhere, the sound of Twist's howl as the screecher birds took their revenge on him for the time he'd beaten them. A huge shadow fell over the Old Town, as if the sun had been blotted out, and Minnie felt bleakness steal into her heart.

'Time to give up?' said Mr Athelstan.

'Not quite,' said Florin Athelstan, beaming, standing proudly beside the giant he'd brought back from the Rubbler District. 'I've brought backup.'

And the shadow that loomed over them didn't seem quite so gloomy – for it had been cast by Sandborn.

'We meet again,' he said, picking up a handful of guards and looking at them contemplatively as they struggled in his fist. His skin was slightly covered in dust, and still completely grey, but he was alive.

'It worked!' Minnie gasped. Beside Sandborn, Florin shone with happiness. He glanced at Minnie. 'It did,' he whispered. 'Easy as anything.' Blade and Sandborn stood close together, staring down at the fighting around them.

'Back in a tic,' said Blade, and he strode off and began to stamp out fires with his bare feet.

Sandborn glanced at the new, shaking servants from the compound, who were staring at him open-mouthed. 'Join us,' he called, holding his hands out towards them.

And then he turned and stared into Minnie's face. 'It's really true then,' he said, grinning at her. 'You were a giant all along. I kept hearing a rumour . . .' He frowned a little. 'And you're taller than me? Outrageous!'

Blade and Sandborn's return seemed to galvanise the remaining No-Go giants and jackals. With their loss of fear came a new realisation of how strong they really were, and that was all the giants seemed to need. Tentatively, one of the training giants broke away from the GMC side and strode over to Speck, and a few seconds later the other apprentices had joined them. The young servants began to pull down the bricks in the wall that were pinning Speck in place. The harder they worked to pull down the wall, however, the faster and thicker the flames flew at them.

The sound and fury of the battle roared in Minnie's ears. She was tired, and despite Sandborn's appearance, still wasn't sure if they would win the battle. She felt dizzy, and as she stared at the scene around her, her hopes began to slip away.

She glanced down at herself, and at the people fighting beneath her. She saw the Giant Management officials, cruel and mean and small in everything they did. A dark cold despair stole into her heart. But then she looked at the giants again, and slowly she lifted one arm, and then the other, watching how she sparkled in the light, looking at the new dimensions of her new body.

I'm a giant now, she thought, and for the first time, the idea pleased her. It did more than please her. It filled her with a huge wave of pride and wonder. *I'm a giant.*

She turned her head and stared down into the eyes of Mrs Primrose. *I'm a giant,* she thought again, and she smiled hugely. And then she strode over to the wagons, filled with jackal torches waiting to be thrown, and began to kick them over, and stamp on the torches, and as she destroyed the remaining weapons, she gave thanks for what she was.

Mrs Primrose, aware now that she was on the losing side, seemed to shrink in her clothes, and as more children bolted away, hurrying off to turn their giants back to life, all the power and authority seemed to seep out of her. She too, turned and fled.

The weakened island seemed to sense this, and decided to give one last quake, and this one rippled under the city walls. This, combined with the efforts of the young compound giants, released Speck from her prison, and she was finally free. Minnie, puffing from her exertions, stood and stared at Speck, and for a tiny moment, it was all she could do.

Speck opened her arms.

Minnie ran into them as fast as she could.

It took a long, long time for Speck to stop hugging Minnie, and when she finally pulled away, her face was streaked with tears. 'I can't believe you made all this happen.' Her voice was soft and wondering. 'You overthrew the Giant Management Company. I never would have thought it possible.'

'I couldn't bear to lose you,' said Minnie.

'You ran away to save me? And you – you stayed away, despite the pain you were in?'

Minnie nodded, unable to speak. Speck smiled softly. 'I love you, Minnie,' she said. She glanced mischievously around, and then raised her voice and said it again.

'I – I – I love you too,' stammered Minnie.

'Do you hear that, Mrs Primrose? We're breaking all the rules! Quick, come and arrest us! Oh, too busy?' Speck was shouting into the air, crying and laughing at the same time, shaking all over, and Minnie *felt it all at once*. Felt how unhappy and trapped Speck had been all her life, and how she'd never been able to tell a soul.

Minnie sat down on the floor, suddenly. She rested her elbows on her knees, put her head in her hands, and sobbed, for it had been a long, long journey for a young girl to go on.

Speck put her hand on her shoulders for a second, and left, as if she knew that Minnie needed to be alone for a while.

Minnie leaned back against a brick and closed her eyes, and a few seconds later, she felt the warm fur of Twist as he nestled next to her. He made a tiny whine in the back of his throat. 'No more fights for you, Twist,' murmured Minnie. 'No more.'

And as the sun's rays grew softer and more golden, they stayed there, resting, taking comfort in each other.

*

By dusk, it was entirely clear that the war was over. The GMC compound was waving a white flag from its roof, and the dungeon's gates had been broken wide open by Blade and Sandborn.

All the giants, wherever they were from, were beginning to mingle, talking and laughing, or going on happy walks through the city, carrying children on their shoulders. Occasionally the silence was broken by the sound of a shop roof being lifted, as the giants pulled out food and drink and handed it around to all.

But a few remained at the battle site. Minnie, still sitting cross-legged on the cobbles, was letting Robin bash away at her handcuffs with a rock. Once he'd broken through, he said: 'That's the last time I ever want to *touch* a stone.'

With her free hands, she reached out for Twist, and began to stroke him, checking for injuries.

There was the sound of footsteps, and Mrs Primrose, Mr Athelstan and Mr Straw appeared, nervously. *How old and frail they look*, thought Minnie, suddenly. *As if they are no match for us. How did they manage to hold so much power for so long?*

For a moment, everyone was quiet.

'We've come to start peace negotiations,' said Mrs Primrose. 'So we can work out a way we can all stay here, with little disruption.'

'Surely we can come to some arrangement?' said Mr Athelstan. 'Maybe the giants who fought today can become our guards? We'd make it worth their while.'

Speck snorted with disgust and looked at Minnie. 'Are they for real? They still want the Giant Management Company to operate?'

'It provided a valuable source of income,' protested Mrs Primrose. 'We're more than happy to make you a part of the company, if you wish, while we train a new generation of giants—'

'Stop talking,' roared Speck, and Mrs Primrose

whimpered, and did exactly that.

Minnie smiled at Speck proudly. *I had no idea she could speak so loudly*, she thought. *I can't wait to find out all the other things she can do – all the things we giants can do, without them around.*

And suddenly, she knew what had to happen.

'Speck,' she said. 'Grandmother? I've had an idea.'

Minnie, Issa and Speck spent a few minutes conferring, and then turned to the terrified leaders of the GMC.

'You've spent your life making giants and rubblers work on your behalf,' said Speck.

'And now it's time for you to work instead,' added Minnie.

'Work?' stammered Mr Athelstan.

'Doing what?' asked Mrs Primrose.

'Mending your ships,' said Speck, smiling widely, showing all her teeth at once (at the sight of which most of the GMC officials made terrified little whimpers).

I was right, thought Minnie, happily. *Speck can look quite scary when she smiles.*

'Fetch your tools,' added Issa, smiling. 'And your suitcases.'

'W-why?' stuttered a guard.

'Because once you've fixed your ships,' said Speck, 'you're going to sail away. The days of the Giant

Management Company are over.' She trembled all over as she said it.

'You had a good run of it,' Blade said, pleasantly.

'But now it's time to leave,' added Sandborn. 'Find somewhere else to live. And give our island back to us.'

Mrs Primrose looked as if she was going to argue with them, but then the fight drained out of her, and, with a nod, she formally signalled that the reign of the GMC was over.

'You win,' said Mrs Primrose. 'We'll rebuild our ships.'

- 54 -
LOVE

Some weeks later, the ships were ready, and everyone gathered on Black Sand Beach to say their farewells. Large snakes of townsfolk hauled suitcases and baskets and trunks of their possessions in a long line down to the shore and on to each vessel. Rubblers and traders, shopkeepers and Quake society people alike – all prepared themselves to board the ships and head away to new lives, without giants, without earthquakes.

As they filed on to the ships one by one, they turned and looked back at the island which had once been their home. Some waved a hand at the giants in farewell.

Some didn't dare.

Minnie stood a little further apart from the giants, as huge emotions battled away inside her.

There was a polite cough at Minnie's feet. She glanced down, straight into the eyes of her parents, and without warning, she began to cry. She got down on her knees so they could be closer and, for a second, the three Wadlows simply gazed at each other, acknowledging what they had once been – a family.

'It's time we left,' said Mama, softly. She swallowed. 'You'll make sure you eat enough, won't you?'

And then her parents both turned and looked in Speck's direction. Speck no longer wore a uniform and had taken to wearing a particularly beautiful tunic of red and gold fabrics. She didn't stoop, either. As if she could sense their gaze, Speck raised a hand in their direction and gave a solemn nod.

'She was always very good at looking after you, Min,' Papa said, quietly. 'Probably did a better job than us.'

Minnie took a deep breath, and said, through trembling lips, 'But you did your best. I know you did.'

The sigh her parents made was almost giant. Papa nodded, and whispered, 'We tried.'

Her parents were flawed, and had made several mistakes, Minnie realised, but they loved her. Of that, she was in no doubt. For a moment, the three Wadlows regarded each other with so much longing and sadness that one could almost touch it.

They smiled at each other. 'Will you write to us?' said Mama.

'I will.'

'We'll always love you,' they said.

'Me too,' whispered Minnie. Then she put both her arms around them, and hugged them tight. 'Are you sure

we can't take your friend Robin with us? We'd be happy to help him when we get to the mainland. He could stay with us for as long as he wanted.' They both looked hopeful.

'He doesn't want to leave the island,' said Minnie, smiling a little. 'Not yet. But if he ever does one day, I'll be sure to tell him to look out for you.'

They nodded, and with one final, searching look, Mama and Papa boarded their ship. A few minutes later, it began to move over the shallow waters, and out into the open ocean.

Minnie watched the ship for as long as she could. When it was just a small black dot on the horizon, she turned and walked back up the beach towards the giants, and the boy and the jackal who were waiting for her.

ACKNOWLEDGEMENTS

I'D LIKE TO thank my friends, neighbours and family for their immense kindness and humour.

Thank you, as always, to Nick Lake, for being exceptionally patient.

Thank you, Jessica Dean, Jodie Hodges and Julia Sanderson, who did a lot of thinking on my behalf.

Thank you, Flavia Sorrentino, for your covers and your stunning illustrations, and everyone involved at HCCB for helping with this book.

Thank you to Struan Murray for suggesting the name 'Robin', and to Hannah Love for the name 'Twist'.

Mum, thank you for being my first cheerleader.

Polly and Ben, as ever, thank you. Some things have changed, but that will never change.

And thank you, whoever left that sign on the road in January 2020 that simply said: GIANT SALE.